'You are possibly the loveliest woman I ever beheld and any man can dream of until he drives himself nigh mad with longing.'

There was something very serious in his steady look that made Persephone's heart thump heavily and then race on.

'Did you do that when you were held and tortured, Alex?' she asked painfully, somehow unable to halt the question on her lips.

'Not then,' he said, with a shake of his head that spoke of honesty and regret. 'Don't forget you were a very cross little schoolgirl when I left for the army, Persephone. I dreamt of someone very like you are now—a someone who could reach inside my tortured heart and join her clean, bright soul to my bitter one. I was getting ready to dream of you and only you every night from the moment I finally did lay eyes on you as a grown-up goddess. I've got so into the way of it now that I don't think even your displeasure will stop me.'

'Maybe I don't want to stop you,' she murmured, and suddenly found it impossible to meet his gaze full-on without a host of huge possibilities humming between them like warm lightning.

AUTHOR NOTE

I fell for the scarred and reclusive Earl of Calvercombe the moment he walked into THE DUCHESS HUNT, the first book in my *Seaborne* trilogy, one dark night. He seemed an ideal hero for a spirited Seaborne lady, and I hope you enjoy Alex and Persephone's story whether you read the first book in the series or not.

Rich Seaborne's story is coming soon, and I hope his family forgive him for all the trouble he's caused them!

THE SCARRED EARL

Elizabeth Beacon

All the characters in this book have no existence outside the imagination of the author, and have no relation whatsoever to anyone bearing the same name or names. They are not even distantly inspired by any individual known or unknown to the author, and all the incidents are pure invention.

First published in Great Britain 2013
by Mills & Boon, an imprint of Harlequin (UK) Limited.
Large Print edition 2013
Harlequin (UK) Limited, Eton House, 18-24 Paradise Road,
Richmond, Surrey TW9 1SR

ISBN: 978 0 263 23710 8

Harlequin (UK) policy is to use papers that are natural, renewable and recyclable products and made from wood grown in sustainable forests. The logging and manufacturing process conform to the legal environmental regulations of the country of origin.

Printed and bound in Great Britain
by CPI Antony Rowe, Chippenham, Wiltshire

Elizabeth Beacon lives in the beautiful English West Country, and is finally putting her insatiable curiosity about the past to good use. Over the years Elizabeth has worked in her family's horticultural business, become a mature student, qualified as an English teacher, worked as a secretary and, briefly, tried to be a civil servant. She is now happily ensconced behind her computer, when not trying to exhaust her bouncy rescue dog with as many walks as the Inexhaustible Lurcher can finagle. Elizabeth can't bring herself to call researching the wonderfully diverse, scandalous Regency period and creating charismatic heroes and feisty heroines *work*, and she is waiting for someone to find out how much fun she is having and tell her to stop it.

Previous novels by the same author:

AN INNOCENT COURTESAN
HOUSEMAID HEIRESS
A LESS THAN PERFECT LADY
CAPTAIN LANGTHORNE'S PROPOSAL
REBELLIOUS RAKE, INNOCENT GOVERNESS
THE RAKE OF HOLLOWHURST CASTLE
ONE FINAL SEASON
(part of *Courtship & Candlelight*)
A MOST UNLADYLIKE ADVENTURE
GOVERNESS UNDER THE MISTLETOE
(part of *Candlelit Christmas Kisses*)
THE DUCHESS HUNT

THE SCARRED EARL
features characters you will have met in
THE DUCHESS HUNT

Did you know that some of these novels are also available as eBooks?
Visit www.millsandboon.co.uk

I would like to dedicate this book to my lovely editors past and present: Maddie West, Lucy Gilmour and Megan Haslam—without their hard work, humour and patience all my books would be very much poorer.

Chapter One

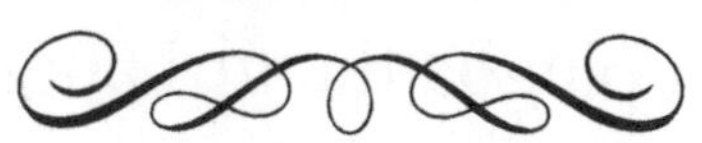

'Your turn next then,' the Dowager Duchess of Dettingham told her eldest granddaughter with a smug nod at the posy of late China rosebuds the bride had thrown into Persephone Seaborne's hands before driving off with her besotted bridegroom.

Suddenly Persephone wouldn't have been surprised to look down and find it made up of thistles and stinging nettles instead of cosseted late blooms, and almost dropped the lovely thing in the dust. Jessica's purposefully accurate throw showed what a schemer her best friend had become since she had fallen in love with Jack Seaborne, Duke of Dettingham, and she wondered at herself for catching it more by reflex than desire to be the next one to marry as tradition demanded. Wondering who her grandmother expected her to marry this time, she coolly returned the Dowager's gimlet-eyed stare and silently fumed about matchmakers of all ages and abilities.

'Please don't plague the girl about such things on my daughter's special day, your Grace,' Lady Pendle, mother of the bride, intervened. Her youngest daughter had just married Persephone's cousin Jack, Duke of Dettingham, yet she found time to rescue Persephone from her domineering relative, and she was truly grateful.

'Anyway, I think Miss Brittles and Sir John will walk up the aisle long before I do. I see all the classic signs of mutual enchantment,' Persephone mused aloud.

She marvelled that a couple so very different from Jessica and Jack could wear the same smitten look whenever they set eyes on each other as the happy couple had been modelling for weeks. Sir John and his lady love seemed to manage to find their mark remarkably often among the large group of aristocrats and friends invited to the wedding of the year, let alone the Season, as well. Realising too late she'd placed them in the Duchess's sights by doing her thinking out loud, she sincerely wished she'd held her tongue in the terrible old lady's presence.

'Hah, that pair are far too old to go about smelling of April and May in such a ridiculous fashion,' the Dowager snapped with a fierce frown in their direction.

Miss Brittles took an involuntary step backwards and Sir John Coulter glowered back with compounded interest. Sensing more interesting prey than her stubborn granddaughter, the Dowager forgot her reluctant companions, so Persephone and Lady Pendle cravenly slipped into the crowd of guests milling about the famous gardens and made good their escape.

'Sir John seems very well equipped to fight his own battles,' Lady Pendle muttered sheepishly.

'And I'm sure Miss Brittles thinks him even more wonderful than usual for defending her from the dragon Duchess,' Persephone replied.

'So it's probably not really chicken-hearted of us to leave her Grace having fun in her own peculiar manner,' Lady Pendle agreed as she led

Persephone to where her second-youngest daughter was standing with her doting husband, holding their baby son in her arms and taking in the finer nuances of a happy family occasion with her usual good-humoured intelligence.

'Never mind, Persephone dear, her Grace can't endure the countryside for more than a day or so and must be pining for the noise and stink of the city by now. Although making her grandchildren squirm is one of her favourite occupations, you do all seem to share a stubborn habit of going your own way. I can't imagine anything more exasperating for the poor, dear Duchess than being saddled with such deeply ungrateful descendants as this latest generation of Seabornes, can you, my love?' Rowena, Lady Tremayne, observed wickedly as she passed his son and heir to Sir Linstock instead of his hovering nurse, who seemed constantly surprised the child's parents were unwilling to leave him to her until he was old enough to be seen and not heard. If that day ever came in the lively Tremayne household, which Persephone doubted.

The dashing Baronet took his child from his

lady with a rueful smile and a shrug that admitted the wild reputation he'd once worked so hard to earn was ruined, first by his uniquely fascinating wife and now the robust little son upon whom he clearly doted. There was a look of quiet contentment in his dark eyes Persephone had never thought she would see and Sir Linstock gently rocked his son as if he'd been practising to become a loving father for years. He had enjoyed a wild career as one of the worst rakes in London until he met Rowena's laughing blue eyes one night in Mayfair and fell flat at her daintily shod feet like any awed boy fresh up from the country.

'I expect the Duchess will shortly decide she's not being treated with the reverence she deserves and demand to be taken home at a breakneck pace she would find deplorable in anyone else,' he observed laconically. 'Her coachman is probably supervising the harnessing of his team as we speak, in anticipation of his call to duty.'

Persephone laughed, but, as she chatted easily with the wider Pendle family and enjoyed their witty but never vicious byplay, she wondered why the idea of even so close a marriage as Rowena's with her Sir Linstock left her shivering. She was nearly two and twenty now and should make a creditable alliance, if only to stop her mother worrying about at least one of her children. Yet she hadn't met one gentleman she could endure being tied to for life during three successful Seasons in town.

Another shiver ran through her at the thought of meeting her imaginary groom in their nuptial chamber on their wedding night to trust him with so much of her true self. It was her parents' fault, she decided, picturing her father and mother together and knowing how desperately hard Lady Henry's life had become without her beloved husband to share it with. Like swans, Seabornes seemed fated to pair for life, with the notable exception of her grandfather. That famously raffish gentleman married for money and kept a succession of exotically lovely mistresses once the heir and a spare had filled the Ashburton nurseries with their robust cries. Persephone often wondered if her husband's careless infidelity was the reason for Grandmama Dettingham's famous irritability, even so many years after his death.

Despite his ramshackle example, the idea of marrying for less than love made Persephone shudder with distaste. She knew the intimacy of the marriage bed would never beckon her unless she was passionately in love, yet couldn't imagine actually being so. She would probably become the family quiz, but even that would be better than submitting to a husband she might grow to hate, just for the sake of children and an assured place in the world as a wife.

To avoid the uncomfortable jar of fear and denial in her heart at the very thought of such a husband, she watched as groups of chattering guests drifted on to the South Terrace, with its spectacular views of the distant Welsh hills one side and the rolling Herefordshire countryside the other. The vast Seaborne and Pendle clans had settled into casual groups and couples, along with Jack's friends and neighbours, and looked happy and relaxed as they exchanged news and enjoyed good company.

Sir Linstock was probably right about the Dowager deploring such simple pleasures and the fact that the company didn't hang on her every word as they clearly should. Persephone met Rowena Tremayne's laughing gaze for a rueful moment when an expected stir came from the Dowager's direction. A goodly part of the Pendle clan and Lady Henry Seaborne's own family moved to surround her ladyship in a protective huddle while she did duty as Jack's hostess once again to bid her exacting mother-in-law farewell.

When the Dowager finally departed, with as much stir as she could whip up to reassure herself of her importance, Persephone returned to the terrace with the rest of her family. The shock of a chilling shiver ran through her and made her want to hide in the crowd from malicious eyes that felt as if they watched her every move. She refused to cower like a coward inside the house, even if the warning instinct raising goose-bumps along her bare arms on this hot August day happened to be right. Trying to look as if she wasn't inspecting the crowd for a source of this odd sense of unease, she drifted about the terrace, greeting friends and acquaintances, and even forgot portents of evil as she met the infinitely complex gaze of Alexander Forthin, Earl of Calvercombe, and found him far more disturbing.

Now here was a man who would never love anyone but himself, she decided tetchily. Even if she disliked him more than any other male she had ever laid eyes on, fairness made her acknowledge he wasn't the one provoking this warning sense of danger she'd struggled with all afternoon, as if she were being sized up for her coffin by some ruthless but invisible enemy. Alex Forthin always provoked a very particular unease in her and it certainly wasn't this shivering sense of impending evil that had been nagging at the edges of her mind all afternoon.

So that was fairness out of the way and it was hard to maintain impartiality about him when the Earl constantly irritated her without any effort at all. My Lord Calvercombe would certainly be declared a deliciously brooding romantic hero by the flightier elements of the *ton*, if only they set eyes on him more often. Such breathless young ladies would be taken faint with delicious *frissons* of panic and desire on beholding his flawed male beauty, but it would take more than a few battle scars and a cynical smile to make the wretched man *her* beau ideal.

Yet she had to admit there was more to him than a wry smile and an intriguingly marred and still very handsome face. He had an ancient title, a suitably mysterious past, a vigorous masculine body that looked fit and hard with sleek muscle and that air of cool command. He somehow defied his own kind to see only the fine scarring over one side of his face and the one damaged, deep blue eye he wouldn't cover to make the world feel better when it looked at Alex Forthin.

She was a fair woman, Persephone told herself, as she wondered why he always made her itch to be an unfair and petty one instead. The man would make a model hero—or villain—for one of the Gothic novels her contemporaries loved to lose themselves in with shivering delight. He would be revolted by the idea of fictional vices or virtues inflicted on him when he had plenty of his own, so just as well she wasn't a susceptible young girl. Persephone almost smiled at the idea, but stopped herself in the nick of time, horrified he might think she was casting lures in his direction when nothing was further from her mind.

Little wonder she was suffering imaginary horrors today with spectres like him drifting about her head, she decided, with a quick frown, and avoided his sharp blue gaze with as much dignity as she could manage. She flitted to the other side of the terrace and did her duty by the cream of local society and half the nobility of the land still milling about Jack's immaculately tended lawns. As most of them were curious about the reclusive Earl of Calvercombe, there seemed to be no getting away from him today even with as much distance as possible between them.

It said much for Lord Calvercombe's love of solitude that he'd escaped the combined attention of gentry and nobility as long as he had. She was surprised he'd risked encountering so many of them today to stand as Jack's groomsman and tried to tell herself it was unfair to blame him for standing in the place where her elder brother Richard should be. If Rich hadn't sauntered out of their lives three years ago, without a single word to reassure them he was still alive from that day to this, Jack would have accepted nobody else but the cousin who had been close as a brother to him. They had raked and larked about Oxford and London until both of them grew bored, after which Rich went off on his adventures and Jack had had to learn the burdens and privileges of being a great landlord and aristocrat, and bear them with style.

Persephone might admire the reclusive Earl for doing his duty by an old friend when her brother failed to turn up and do so, but that didn't mean she was attracted to the wretched man, or even had to like him. Luckily she had more sense than to want a lone wolf focusing his formidable attention on her and shot him an exasperated glare to prove it. How unfortunate that he was looking her way and raised a quizzical eyebrow, as if there was no point blaming him for her wayward thoughts. Turning her back on the annoying creature to prove he meant nothing, she went back to charming Jack's guests.

Their conversation might have revolved round Richard Seaborne's odd disappearance, if the occasion hadn't been Jack's wedding and she hadn't been Rich's sister. Few guests dared ask where he could have got off to, but the question was in many eyes—from sharply curious to genuinely sympathetic. Despite his absence, Lady Henry Seaborne had organised this joyful celebration so flawlessly that everyone who came to be charmed by the happy couple seemed content and even Grandmama had enjoyed herself in her own peculiar fashion.

Persephone's eyes threatened to tear up if she gave herself time to think how deeply her beloved father would have enjoyed it all. When Jack's father broke his neck shortly after his Duchess died in childbed with her stillborn daughter, her own parents had moved to Ashburton New Place to help sixteen-year-old Jack grieve, and then enjoy his minority with as few cares as possible resting on his young shoulders.

To her shame, Persephone recalled being acutely jealous and sulking about the changes in her own life and the new burdens on her father and mother as Jack's guardians. She wondered if her brother Richard had felt the change even more acutely, at fifteen years of age, to her eight. No, she refused to think any more about the significant gaps in their ranks while there was so much still to be done, so she wove through the crowd as if she hadn't a care in the world and smiled and laughed until her face ached.

At last the company began to disperse to rest before dinner, or return home if they lived nearby, and Persephone was able to escape. Once she was out of sight of the house and terrace she gave a heartfelt sigh of relief and sped towards her favourite sanctuary. She was delighted for Jack and his new Duchess and exasperated with herself for feeling acutely uneasy on such a joyful day, but that didn't stop worry nagging at her like a sore tooth.

Even on this brilliantly sunny late-summer day there was the whisper of autumn in the air and she could almost scent something dangerous trying to blow in on the dusty south-west breeze along with it. She shivered despite the heat of a sunny August afternoon and felt everything was changing around her. Instinct was warning her again that an undefined evil was nipping at the safe world the Seabornes built here and it would damage them ruthlessly to achieve its purpose.

At least she managed to wave Jack and his new Duchess off with only a laughing injunction not to enjoy their tour of the English Lakes so much they forgot to come home before Christmas. Despite his eagerness to get his bride to himself at long last, Jack would never have gone if he thought aught was amiss here, so Persephone met his gaze with unclouded serenity and ordered him to go before Jessica left without him. Anyway, there was nothing tangible to worry him with, no convenient enemy to focus her unease upon.

Better if there had been, she concluded, as a tall figure blocked the entrance to her sanctuary. She needed a distraction from Jack's groomsman, she thought, as she watched Lord Calvercombe pause, eye her with mocking irony, and come on. Anyone would think he had the right to plague her with unwanted advice and the sceptical looks he kept especially for her. She wondered why the lone wolf Earl of Calvercombe couldn't leave *her* to enjoy some solitude for once.

Apparently oblivious, he sauntered towards her as if he owned Ashburton as well as an astonishing variety of old-fashioned houses inherited from his ancestors. Persephone wouldn't put it past him to exaggerate their ramshackle state to scare off visitors or eager young ladies intent on becoming his Countess. But he had come out of seclusion to support Jack, which shot down her belief that he was the most selfish man she'd ever come across.

She hoped he would leave her to it, but he loped fluidly towards her as if he had no idea he wasn't as welcome as the flowers in spring. He was the second most irritating man she knew, after her brother Richard, she decided crossly. And hadn't it been stupid of her to hope Rich would hear of Jack's wedding to Jessica Pendle and find a way to attend it? Somehow her brother would be here today, her imagination had assured her earnestly before it all began, but Jack and Jessica had been blissfully wed in Ashburton Church earlier today and no heavily disguised stranger had crept in while everyone else was distracted, only to watch furtively and leave before any noted he was there but her.

Chapter Two

Drat, hadn't she promised herself she wouldn't think about her stubborn, wild and absent brother any more today? Persephone made herself breathe deeply and balled her hands into fists as she tried to blot out that widest of gaps in the Seaborne ranks on Jack's wedding day. Idiot, she chastised herself, as she felt it more acutely as soon as it was forbidden and glared at the nearest available distraction—Alexander Forthin, Lord Calvercombe—to give her thoughts a new turn. Just her luck, Persephone concluded with disgust when the wretch returned her hostile glare with raised eyebrows and a cool stare, as if she was being fractious and difficult and unwelcoming, which of course she was.

It seemed to her he could see as well with his

damaged eye as he did with the one still as clear and piercing as a watchful predator's. His injured eye was clouded by that streak of opacity, almost as fine as the faint lines scarring that side of his face, but however much, or little, he saw with it, insolence and hauteur glared out of that blue orb as notably as from the other. Of course the man would never explain what he saw and didn't see, but he certainly hadn't got those injuries in battle. Chance didn't inflict such fine cuts day after day on a man too strong to cave and say what he'd been tortured to tell, she decided, with sneaking admiration for the dogged courage it must have cost him to hold out against the wicked torture his face revealed.

'Well, Miss Seaborne?' he asked at last, as if she must know what he meant by his satirical question and the hint of a cynical smile on his lips by sheer instinct.

'How could I be otherwise on such a happy day, your lordship?'

'Quite easily, I imagine. You will have to concede precedence to Jack's wife from now on and your mother tells me she is intent on returning to your old home as soon as they get back from their bride trip. However comfortable it is, Seaborne House can hardly rival the freedom and luxury you must have enjoyed here as Jack's cousin and honorary sister.'

With any other man she might take his statement as a mild expression of sympathy, but this was the rude and insufferable Lord Calvercombe, so there was no point hankering after such consideration from him.

'I dare say I'll amuse myself perfectly well, despite the drawbacks,' she said coolly, determined not to tell him what she thought of his barbed comments and superior smile and give him even more of an advantage. 'You must remember I am still the eldest daughter of the house, which gives me endless chances to preen on being granddaughter, niece and cousin to various Dukes of Dettingham.'

'Which will help salve your sad drop in consequence, I suppose,' he said as if consoling a sixty-year-old spinster.

Persephone remembered why she found this man so annoying—he even outdid Jack, Rich and her second brother Marcus all rolled into one irritating being—and she itched to take him down a peg or ten.

'You really have no idea how much,' she drawled as if she really was a bored society beauty. 'In a few weeks the Little Season will be on us and I can blithely skip off to town and leave others to open up a house that's been unlived in, if not unloved, these ten years and more while I selfishly enjoy the social whirl as I deserve to.'

'Being too frivolous to worry yourself over hiring suitable staff, supervising any redecoration and reupholstering found necessary, and any general interfering that will entail? Please don't mistake me for a flat, Miss Seaborne. You will jump at such a golden opportunity to impose your iron will on your world, social whirl or no.'

'Not as high as I might at the chance of reordering yours,' she snapped, and if he had any illusion she meant for the better, he was more naive than he looked.

'I have no desire to find the mouldering splendours of my ancient state rooms in the dungeons or on the nearest handy midden, so you'll certainly never be asked to spruce up any of my houses.'

'Why on earth would I want to?' she asked with as much disgust as she could fit into so few words.

'You tell me, my dear,' he replied, and suddenly he was too close for comfort and even more impossible to ignore.

'I suppose I *might* want to murder you in your bed.'

'I sleep so lightly not even a sleek little hunting cat like you could slip into my bedroom without my knowing. You would be in far more danger than I if you ever tried it, Miss Seaborne, and it wouldn't be murder I had on my mind.'

All she had intended was to make him see she disliked him, but he'd turned her words on her. She shivered with apprehension and something more disturbing as his softly muttered threat seemed to fill the air between them with false promise.

'If I were such a discerning animal, I doubt I would look to you for comfort by night, or any other time of day, Lord Calvercombe. Cats of any sort are too wise and independent to need aught from such as you,' she managed to say, as if the idea of purring under his stroking hand didn't send a dart of something hot and uncomfortable shivering through her, as if her body had plans for Alex Forthin the rest of her didn't want to know about.

He smiled blandly at her defensive words and she cursed the man for seeing too much, whatever he could physically see or not see. More civilised men would realise she wanted to be alone when they found her in this quiet garden. A true gentleman would turn and leave at first sight of her staring at the statue of her namesake at the heart of a garden intended to glorify spring and its goddess. As the garden was long past its best and waiting for next spring's abundance to be astonishingly lovely again, why would he come in here if he didn't want to speak to her? Yet now he was here, he infuriated her with his aloofness and looked as if he preferred her room to her company.

'I wouldn't believe anything you heard about

me until you know me better than you do now, Miss Seaborne,' he warned silkily.

'Why on earth would I gather gossip about you?'

'I can think of one very earthy reason,' he said softly and suddenly there was a different danger in the air from the one that had frightened her earlier.

'Then think again. I wouldn't tangle with a bitter and disillusioned man like you if you came gilded and anointed by the gods,' she told him militantly.

'I wonder if your namesake argued with Hades before he bore her off to join his dark world?' he mused with a nod at the artfully carved Persephone nearby.

It felt as if he was drily discussing classical mythology with a tutor at Oxford or Cambridge, except she was sure he'd never looked at one of them with lust in his fathomless deep-blue eyes. There was a spark of something more dangerous than mere need lurking in them to disrupt her peace of mind as well, and she struggled to free herself of a spell she was sure he hadn't wrought deliberately, since he seemed to dislike her almost as bitterly as she did him.

'Persephone's mother raged after her daughter to wrest her from her dark lord and his underworld,' she managed to argue, despite a fast-beating heart and this odd feeling of being cut off from the real world in here, with him.

She ought to turn and walk away, of course, but the reckless Seaborne spirit had got into her along with her fidgets, so she stood her ground and met look for look. Trying not to acknowledge a terrible heat had sprung to life deep inside her and was making her a stranger to herself; she reminded herself he was a stranger and would remain one if she had any sense.

'Only for half the year, remember?' he argued. 'Do you think she was content above ground and missing her lover until winter came back and she could join him? I suspect she couldn't wait to lie in his arms again while the earth rested and she could escape the constant pleas and botheration of mere mortals.'

'It's just a myth, a neat story to entertain simple people and explain away the seasons without need for deep thought,' she replied in a breathy voice so different from her usual tone that she scolded herself for being a fool and letting him unnerve her.

'Persephone was a fertility goddess, Miss Seaborne. Her cult wove deep into the fabric of ancient Greek life and held her responsible for far more than a little extra daylight and the wearing of lighter clothing for a few months.'

'I understood that Greece, being a Mediterranean land, enjoyed little change in climate between summer and winter, Lord Calvercombe,' she said in as unemotional a tone as she could manage.

He was so close it seemed almost a crime not to touch his scarred face and explore the smooth firmness of the unmarred side. He seemed to be two facets of man: one smooth and bronzed and as perfect as man could be, the other battle-scarred, cynical and deeply marked by the terror and evil he must have met. Intriguing to find out how a young Apollo like Lieutenant Forthin had become bitterly reclusive Lord Calvercombe and if much of one remained in the other, despite his hardened exterior. Also incredibly dangerous to her peace of mind—she had enough to worry about without him fascinating and infuriating her by turns.

'Tell the men of the mountains there's no winter there when they battle feet of snow, Miss Seaborne, and all their kin and cattle crowd in the house for warmth and travellers and luckier souls stay by the sea to seek what warmth there is. Winter exists everywhere, Persephone, even if sometimes it lives only in the souls of men.'

'How do you know?' she had to ask softly, sensing the real Alexander Forthin beneath all the armour and scepticism and wanting to know him better.

'I've seen it,' he said, seeming continents away, lost in a bleak place where men carved their hatred of others on the faces of their captured enemies, either to extract their secrets, or for the twisted pleasure of torture itself.

Her fingers itched to soothe those silvery, healed scars of his and assure him he wasn't at the mercy of merciless men any longer. He seemed to remember where he was and who he was talking to, and stepped away as though he could read her mind and her thoughts burned him.

'You have a way of extracting secrets that could be a potent asset, Miss Persephone Seaborne,' he accused, as if she had broken his solitude and peace after a hectic day, not the other way about.

'It might indeed, if I wanted to know them in the first place,' she said as icily as she could.

'*Touché*, my dear,' he said with a rueful smile that almost disarmed her.

'Go away, Lord Calvercombe,' she ordered coldly.

'If only I could, Miss Seaborne,' he said regretfully, 'but something evil this way comes, to paraphrase those witches in *Macbeth* you probably know all about, given your erudite education. I can't let it harm you whilst Jack is otherwise engaged.'

'Why not?' she said childishly. Though she was acutely disturbed to know he felt as if a dark blight was eating at the edges of Jack and Jessica's glowing happiness as well, she was unwilling to acknowledge she and this apology for an

Earl might have more in common than either of them desired.

'I've seen what a man's worst enemy is capable of, more often than I care to recall in India. Do you think you're immune to the evil we humans do each other purely because you're lovely, rich and well born? You could only cling to that belief for seconds after stepping on to a battlefield, unless you really are as impervious to the lives of mortals as yon stone depiction of your namesake,' he told her, as if she were the unreasonable one and he temperate as a May morning.

'No, I'm not so arrogant, whatever poor opinion you may have cobbled together from second-hand gossip and supposition. Nevertheless, I have a brother out in this wide and weary world somewhere and I fear deeply for him, Lord Calvercombe, despite my selfish, shallow and hard-hearted nature. If facing whatever threatens Rich is the only way to find out what happened to him, and why he either can't or won't come home, then I will face it. I certainly don't need your help to do so.'

'Then you really are a fool,' he said harshly,

and she couldn't resist giving a shrug, as if his opinion didn't matter.

'Not fool enough to put faith in a man who sneaks about in the dark to meet his old friend as if he doesn't trust him. Jack would welcome you joyfully if you came up his drive in rags with not a penny to your name.'

He had the grace to blush as she spoke of the hurt her cousin had felt when Lord Calvercombe didn't trust his generosity of spirit to face him by daylight. She recalled the June night when Alex Forthin met the Duke of Dettingham at midnight and they found more in the dark than either had bargained for.

Independent of each other, she and Jessica had stalked them in brilliant moonlight. Whilst Jess had met her match in the enchanted depths of the wilderness walk in full midsummer bloom on the way back that night, Persephone came away from her first sight of the man she remembered from Rich and Jack's schooldays as fabulously handsome, if arrogant, with a vague sense of disappointment. He probably would have annoyed her even if she weren't already furious that he could think any Seaborne would turn from his scars in disgust.

'I was misinformed,' he defended himself, but this wasn't the time to find endearing his gruff reluctance to admit he was wrong. 'The Duchess told me I was unfit to be seen by light of day.'

'Jessica said that? No, she would never spout such rubbish, any more than she could revile you for a hurt that was none of your fault.'

'That's debatable,' he said ruefully. Then, catching sight of her renewed fury at his dismissal of Jessica's generosity of heart, as well as her extra sensitivity to society's uneasy reaction to her own damaged leg, he held up his hand to stop her tirade. 'I mean it's a moot point that this was not my fault—' he flicked an impatient finger at his damaged face and eye '—if I'd obeyed orders and not been an arrogant young idiot, I would never have been captured in the first place. Perhaps life would then have been very different for me if I'd done as I was bid, Miss Seaborne, but you leap keenly to the defence of relatives or friends others dare to criticise, do you not?' he asked almost as if it were the first admirable quality he'd found in her and common justice made him admit it. 'It was Jack's grandmother, not his new wife, who informed me I should not bother him or the ladies of the house party he was hosting with my repulsive countenance. I can see for myself Jack and his Jessica will be likely targets for every enterprising beggar in the Marches, once word gets out how good and benevolent both are. Hopefully Jack's to-hell-with-you manner will disguise it well enough for them to keep a few guineas in their coffers to feed their family when it comes along.'

'I think it might manage that,' she couldn't help responding with a rueful smile at the idea of the fabulous wealth of the Seabornes being dissipated by her shrewd, if sometimes soft-hearted, cousin. 'And can't you see for yourself that's just the sort of thing everyone expects the Dowager Duchess to say? If you haven't realised by now that's half the reason she goes on saying such things, then you're a bigger fool than I thought you to be that night.'

'She's *your* grandmother,' he replied as if that explained a great deal.

'We all have our crosses to bear,' she said lightly.

She refused to see any of herself in the famously rude old lady, who had terrorised her husband and both her sons and their wives as Duchess in power, until her husband died, annoying her more in death than he had in life. The Dowager Duchess had retired to the mansion in Hanover Square and a lofty house near Bath she had inherited from her nabob father, rather than yield precedence in her former domain to a mere daughter-in-law, or endure living in Ashburton Dower House for the rest of her days.

Since she had decamped for her own houses, the Dowager refused to discuss events at Ashburton, or Dettingham House in Grosvenor Square, much to her sons' relief. Or at least she had until Jack was rumoured to have done away with Persephone's brother Richard. Then the Duchess had decreed it was high time Jack wed and put that silly story down as the fairy tale it was by siring direct heirs to replace Rich in the succession. Persephone wondered if it annoyed her haughty grandmama that Jack then went about it in his own unique fashion and fell head over heels in love with Jessica Pendle. She surprised herself with the conclusion the Dowager was almost smug about that very outcome, as if she'd planned it all along, and learnt to distrust the wily old tyrant more than ever.

'At least you *are* blessed with a close family,' Lord Calvercombe interrupted her reverie and the uncomfortable notion her grandmother was omnipotent after all.

'Sometimes that's more a curse than a blessing,' she said, trying not to feel sympathy for a man who was as alone as a powerful aristocrat could ever be.

'I could certainly curse your brother up hill and down dale at times.'

'If only you would find him safe and well while you did it, I might join you.'

'Yet from what you said just now, you would put yourself in danger for him if there was any prospect you might find him by doing so, or did I mistake you?'

'Yes, I would, but even when he makes me wish I was strong enough to shake him until his teeth rattled, I still love him. Richard is my big brother after all, Lord Calvercombe, and can't help being annoying at the best of times.'

'It doesn't mean you have to love him for it, Miss Seaborne. I can't recall any love ever existing to be lost between myself and my own half-brother, or between my father and his elder brother for that matter. Rivalry over an empty thing like a title, especially when the estates that goes with it are in the condition mine were after they all finished quarrelling over them, apparently transcends brotherly love so far as we Forthins are concerned.'

'Being raised in such a nest of rivals, I suppose it is little wonder you don't understand how deeply we Seabornes feel about each other, my lord. Your example proves how very lucky we are to do so, I suppose.'

'Or that you are better and more generous people than we are.'

'Far be it from me to suggest it,' she said innocently, then wondered why there was a flash of some powerful emotion in his eyes, as if he had an impulse to do something very foolish indeed.

'Perhaps it's because my cousin Annabelle

wasn't born a Forthin that I loved her so much,' he said almost as if he was reasoning something out loud, rather than confiding in her. 'And why I must find her, or at least know what happened to her, while I was too far away to help. She is the only child of my cousin Alicia and her nautical husband, Captain de Morbaraye, and she came to live at Penbryn once she was considered in need of an education, while they carried on sailing the seven seas.'

'Penbryn was your father's house?'

She was interested because his precious Annabelle disappeared at the same time as her brother Richard. This discovery had provoked his midnight visit to Ashburton—and there was nothing personal about her memories of that night, she excused herself. She wasn't intrigued by this complex and contrary man; she only needed to know Rich was alive and well, and if his search helped prove it then all well and good.

'Penbryn was my mother's home,' he replied with a puzzled shake of his head and a distant look in his eyes as if trying to recall her. 'It was probably only because she was heiress of Penbryn Castle that my father married her in the first place, since my uncle didn't have a Welsh castle and it must have annoyed him to know his younger brother would live there with his second wife. You can probably only imagine how my brother hated me for inheriting the castle when he was the eldest son. In his own opinion, as well as that of the law, he should have had everything, although he had no blood ties to my late grandfather, the Earl of Tregaron, whatsoever.'

'If the castle is yours, why did you join the army and leave it for India?'

'Have we not discussed the fact I'm a fool already, Miss Seaborne?' he asked with a wry smile that set her heart skipping all over again when it made him look boyish and almost lovable.

It should not be allowed. She could cope with him bitterly furious at life; could easily endure arrogant and aloof Lord Calvercombe with little more than an irrepressible flutter of girlish excitement; but the complex man underneath made her long for all sorts of things the Earl would never countenance.

'My grandfather tied up my inheritance until

I attained the age of five and twenty,' he went on. 'Since my legal guardian was to administer the trust and my brother became that guardian when my father died, I could not endure seeing him play ducks and drakes with my inheritance whilst I waited impatiently for that day. I decided I'd better put a few thousand miles between us, before I gave in to the urge to strangle him before he did more damage.'

'How could the other trustees sit back and let him ruin your future?'

'It was easier than arguing or taking him to law,' he said ruefully.

'Cowards,' she muttered furiously and surprised some intense feeling in his eyes, before he clamped down on it and it was gone.

Chapter Three

Lord Calvercombe shrugged dismissively.

'My brother is dead, Miss Seaborne. The law is quite strict in its refusal to prosecute dead men.'

'At least he didn't inherit the estates that go with your title,' she said consolingly, but from his moue of distaste that wasn't much of a blessing.

'There was little my predecessors hadn't already done to impoverish them. If not for the revenues from my grandfather's estates that even my brother Farrant couldn't quite dissipate during his five years of trusteeship, I would be in hock to every moneylender in Greek Street to pay the wages on my new estate, let alone redeem the mortgages.'

'How profligate of your predecessors,' she said and wondered at so much wealth and power being so spectacularly wasted.

'That's what happens when jealousy and pride come before love or duty. One branch of my family litigated against another, solely for the joy of a good argument so far as I can tell. The Seabornes have a more pragmatic approach to inheritance they would have done well to share.'

'How odd that the first male heir born in the Duke's bed becomes Duke in turn, God willing.'

'So it would seem, Miss Seaborne.'

'Your mother must have been furious at being caught in the midst of their quarrels and petty rivalry.'

'My sainted mama ran off to Naples with a poet about a year after I was born and died of typhus fever in Rome a few years after that. I doubt she cared one way or the other what became of me. She clearly couldn't abide my father, yet she left me in his so-called care when she ran off with her lover.'

He said it with such matter-of-fact composure Persephone might have wept for the lonely child he'd once been, if that child hadn't grown into the latest Earl of Calvercombe, who clearly didn't want or need anyone's tears.

'Who have you got left to argue with now then, my lord?'

'That's the beauty of it—apart from one childless and ancient great-uncle who refuses to have anything to do with me, or anyone else so far as I can tell, I am the last of my line. Apparently we Forthins have litigated one another into oblivion.'

'I suppose there's plenty of time to remedy that situation,' she said, wondering why the idea of him setting up his nursery as soon as some poor innocent girl would marry him made her shiver in the enclosed warmth of her namesake's garden on a hot, late-August afternoon.

'No, we've run our race,' he said, his expression closed and even a little bleak.

All sorts of unsuitable questions raced to spill off her tongue and he must have sensed them teetering there outrageously in an unmaidenly rush she somehow managed to contain. His austere expression gave way to the mocking grin she was beginning to loathe and any compassion she felt for the lonely man vanished like mist in the sun.

'My captors made the mistake of saving that particular form of torture as their ultimate threat, but ran out of time or chance to carry it out, Miss Seaborne. You can restrain your unladylike imagination on that front at least.'

'I have no idea what you mean,' she said distantly.

'Oh, come now, my dear. I prefer your open curiosity to the soulless propriety of most of your kind. Don't disappoint me by becoming as mealy-mouthed as any other well-born single lady I would go well out of my way to avoid.'

'If you shun such correct young women, I'd best polish up a suitably outraged expression and work harder on my simper.'

'At least then I wouldn't have to worry about you getting in the way while I search for my ward and your brother, even if it would be a crime against nature to meddle with your more strident character. I can't imagine such a properly nurtured female squawking and swooning and disapproving her way about the countryside without an entire army of villains knowing she was on her way, so if you could arrange to become one as soon as may be I shall be enormously relieved.'

Tempted to flounce away and let him believe

whatever he chose about her whilst she conducted her own investigation into Rich's disappearance, she was held back by the frustrating certainty that a lady on her own would never get far with such a quest. She was too hedged about with constraints not to need a man of power on her side to forge through or round any obstacles thrown in their way.

'Whatever your opinion of me, I'll not rest until I know where my brother is and what has made him conceal himself so completely from those of us who love him, Lord Calvercombe. Despite all Richard has done to put his family off the notion of owning up to him, let alone loving him, we stubbornly insist on doing so,' she told him with as much icy dignity as she could muster.

If not for the habit he had of watching her with cynical incredulity—as if he were about to have her stalked and captured to be displayed as a public curiosity—she might have turned and walked away, but as it was she didn't trust him not to go straight to her mother and warn her that her daughter was intent on seeking out her errant eldest son, if only to get Persephone out of his way and carry on searching for Rich and his precious cousin Annabelle unopposed.

'At least I now know I read you right in the first place,' he muttered with a formidable frown to tell her he'd hoped he was wrong, for once in his life.

'I'm a Seaborne—what else did you expect?' she said scornfully.

'Some common sense and a smidgeon of ladylike self-restraint to make you more endurable?' he asked as if he already knew that was too much to ask.

'That would be your mistake, my lord, not mine.'

'So I see, but would you truly risk your unfortunate mother losing yet another of her offspring in such a reckless fashion, Miss Seaborne? I dare say she'd miss you as much as she does her eldest son, even if I can't currently fathom any reason why she should find your absence aught but a blessing,' he replied, as if only his talent for merciless words kept him from physically shaking her.

'It's because she's our mother and a darling,

something you clearly wouldn't understand,' she declared, informing her conscience it wasn't a low blow if it got her out of here with her dignity intact.

She would *not* lose the blazing Seaborne temper she had inherited in spades from her passionate and often restless sire and make this infuriating idiot happy that he'd bested her in an argument. She didn't need his admiration or approval, but letting him brush her off as a feminine irrelevance was not an option she could allow, either.

'No, I wouldn't,' he admitted. 'Although I do have an imagination,' he went on, 'even if it's a quality you clearly lack. Being cursed with such a questionable gift, it tells me you could end up as alone and beleaguered as Rich Seaborne if you carry on pursuing this mystery. You risk losing everything you have, Miss Seaborne—your health, your safety and even your sanity—if you try to pick up their trail where I left off, and that's a risk too far for a gently bred female.'

'How would you know?' she demanded, stung

by the assumption he knew better than she did what was good for her.

'You can really ask such a question of a former soldier like me? How naive are you in this ridiculous quest to outsmart your brother and the enemy he and Annabelle must be hiding from? Rape and slavery are weapons of war, Miss Seaborne. Pray that you never have to watch the sack of a conquered city or face the wrath of a triumphant enemy.' He fell silent as appalling images flicked through his head in a kaleidoscope of horror she could only imagine.

Persephone hesitated between keeping out of whatever battles might be coming, as he wanted, and following her instincts to find her brother and help him come home at long last. At times she knew he was in trouble almost as if she were there with him, while at others his fate was obscure as a brick wall. No, even if it meant losing some elusive something she should never want and couldn't have with this man, she still had to find Rich. She shook her head sadly and met his eyes with something she feared was very close to an apology in them.

'Would you give up trying to find your cousin Annabelle if someone warned you it could be dangerous and tried to make you stop?' she asked.

'No, but I'm a man and a former soldier. If you have it in you to look beyond the end of your own nose, imagine what a bitter enemy might do to the lovely young sister of a man he's set out to break and overcome. Rich Seaborne has enemies who would love to hold a trump card like his sister in their hands, so why not show some crumbs of common sense and stay here while I track them both down for you?'

'You must do as you please, my lord,' she made herself say as distantly as she could manage when he was so close that every sense seemed on edge.

Apparently he expected her to behave like some passive maiden in a story, waiting for the prince to slay her dragons and retrieve her when he wasn't busy. She told herself this hollow feeling she was fighting wasn't caused by the disappointment that he could misread her so radically, or want her to be so different from the real Persephone Seaborne under her fine lady gloss.

'While you do exactly the same?' he asked as if he'd like to shake her.

'I must,' she said quietly.

'From where I stand, you absolutely must not.'

'Ah, but you've got your feet firmly planted in those trusty male Hessians of yours, haven't you, Lord Calvercombe? Standing in them, I doubt I'd see how anyone could go their own way without your interference, either.'

'Nonsense,' he said gruffly, with a look that told her he knew she was right, under all that temper and frustration, and it only made things worse.

Something inside her shifted, almost softened, and since that would cause all sorts of chaos if she let it, she refused to consider the notion they might do better together than they would apart. 'How is it that men always accuse us women of speaking rubbish whenever we're in danger of winning an argument?' she mused, doing her best to guard her inner thoughts and fears from him with a superior smile.

'I don't know,' he said after what looked like a mighty struggle. 'Could it be because you talk such illogical claptrap we can't help but be driven half mad? Maybe it's because when a woman risks having to admit a man could be right, she deploys every weapon she can lay hands on to avoid doing so?'

'What a very odd opinion you do have of my sex, my lord,' she said sweetly, deciding that since she wasn't going to find peace today, perhaps she ought to leave him to his instead.

'I'll admit I find many ladies empty-headed and silly, but that's mostly the fault of unequal upbringing and low expectations. In your case it can only be wilful stupidity though, since your family seems to expect a great deal of both its male and female members. Your little sisters behave themselves with grace and intelligence, after all, so I can hardly blame your parents for your own lack of manners, can I?'

'Penelope and Helen are good, dear girls, my lord. You'll not succeed in driving a wedge between us by praising them and slighting me. You clearly never had a brother or sister you would walk to the end of the world for if you had to, so I can only feel sorry for you for that lack,' she said, hoping he would see steady purpose in her eyes when they met his, rather than a fear they were both up against a force hellbent on making sure his family never set eyes on Rich again this side of the grave.

'It won't do Rich a mite of good if you sacrifice your peace of mind, personal safety and reputation and achieve nothing. Can you imagine how he would feel if he knew you were pitting your wits against the enemy he disappeared in order to avoid?' he asked, running his hands through his hair, making it curl wildly. He turned away from her to stride up and down the path as if it were the only way to stop himself laying hands on her and physically shaking her this time.

'It may surprise you, but, yes, I can see that,' she told him quietly.

'And it makes no difference? You're bound and determined to go your own way, whatever the cost to the rest of us might be.'

'It will cost you nothing, my lord. You clearly don't like me and will not care a snap of your fingers what happens to me.'

Somehow that stopped him in his wolf-like pacing and he turned to glare back at her as if she'd accused him of some terrible crime. 'I might not like you, woman, but that doesn't mean I can't worry about you—donkey stubborn and as wilful as a three-month-old puppy as you clearly are. You need someone by who isn't blinded by charm and physical perfection to the heart of a vixen that lies underneath it all.'

'I could be just like you, then,' she said unsympathetically, trying to fight a ridiculous feeling inside her that something astonishingly promising had just fallen empty at her feet like a deflated hot air balloon.

'Hah!' he raged on, resuming his pacing again, except now it was more of a wild-cat lope than a wolfish fury as he worked himself up about her shortcomings instead of Rich's plight. 'We're not in the least alike, you and I, not in the least similar in any way,' he accused as he kicked a skewed edging tile, then had to pretend it didn't hurt as it proved to be a lot more fixed in place than it looked.

'Well,' she said sarcastically and folded her arms to stop herself going up to him and holding on to halt his frustrated activity, 'we certainly have a foul temper in common, if nothing else.'

'I've enough to make me foul tempered; you could infuriate a whole regiment without even pausing for breath.'

'No, I couldn't,' she argued for the sake of arguing as much as to prove a point now. 'Even I can't shout loudly enough to make that many bone-headed, born-stupid, stubborn-as-rock men hear me all at once.'

'Ah, but they'd hush long enough to listen to the likes of you, Persephone,' he told her, as if saying her name softly like that ought to cancel out his unflattering opinion of her up until now.

'Why?' she demanded, uncrossing her arms so she could fist her hands and pretend he was wrong.

'Because you're as lovely as half-a-dozen goddesses put together,' he told her with a wry grin that acknowledged it was a silly thing to say and almost made her long to melt into the sort of weak-kneed female he obviously admired.

'With a dozen fists to hit you with and as many feet to kick you, I think I could support being that lovely,' she said and tried not to laugh at the very idea of it.

'You'd fall over,' he informed her solemnly. Oh, the temptation of him as he stood there, suddenly as light-hearted and heartbreakingly handsome as Mother Nature had intended him to be.

'True, but at least I'd do it happily, knowing you were sure to be hurting far more than I was,' she said, determined not to be charmed into a quieter, more accepting frame of mind.

'I bet you were a devilish little girl, ready to lash out at anyone who told you not to do something merely because you were born a girl,' he said reflectively.

If he but knew it, he was in danger of succeeding by using his acute mind to read her true character where all his raging and charming and unreasonableness had failed to persuade her. Mainly because he was right, she told herself. His knowing all her frustrations at being born a girl in a world dominated by men, when every time they met they quarrelled and struck sparks off each other, felt oddly disarming.

'Please don't think me so changed I won't do

it again, Lord Calvercombe,' she told him rather half-heartedly.

'Yet it would have been such a shame if you had been born one of us unsatisfactory males instead of a goddess-like female, Miss Seaborne, for then I would be denied the sheer pleasure of looking at you,' he told her as if it were no more than passing the time of day.

'I'm not a cold collection of limbs and good enough features to be gawped at like yonder statue, my lord. I am a human being with all the faults and failures and hopes and dreams we earthly creatures are subject to.'

'But it doesn't hurt the rest of us fallible beings that you're a sheer pleasure to look upon, Miss Persephone Seaborne,' he informed her quietly and strode dangerously close again, to look down at her as if he'd find out all the secrets of her inner soul she'd managed to bury deep inside.

'And if I was to be as rude and bold as you are, I'd have to admit you're no hardship to behold yourself, Alexander Forthin,' she countered, meeting his disconcerting gaze as if it were normal for a lady to compliment a gentleman.

For a moment he looked shocked, then almost flattered, before his insecurity about his scarred face and marred eye surfaced and he merely looked offended—as if she were mocking him for being less handsome, at least in his own eyes, than he'd been once upon a time.

'I do remember you from before, you know,' she said softly and, as he appeared to want to step back, she took a step nearer so she could meet his eyes to show him she meant what she said. 'You were handsome and arrogant and proud as sin back then, when Rich and Jack left Eton for Oxford and you got your commission and a scarlet coat to dazzle schoolgirls like me out of the few wits I had left me. To my mind you're a great deal better looking now than you were back then and considerably less vain.'

'Then you're still dazzled?' he asked as if that was all that mattered to him in her shaming admission that she'd once cherished a fiery and fearsome crush for him, even though she'd only set eyes on him once or twice when she was supposed to be minding her lessons.

'I'm no longer a schoolgirl who can be easily enchanted by a devil-may-care manner and a pair of knowing blue eyes, Lord Calvercombe,' she claimed primly, but inside she wasn't quite so sure.

'If you first set eyes on me when I was still a boy straight out of school, I doubt they were as knowing as either of us thought at the time,' he admitted and disarmed her all over again.

'Whatever you knew, it was a lot more than I did,' she admitted. Since he was about the same age as Jack and therefore eight or so years older than herself, that was a safe enough bet at least.

'Not that you would ever have admitted it.'

'No, not then,' she acknowledged.

'Or now,' he said flatly, and since she'd dug that trap for herself, she supposed she couldn't blame him for using it.

'Nine or ten years have gone past since we first set eyes on each other and I've learnt a lot in the meantime, Lord Calvercombe.'

'Then you're prepared to rashly lay claim to

having become a woman of the world since then, are you, Persephone? I suppose you are an experienced female with three, maybe even four Seasons at your back by now and still no husband to make them into a triumph,' he observed, and she wasn't going to admit the cutting edge of that conclusion, coming from him instead of her few known and familiar enemies among the *ton* as it did.

She knew he was using temper to set her at a distance, but it hurt her far more acutely than it should. He'd slyly trailed the outrageous possibility she might have become worldlier than a respectable young lady should be, as well as reminding her the world might one day mock her looks and birth and comfortable marriage portion if she refused to wed. He deserved to have his face slapped before she flounced away, but she wouldn't give him the satisfaction.

'Only three Seasons actually, my lord, and that really doesn't mean I'm either desperate for a lover or considered to be at my last prayers quite yet. I happen to be very particular about the man I might one day decide to marry.'

'After you've had your pick of the bachelors to flirt and test and measure against some impossible ideal of perfection, I suppose? Please don't tell me how he must be, let me guess. The poor man will have to be rich if he's to afford you,' he said as if about to count off on his fingers all the things she must demand in a husband, when all she really wanted was to love passionately and be loved in return one day or not wed at all. 'Then there's all that ducal blood flowing proud in your veins to measure up to. I doubt some ancient old noble will do for such a lovely and fastidious young lady as you, either, so he must be smoothly god-like and haughty as a Roman senator with all except his lady. He'd better be a fine horseman, or strive to become one, since you're reputed to possess a fine seat and a good eye for a horse that he'd do well to match. All in all, the man must be a paragon, don't you think? Little wonder it's taking you so long to select the poor fellow; such a pattern card of perfection can exist only once in a generation.'

'Even more of a wonder if he actually exists at all. What right have you to think you know me so well that all my most private thoughts are an open book to you, Lord Calvercombe? I'd sooner stay a maid all my life than go about the business of finding a husband in such a cynical and chilly fashion and, if that's the best you can let yourself think of me, I'll thank you to avoid me in future for our mutual comfort.'

'It would certainly help mine,' she thought she heard him murmur as if she made him acutely uneasy somehow by breathing the same air as him.

'Consider it done,' she declared airily and would have strolled away from him as if nothing about him interested her, if he'd let her.

'If only I could,' he rasped as he grasped her arm and his touch burned through her like wildfire and froze her in her tracks.

'Take your hands off me,' she hissed with all the passion she could muster, since the very air seemed to hum with a warning that he was now far too close.

'Gladly, if only I could believe you will dutifully return to your mother's side and leave me to find Richard Seaborne and my ward.'

'Do you think Mama would want me to do that

if there's a chance we can find Rich and have him back here in his true home once more? Or do you assume she doesn't miss him every minute of every day? I suppose you see the serene face she shows the world and imagine Lady Henry Seaborne either doesn't feel deeply, or knows very little of the world beyond the safe boundaries of the Seaborne estates. My mother longs desperately for Rich every moment of every day he's away, Lord Calvercombe, as she would for any of her children should they disappear. My big brother is her first child, the one she and my father made in the heat of first love and he will always be special to her. And, no, before you imply it, I'm not jealous of the strong bond that exists between them.'

'You really do have a low opinion of me, don't you?' he asked with a look that seemed to hint he was hurt by such a harsh summary of his possible thoughts.

'I merely reflect what I see in your eyes when you look at me, my lord.'

'Then you see something I didn't put there,' he responded rather bitterly, as if that blurred line of scarring troubled him far more than his arrogant manner and to-the-devil-with-you glare allowed for.

'Can you blame me when you've done nothing but snap at me since we first met again by moonlight that first farcical night you came to Ashburton?'

He looked down at her as if he'd almost forgotten she was there that night and didn't relish the reminder. 'You're certainly a thorn in my flesh, Miss Seaborne, but I don't suppose you mind if I consider you irritating and prickly, since you have done nothing but abuse and rebuke *me* from that moment to this.'

'Of course I have—you manhandled me like a sack of potatoes.'

'And that still rankles with you? What a veritable goddess you are, Miss Seaborne, to expect reverent awe from the opposite sex at all times of the day and night, however ungoddess-like your own behaviour might be at the time.'

'Enough, my lord, I've had more than enough of your illogical arguments and irrational prejudice against my sex. I'm going to find my family now and no doubt I shall see you at dinner, whether I wish to do so or not,' she said ungraciously and, tugging her arm from his slackened grasp, marched off like an offended queen.

Chapter Four

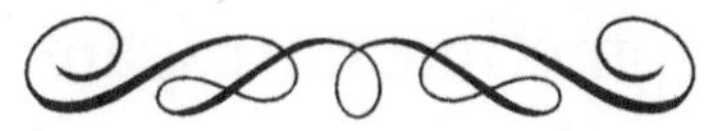

'Well, that certainly told me,' Alex Forthin muttered ruefully.

Of course he recalled coming here one moonlit night in June to vent his wrath on Jack Seaborne, because Jack's errant cousin had spirited Cousin Annabelle away so effectively. Back then he'd been so full of wild plans to avenge himself on Richard Seaborne and rescue his vulnerable young cousin that it had never occurred to him that she had wanted to disappear and Rich, gallant fool that he was, insisted on going, too.

Now he knew it was an idea born of pain and suffering in a war that brought little glory to either side—a ridiculous scheme he'd thought up to try to redeem the aching darkness in his own soul. He had needed Annabelle's gift for loving the unlovable too much to consider why she had gone and what looking for her might stir up, but facing Jack across that would-be Grecian temple down by the lake had jarred him into reality somehow. Jack was so completely his old complex and sometimes arrogant self that Alex realised he was the one who had changed into someone he didn't want to know.

He'd let the fanatics who had tortured him to the edge of madness cloud his thoughts and colour his actions. His cousin's absence had taken any gloss there might have been off a homecoming only a few old servants were left to rejoice in, but he should have realised Rich wouldn't run off with an innocent like Annabelle. Clearly there had been a pressing reason for them to disappear and it remained urgent enough to keep them away three years on. How could he have wasted so much time suspecting his friends when he could have been looking for real enemies all along?

His cousin Annabelle had an independent spirit, as well as a truly loving nature and sunny optimism she must have got from the other side of the family. She would never have stayed with

Rich for so long unless she truly wanted to and there was the crux of another conundrum. If Rich knew how Alex lusted after Persephone, he might suspect him of wanting to avenge himself on Rich through her for carrying off his own innocent young cousin. Truth to tell, he would hide at Penbryn himself and try to forget the beautiful virago existed if he could, but he must stay here and risk what little peace of mind he had to make sure she didn't risk her lovely neck on some harebrained scheme to track down the missing pair.

At least being armed against a vain hope she would come of her own accord would guard him against wanting her so badly he'd risk asking her to go with him. He was a fool like all the other idiots who desired the unobtainable Miss Seaborne and pined for only a sight of her across a crowded room. After today she would avoid him like a noxious disease, which might keep her safe and dutifully by Lady Henry Seaborne's side for the next few weeks, while Jack was away and Alex was busy searching the length and breadth of Britain for Belle and Richard without their enemies noticing he was doing it.

Something told him Miss Seaborne was more likely to dash off on some reckless adventure—giving him three people to rescue instead of only two—if he didn't fool her into playing the docile young lady somehow. He shuddered at what trouble she might bring on herself if he didn't divert her and decided he couldn't ride off into tomorrow's sunrise without a backward glance at the Seaborne lair and all those supposedly safe inside it. Wondering how to keep an eye on a single lady whilst she decided which way to jump into the lion's den, he paced the quiet garden. Only once did he catch himself wondering how such a sanctuary could be created at his Welsh home for a lady of his to roam, so that she might stay and make Penbryn Castle and his other rundown homes less spartan.

Deuce take it, he wasn't going to have a lady. Even before he set foot on home soil again, he'd decided the Forthin name would die with him. It was a cursed line—a supposed family where hate and greed and jealousy stood in for the love, generosity and solidarity that seemed to bind the Seaborne clan together. Belle would inherit everything he had to leave. And when he found he'd become Lord Calvercombe, it seemed the final joke of fate to come home and find his cousin gone and no clue to her whereabouts. So any hope he still had for the future was wiped out.

He didn't dare let himself think her truly lost—the one hope of redemption for his whole rotten clan. So he had to find her, rather than succumb to the ridiculous hope that he might build a life on shaky foundations with some spoilt society lady and see it crash round his ears when she laughed in his marred face.

'Wherever have you been, Per?' Miss Helen Seaborne demanded a little too loudly as Persephone did her best to slip into the dwindling crowd as if she'd never been away.

Silently cursing little sisters and their over-eager tongues, Persephone shrugged with would-be carelessness. 'I went for a walk in the gardens to clear my head, sister dear. Since it's been a long and exciting day, I needed a little peace to gather my senses. You dare to call me Per again and I'll retaliate in kind, Hel,' she added in a fierce aside meant for her sister's ears only.

'Neither of you will do any such thing,' Lady Henry informed her daughters with a look neither of them quite managed to meet. 'This is still Jack and Jessica's special day and I won't have you two arguing like fishwives just because they can't hear you at the moment.'

'They can't hear anyone but each other when they're together nowadays,' Penelope Seaborne put in with obvious disgust at such mutually obsessed lovers.

'Which is exactly how it should be when two people love each other as deeply as those two clearly do,' her mother said with an understanding smile at her youngest daughter's moue of distaste. 'One day you will understand, my love,' she said and laughed when Penelope gave a disgusted shudder and fervently declared,

'Never!'

'Well, I think they're very lucky and I wish I might love any man half as much as Jess does our cousin, even if I can't quite understand why anyone should,' fifteen-year-old Helen declared, halfway between the romance of being almost grown up and the brutal frankness of nine-year-old Penelope.

'What, love a man, or love Jack specifically?' Persephone asked, reluctantly intrigued by the workings of her little sisters' minds and the changes maturity was threatening before she felt prepared for any of them to move on.

'Jack, of course. He's all very well and I know he's a Duke and fabulously rich and not particularly ugly, but he's only Jack when all's said and done.'

'True,' Persephone agreed seriously enough, 'but Jessica has known him for ever and still thinks he put the stars in the sky, so I suppose love must be blind.'

'Wait until you're in love, my dearest, then you can tell me how it feels to trust a man to do so for you,' their mother advised, too seriously for Persephone.

A moment later she wondered why his lordship the Earl of Calvercombe had chosen to emerge from the spring garden at the worst moment possible and felt her mother's eyes on her when she refused to meet his gaze or Lady Henry Seaborne's.

'I doubt I shall ever love a man so completely,' Persephone argued as she squirmed at the very notion of ever loving such an aloof and cynical one.

'I don't think a woman can sensibly consider herself immune to such folly until she's cold in her grave, my love,' Lady Henry objected mildly enough, but her eyes dwelt thoughtfully on Lord Calvercombe while she did so.

The shock of seeing her wise, sensible and almost cynical best friend tumble fathoms deep under Jack's rakish spell had been bad enough, Persephone decided, but he'd made bad worse by stumbling so totally into love with Jess it sometimes seemed as if he could scarcely string two sensible words together for enchantment. The whole mad business had shaken Persephone's confidence in her own cool judgement and well-guarded heart. If Jack and Jessica could fall so comprehensively in love with each other, nobody was safe from the malady.

Well, almost nobody. She really couldn't imagine the Dowager Duchess of Dettingham falling in love, even in her salad days. The unlikelihood of her grandmother considering the world well lost for love made Persephone smile ruefully, then curse her abstraction when she realised she was beaming idiotically at the Earl of Calvercombe as if he were the light of her life. Berating herself for a fool, she frowned fiercely at him, then felt a prickle of what must be fear run up her spine when he seemed to read her confused thoughts and flashed a crooked smile of understanding at her. He was far too dangerous to exchange perceptive glances with and she told herself to look away when there was any danger of him looking back at her from now on.

The chambermaids of all the inns from here to London who'd been gifted one of Lord Calvercombe's devil-as-angel smiles must spend their working days yearning for him to come by and lavish another on them. She told herself she was made of far stronger stuff and tried not to wonder if his lordship currently kept a mistress to charm and seduce and puzzle. No point wondering how it felt for the unfortunate female to have such intense masculine attention concentrated solely on her.

He was such a self-contained puzzle of a man the poor woman was probably left to yearn and yawn the days away until he felt the need of her so strongly he would lavish all his passion and attention on her once more, for as long as she could hold his restless attention. Then he would be off back to his splendid isolation until next time. Glad she would never need to charm, caress and fawn on a man to know there would be food on the table or clothes to render her decent, she shot the object of her half-furious speculations what she hoped was a coldly quelling look.

On the hill above Ashburton New Place the observer snapped his telescope back into its case and let his fist tighten into betraying fury. He was alone up here, after all, and could afford to reveal his feelings for once. The original baron who built Ashbow Castle on this patch of high ground would despise the Seabornes as fools for letting themselves be overlooked like this, but the watcher knew it was a deliberate statement of power. The Tudor pirate who had made his fortune at sea under Good Queen Bess's flag, if not exactly at her direct order, sited his new mansion on the side of the valley precisely because nobody dared challenge him at the heart of his ill-gotten estates. The whole breed of Seabornes were so arrogant they considered themselves beyond the reach of their enemies, but he was here to prove them wrong.

Up here on the defensible ground others had fought over for generations before the Seabornes claimed it *he* seemed face to face with failure. A vantage point was useless when the enemy wouldn't emerge from hiding to give battle. He longed for the lawless days when a rival lord and his army could camp up here while they destroyed the arrogant Seabornes to every last man.

Taking a deep breath to steady himself, to fight off a reckless, cleansing fury at the thought of all he wanted being ripped away from him, he slunk back into the cover of the trees. Forcing himself to watch the nauseating spectacle of the Seabornes joyously *en fête* for so long had all been for nothing, he concluded bitterly. Richard Seaborne had stayed away from his cousin's nuptials and outfoxed him once again. Overcoming the need to lash out at something to relieve his frustration, he forced a mask of calm on to his face and strolled along as if he hadn't a care in the world. Experience had taught him that the man who looked as if he didn't care if he was seen or not was less noticeable than the one slinking along furtively with a guilty look.

It was time to take the fight to the enemy, he decided as he went. Three years waiting for Richard Seaborne to show his hand was more than enough patience for any man. Time to see how the elusive devil felt when everything he valued was under threat and an enemy held *his* fate in the palm of his hand.

Later that day Mr Marcus Seaborne was expecting to be on his way to heaven in the arms of his mistress, keen to shake the dust of Ashburton off his feet and get to that lovely armful as fast as a good horse would take him. He was three and twenty, vigorous, healthy and generally held to be a handsome, if currently rather unsteady, young gentleman with the world at his feet. He was almost as happy as he knew the bridegroom would be on this fine August evening, as he rode away from Ashburton with a picture of the beauty he was intending to bed tonight in his head.

His frivolous and sweetly rounded Clarice was no Jessica Pendle, of course. There was only one Jess, and if not for the fact she had grown up with him and he saw her as another sister, he might feel a twinge of jealousy for all she and his Cousin Jack had tonight. As it was, he blessed them both and whistled softly between his teeth as he rode towards his current love with the certainty he had plenty of time to find one to last for ever, when he was creeping up on thirty like poor Jack and called upon to take life seriously.

He wasn't as intense about anything as his brother Rich either and growing up with the ducal succession at two removes hadn't felt like a hardship to him, but he still felt smug about the fact Jack clearly couldn't keep his eyes, or his hands, off his new wife. Soon there would be a pack of little Seabornes crowding the Ashburton nurseries and when he got to that solemn age himself there would be no need to search for his Mrs Seaborne with the driven urgency Jack had been pushed into earlier this summer. Marcus was free—not as free as he would be if Rich had stayed home and done his duty as well, he recalled with a frown, but free enough. With luck, Rich would come back now Jack was wed and would take his own responsibilities off his little brother's shoulders.

None of them seemed to matter when lovely Clarice, with her inviting smile and tightly luscious curves, was waiting for him in the nearest town she considered remotely civilised. He dwelt on happy memories of her dancer's body and the eager glow in her sloe-dark eyes when she slanted one of her come-and-get-me looks his way, and felt so on fire with desire he tightened his knees and urged his grey into a smooth canter and then a downright gallop. At this time of year daylight lingered long enough in the sky to get a lover to his lady before pitch dark, he decided with a cocky grin, as he calculated how much riding he had to do before sunset finally thickened into darkness.

'Givage, wherever are you off to in such a mighty hurry?' Persephone asked the morning after Jack's wedding when she saw the usually dignified steward close to running towards her towards the main staircase.

'Let me pass, Miss Persephone, I must speak with Lady Henry.'

'My mother is very tired after the wedding and hasn't left her bedchamber,' she informed him briskly, refusing to step aside so he could hurry upstairs and worry her mother with some crisis Persephone could deal with just as well.

'Then I really don't know what to do,' Givage said despairingly and Persephone's heart began to thump with fear as she took in the white line about the man's mouth and the look of despair in his eyes.

'About what precisely?' she asked abruptly.

'This,' he replied, holding out what should have been a jaunty beaver hat.

She stifled a horrified gasp as she took in the

battered state of her second brother's favourite headgear. It looked disturbingly as if someone had taken a cudgel to it whilst it was still on his head, or perhaps he'd taken a headlong tumble off his horse. That was a thought she hastily decided to ignore, since she doubted even her brother's hard head could survive such a bruising fall without desperate injuries.

'Where did you find it?'

'Well, it was under the Three Sisters' Oak first thing this morning. Joe Brandt brought it to me, since he didn't know if her ladyship was aware Mr Marcus had left Ashburton after dinner last night and didn't want to make bad worse, so to speak.'

'Did he indeed?' Persephone asked disapprovingly, having a very good idea why her brother would sneak off when the company were occupied with discussing the wedding and the business of everyday life Marcus always did his best to avoid.

'Mr Marcus asked the stable boy who saddled his horse to keep the news of his departure to himself as long as he could.'

'I dare say he would have done,' she said absently, wondering if the opera dancer she suspected he had waiting for him nearby had any idea where he was now.

'Joe said the hat was placed on the ground with this underneath it, Miss Persephone. Not even Mr Marcus would do such a thing as a prank,' Givage said and delved in his waistcoat pocket to produce a heavy signet ring for her inspection.

Persephone looked at the distinctive stone with a fantastic sea creature resting on the waves engraved into its surface and gasped. Halfway between affectation and joke, with its pun on a sea-borne monster, it was her late father's signet ring. Richard had reluctantly slipped it on his own finger after Lord Henry Seaborne's funeral and that was the last time she had seen him or her father's ring. Knowing a fine manor house and large estate were now his, Rich had ridden away from them all that day as if pursued by devils. Intent on going his own way as usual, Persephone reflected bitterly now, and had succeeded so well this was the first sign of him she'd seen from that day to this.

'Please don't tell my mother,' she asked, her gaze hard on her old friend as she silently pleaded not to add to Lady Henry's burdens.

'How can I not?' the ageing steward asked.

'It will break her,' Persephone said bleakly. 'She's borne enough since my father died and Richard went missing. She must not know that both her sons could be in danger until we're certain this isn't a mare's nest.'

'We can't pretend nothing has occurred, Miss Persephone. Not when he could be in the power of some shameless rogue.'

'Let me think about it properly before we make any over-hasty decisions,' Persephone insisted and held out her hand for the hat and ring, her gaze steady on her old friend's until he gave a faint shrug and passed both into her keeping.

She sighed in what should have been relief, but felt the heavy burden of what could be both her brothers' safety on her shoulders. 'Please speak to Joe and the stable lad, Givage. I'm sure you told them to be silent until you had spoken to Mama, but they must stay so until we know for certain what's to do.'

'I'll do it, Miss Perry, but we can't sit and do nothing about this for very long,' he cautioned, slipping back into that childhood nickname.

'We won't have to, but someone clearly wants us to panic and I intend to plan our response rationally, if only to spite him.'

'Please don't delay until there's no hope of us finding a trace of Master Marcus though, will you, Miss Perry?'

'I hope I have more Seaborne blood in my veins than that, Givage,' she said and let her steady gaze hold his so he would see how serious she was.

Her instincts had been proved right, Persephone reflected without satisfaction as she resorted to Jack's bookroom to prowl, as he was on his way to the Lakes with his new Duchess. If only she'd raised the alarm yesterday, this calamity might have been prevented. Impatient with herself for dwelling on yesterday, which couldn't be altered, she felt panic threaten after all. Perhaps the magistrates should be informed and their constables, maybe even the Bow Street Runners, set on the trail of Marcus and his abductor? She shuddered at the idea of whoever had left her father's ring and Marcus's hat for them find. It spoke of a cold and calculating mind to leave objects the family would know were removed against their owners' will and imply a threat she couldn't let herself explore completely just now.

'What else can you tell me?' she asked those objects.

She set them on Jack's desk to puzzle over and stopped pacing at last, still with the long skirts of her riding dress draped over her arm to free her feet for action.

Chapter Five

'What's to do?' an irritated male voice demanded before she could say anything else to a pair of inanimate objects and seem even more of a fool.

'What the devil are you doing in here?' she asked, glaring at Alexander Forthin for interrupting her thoughts at such a crucial time.

'I was invited, remember?' he replied brusquely and she recalled that Jack had given his groomsman the run of his own apartments for the duration of his stay a little too late.

Jack wouldn't need them himself after the wedding, so he had invited Lord Calvercombe to use them and pretend he was alone in his Welsh eyrie, if that made him more resigned to leaving it. She knew her cousin was sensitive to his friend's desire to avoid the eyes of the curious whenever possible. Jack didn't usually pander to the foibles of his acquaintance, but she grudgingly accepted that his lordship's aversion to being stared at or pitied went deeper than a mere whim.

'So you were,' she agreed absently and wished he would go away so she could think without him looming over her like some battle-scarred Roman general.

'Are you going to tell me what's happened?' he demanded as if he'd taken on Jack's authority along with his private rooms.

'Why do you think anything has?' she challenged irritably.

'How could I not? First Jack's head groom's son rode hell for leather to the steward's house, then his steward ran into the house on some urgent business that couldn't wait,' he replied, refusing to pretend it wasn't his business as a more accommodating guest might.

'Well, I'm busy,' she excused her ill manners brusquely.

She didn't have time or inclination to tread on eggshells round her cousin's most prickly and disturbing guest this morning, she decided impatiently, squashing an impulse to confide the whole terrifying story. He raised his eyebrows at her bunched skirts and the riding boots revealed in what she supposed was an unladylike fashion. But she refused to let her long skirts drop and risk tangling her feet in them just to reassure him she was a proper young lady.

'If you're going to pace Jack's bookroom and wring your hands, I suggest you change out of your habit before you trip,' he said as if she were a slow-top.

'And I suggest you play the gentleman for once and leave,' she snapped.

'Not until you've told me what's to do,' he said, leaning on Jack's desk as if he had all day set aside.

'It's none of your business. And why should you care? You thought Jack was involved in abducting your precious cousin when you came here so furtively in June, didn't you? I really don't care what you think of the rest of us, my lord, but Jack is far too honourable to kidnap or imprison any lady against her will.'

'A little brutal and lacking finesse, but it's a fair question, I suppose,' he allowed as if talking to himself.

'Thank you. So what is the answer?'

'My family is caught up with yours, somehow, and I know I was mistaken,' he conceded gruffly.

'I'm sure Jack would be deeply gratified to hear it.'

'He already has heard it, and a lot more gracious about forgiving me he was, too. So are you finally going to tell me what's to do, Miss Seaborne? Time is clearly a-wasting and you must be keeping some sort of crisis from your mother, since nobody is rushing about in response to Brandt's news and Givage's urgent mission to consult whoever is in charge in Jack's absence.'

'Good of you to remind me,' she said impatiently, so wanting to pace again she wondered about punching him in his stonewall of a chest, since he wouldn't get out of the way and leave her be, but decided she would end up hurting only herself.

'So what's occurred, then? If you knew what

to do about whatever it is, you would be out and busy doing it by now.'

'How do you know I'm not? One wrong step could ruin everything,' she added, feeling the weight of her dilemma lie heavy on her shoulders once again.

'Tell me?' he urged softly, offering her his strength and experience of dealing with impossible situations and allowing her to glimpse the real man behind the façade of cynical indifference for once.

He was sure to snatch the whole business out of her hands if she did as he asked and confided the whole sorry tale though, wasn't he? Wondering if that wouldn't be a very good thing, she reminded herself he had his own very strong motives in all this. He might chase after Rich and his cousin rather than helping to find Marcus if she revealed the whole story, but Givage or Joe Brandt would soon tell him about Rich's ring if she left that bit out. He was a warrior, even if he sometimes looked as if he hated himself for it; it was his job to take on impossible odds and win.

'Why on earth would I do that?' she said to gain more time to think.

'Because I have been a reconnaissance officer and will find out anyway. It will be much simpler if you save us both time and tell me the truth to start with.'

'It's not only my story.'

'Ah, so your family are tangled up in some new escapade, are they?' he asked cynically. And that was exactly why she hadn't tumbled this affair into his lap and gone off to lie to her mother while he dealt with it.

'No, my family have become entangled in *your* business, my lord. Why else should whoever is behind my elder brother's disappearance endanger Marcus? He was content to let Rich and your cousin lie until you began asking questions.'

'So whatever has happened to young Marcus is my fault as far as you are concerned?' he asked incredulously.

'How do you know anything happened to him?' she demanded irrationally, resuming her pacing as frustration and anxiety demanded an outlet.

'Because you just told me so and from the state

of that questionable piece of headgear he insists on wearing when your august grandparent is not here to forbid it. The lad would not be willingly parted from his supposedly dashing and expensive favourite hat, so why not tell me the whole tale and see what two heads can make of it instead of only one, Miss Seaborne?'

'I don't know more than half of it,' she informed him as she did her best to unclench the fisted hands that seemed to have a will of their own this morning. 'I have no idea who has kidnapped my little brother, but he left us a very strong hint that his true interest is in finding Rich. How can I be sure you won't rush off after my elder brother instead of finding Marcus, who is certainly being held against his will?'

'Enough!' he snapped. He stood in front of her and had the temerity to physically stop her agitated pacing by grasping her wrist in his strong, supple fingers.

'More than enough,' she raged at him. 'How dare you take such liberties with me, Lord Calvercombe?'

'Because this shilly-shallying only helps our

mutual enemy. Gather your wits and tell me about Marcus's disappearance, before all traces disappear.'

Giving in to her baser side and doing her best to thump or kick him would cause an even more undignified struggle while he did his best to restrain her without hurting her.

'Oh, very well,' she agreed and felt contrarily bereft as he sighed and let her go, so he could stand a little further off and watch her warily.

'Young Brandt and Givage believe your second brother has met with foul play of some sort, don't they?' he prompted gently and she knew she was more shaken than she'd realised when tears threatened.

'Marcus keeps his lady-love somewhere close by. Please don't expect me to pretend ignorance of such dealings when his life is at risk. I refuse to play the innocent whilst my brother is in such danger.'

'Perish the thought,' he muttered, then gave her a bland, blank look that set her at a distance and impatiently ordered her to get on with it.

'I could easily learn to hate you, my lord,' she

told him, but finally decided to trust him with the whole story all the same. 'Even so, you're right and at least you have the experience to help me find him. Joe discovered Marcus's favourite hat placed on the protruding roots of the forked oak tree you probably noticed in the outer reaches of the park. Whoever took my brother put it where it could be seen by anyone who passed that way. As well that it was not on the direct route the staff who live out usually take, so Joe found it and not one of the maids or gardeners, otherwise the tale would have gone the rounds before any of us knew about it.'

'Why are you so convinced Rich is tangled up in the affair? Perhaps a poacher found the hat and considered it the only way to draw attention to Marcus Seaborne's plight without betraying who he was and what he'd been up to.'

'This was placed very deliberately under Marcus's hat,' she finally admitted, holding out the heavy, old-fashioned ring for his inspection.

'Theatrical of whoever is behind this, since it clearly has great value and might easily have been purloined by whoever found it instead of being brought to you. He was lucky it worked, but our enemy shows himself up as being a little less clever than he thinks. By using such a grand gesture to draw your family into finding Rich to get Marcus back, he risked his whole enterprise,' he said, weighing the expensive ring in his hand as he eyed it sceptically.

'Maybe so, but it has served his purpose very well so far as I'm concerned,' she agreed with a shudder. 'It was my father's ring and the last time any of us saw it was on the day my brother Richard rode away from Seaborne House after our father's funeral. Papa always wore it—I think it was some sort of private joke between him and my mother.'

'I can see how it would be,' he said absently, his attention obviously more on the significance of the ring than its sentimental value to Lord Henry Seaborne's wife and family. 'Could Rich have sold it or pawned it, do you suppose?' he asked at last and she bit back an urge to ask if he'd known her brother at all during their school-days and wild youth.

'Not unless his life depended on obtaining the money.'

'Or that of someone he cared very deeply about?' he mused aloud. Perhaps he knew Rich after all.

'Maybe,' she said and wondered if he was right about Rich running off with his precious cousin Annabelle.

If he truly loved the girl, Rich might even part with this most tangible reminder of their father for her sake. Perhaps they needed money to make good their escape from their enemy. If this latest scheme of his was an indication of how ruthlessly he wanted to track them down, maybe Rich and Annabelle had been wise to vanish so completely.

'It's very distinctive and, if they truly wanted to disappear, I suppose they would have to be utterly ruthless in ridding themselves of anything so traceable.'

'Aye, and if they couldn't rely on Rich's acres or private fortune, they would realise as many assets as possible before they went.'

'Maybe, although Jack did succeed in getting Rich's bankers to reveal he withdrew an entire quarter's rents from his account before visiting his lawyers to sign over control of all his property and income to Jack until further notice.'

'Did the man not find such a move at all odd?'

'Not really, Rich had done it before, when he intended going off on one of his rackety adventures and knew he would be out of touch for a long while. I was surprised he chose to go on one of his wild starts once he inherited my father's rights and responsibilities. It meant landing Jack with a much greater burden, but none of us were unduly disturbed by his actions at the time. Rich resented the responsibility our father's death left him with, but he wasn't quite as irresponsible as the wider world chose to believe him and, looking back, I should have been more suspicious about his last disappearance than I was at the time.'

'If he was determined to fade out of public and private view, I suspect there was nothing you could have done to stop him,' the Earl informed her coolly.

'Why, thank you, I feel better now.'

'So when *did* you realise there was something

odd about your elder brother's latest disappearance?' he carried on as if she were irrelevant except as a means to find his cousin and ward. If he loved Annabelle de Morbaraye as sincerely as Persephone loved her big brother, she supposed he was right, but that didn't make up for a sly nag of hurt that she was only an obstacle in his way.

'We received no word from him for month after month. All the other times he went off, he would manage to snatch a few moments from his latest adventure to send Mama a terse note saying he was whole, hale and hearty and not to set the Runners on his trail. If he was trying to distract her from her grief for Papa he did a sterling job, since she had the task of playing hostess for Jack, as soon as he would allow her to take it up again, as well as caring for the children and all the pensioners on the Seaborne House estate, since Jack could not do it all as well as control his own vast interests. You have no idea how often I have cursed Rich for his selfishness in riding away that day and turning his back on his responsibilities.'

'Which is why you feel so guilty about his disappearance now it has proved to be more sinister than you thought, I suppose. It's become your duty to find him and make amends, don't you think?'

'You could be right.'

'Don't sound so surprised,' he said with a disarming grin that suddenly made him as dangerous as the most notoriously charming rake.

'However I feel, he's still missing and now Marcus is being held into the bargain. The ring was clearly put there to spur us into finding Rich and your ward, if they truly disappeared together, and we have no way of knowing if Rich or your cousin are his true quarry. The implication is plain enough: we must find Rich in order to get Marcus back.'

'Which speaks of desperation don't you think?' the Earl of Calvercombe said contemplatively, his brooding gaze on the Seaborne ring as if it might tell the story of its adventures if he stared at it long enough.

'Desperate men do desperate things, my lord,' she agreed grimly, wishing it was as easy as wanting to know where the thing had been these last three years and having the answer miraculously pop into her head. 'At times like this it would be good to believe in magic, don't you think?' she asked rather absently.

'Only if there happened to be a way of controlling each aspect of it, since the white side apparently carries a very black opposite. It always seemed to me there must be a vast price to pay for supernatural gifts, even if I did happen to believe in them.'

'Being a Welshman you might more easily do so than most.'

'Why? Because Shakespeare put supposed sorcery in Owain Glyndwr's mouth it has to follow all Welshmen believe they can "call spirits from the vasty deep" if they so desire? I can't decide if it's worse to be thought deliberately fey or deeply credulous by right of birth.'

'Why do some of your countrymen foster the impression your homeland is magical, then?'

'It seems lovely and challenging to me without extra enchantment, but I'm only a bastard Welshman. My father was solidly English and so are my titles and most of my lands. I only suppose that when a people lose the chance to determine their own destiny they escape into a past of legend and power to avoid their day-to-day lot.'

'I don't seek to diminish the legends or suffering of your countrymen because I made an idle remark, Lord Calvercombe. I was brought up in these Marches, don't forget, my nurse used to tell me stories of magicians and fierce dragons as well as the great princes of Gwynedd. Wales always seemed a green and enchanted land to me, as well as sometimes a very wet one—a caveat you must grant me from experience. I used to stay with my mother's cousins in Pembrokeshire as a child, if I'd been good enough to deserve such a treat.'

'I warrant that didn't happen very often,' he said with a look that might be admiring if it didn't come from him.

'No, I was a sad romp in those days.'

'Only in those days? How you do surprise me, Miss Seaborne.'

'Good, I should hate to be predictable.'

'Believe me, there's very little risk of it. I consider myself lucky if you fail to attack me on sight these days.'

'I thought you were trying to harm Jack that night in the park and I wasn't so very far wrong about your motives, was I? You may not have come here to hurt him physically, but you would have fought him if he took exception to your wandering about his estate as if you owned it, wouldn't you?' she challenged, trying to control a blush when she recalled her conduct the first time they met this summer, outside the summerhouse by the lake where Jack had gone to confront the elusive intruder stalking his lands by night.

'I was frustrated at not being able to find a trace of my cousin Annabelle once they apparently left London together,' he muttered gruffly, clearly ashamed of a lapse of judgement.

If that was the only reason he had agreed to take a role in Jack and Jessica's wedding, Persephone couldn't help admiring Jack's ruthlessness in using any weapon handy to persuade his old friend to stand shoulder to shoulder with him when he needed him there most.

'I still can't find her and we're wasting precious

time arguing whilst the trail is going cold and both your brothers are now missing,' he pointed out.

'How do you suggest we change that state of affairs, then? I doubt Marcus's kidnapper left us a convenient trail of breadcrumbs to follow to his lair.'

'I intend to make use of the talents nature gave me and Sir Arthur Wellesley and India refined when you finally take me to the place where Marcus's hat and Rich's ring were found and leave me to look and think,' he told her irritably. She supposed it was the only course of action available given that Marcus and his captor must be long gone by now.

'Very well,' she conceded, but again that vital grip of his tightened without hurting her and stopped her in her tracks. 'What? You demanded action and now you hold me back from taking it? You really are the most contrary as well as the most infuriating man I ever came across, my lord.'

'You will take no part in this affair apart from showing me the place Marcus's hat and Rich's ring were left,' he said as if he had the right to dictate to her.

'Intending to kidnap and imprison yet another of my unlucky mother's brood, are you, my lord?' she demanded hotly. 'That's the only way you'll keep me from doing everything I can to find Marcus and then bring the black-hearted rogue behind his abduction to justice.'

'Don't tempt me,' he rapped out furiously, glaring down at her.

'Shall we get on? You're the one impatient to be going.'

'And you didn't have a stern enough beating when you were young to make you tolerable to your fellow man now.'

'Only a bully resorts to such ridiculous theories when logic fails to get him what he wants from life,' she informed him in what she hoped was a superior tone as her heart thudded in her breast. She wished she was half as confident as she sounded that she must take a part in the search for her brothers.

'Then let's away, before I give in to my baser instincts and drag you upstairs and tie you to my bed to stop you plunging headfirst into whatever danger is on offer.'

'Let's, I've no time to stand here listening to the raving of a lunatic.'

'If I spend much longer with you, no doubt I *will* be mad as a March hare, madam, since you would try the patience of a saint,' he muttered darkly and, keeping her hand firmly in his, urged her out of the room and towards the stables before either of them could think better of the expedition.

Somewhere between Jack's private domain and the vast ducal stableyard, the Earl of Calvercombe's grip became merely the comfort of hand on hand and, despite her determination to hate him as fiercely as she had it in her to loathe a man who didn't actively wish her harm, she found the contact reassuring. He was uniquely irritating, but he was also a capable and battle-hardened ex-soldier. The closeness of him felt nigh irresistible to a wilder self usually buried under her serene exterior as well, and she did her best to ignore the silly creature.

It was folly to turn to the Earl of Calvercombe for comfort, but she needed a man of action. She had even thought about sending Joe Brandt after Jack and Jessica for perhaps half a minute. If she thought it would do any good, she wouldn't hesitate, but all it would achieve would be to give their unseen enemy the satisfaction of knowing they had been dragged back from their wedding journey for no useful purpose. While there was a stubborn and arrogant overlord on hand, why bother landing herself with another imperious aristocrat like Jack to stamp about the place being masterly?

No, Alex Forthin was the ideal man to outfox their mysterious enemy, and she prayed nobody would send for her cousin behind her back and ruin his honeymoon. As they waited for the horses to be saddled, she made herself stay by the mounting block while the Earl went to help, telling herself it would make him even more impossible if she shared that conclusion with him.

She sighed for some sensible female company and wished Jess home after all. At least she would share her driven anxiety for Marcus and the frustration of being a 'mere' woman who was supposed to sit and await the warriors' return like a sweet little heroine in a story. At last the horses were ready and she tried not to feel like a fragile and fairy-like débutante as his lordship arrogantly tossed her up into the saddle before she could manage for herself. If she didn't assert herself, she would end up on the sidelines, forlornly awaiting news while he took over.

Chapter Six

Silence reigned while they rode across the park absorbed in their own thoughts. Persephone racked her brains for a clue as to where her second brother could have been spirited off to. Fifty years ago the roads had been so bad no stranger would have got far along the road without half the neighbourhood knowing where they were. Now the post roads were fast and it had been a dry summer, so Marcus could be halfway to Ireland or London by now. She tried to put herself in the shoes of his kidnapper, but found it impossible, and frowned gloomily at the broad shoulders of Lord Calvercombe instead.

She wondered if Annabelle de Morbaraye had been glad her youthful guardian was a few hundred miles away and preoccupied once she was old enough to want a life of her own? Persephone contemplated how it must feel to be so alone in the world and decided with a shudder that, no, Annabelle would not have been grateful for his absence. From the sound of it, Alex Forthin's half-brother and father had been selfish men who cared for nobody. Persephone thanked God she had grown up surrounded with love.

'That's the Three Sisters' Oak,' she pointed out as they took the undulating rise from house to deer park and saw the venerable tree in the distance. 'I don't know if you came here with Jack and Rich when you were still of an age to climb it. My sisters consider themselves far too aged and ladylike to tear their skirts and dirty their slippers on it nowadays, but I suspect Marcus wouldn't be above doing so even now.'

The mental picture of her scapegrace brother unconscious and ill in the hands of a desperate man tripped her up and she forced back hot tears that would only confirm all his suspicions about weak females.

'He'll soon be back here plaguing you again,' he said, as if he knew how she was feeling, which seemed unlikely when he'd clearly loathed his own half-brother.

'You can't say that, you don't know.'

'I can use the brains I was born with. Marcus is more boy than man yet, despite twenty-three years of life and the ladybird you suspect he has installed nearby. I dare say he enjoys the status of the Seaborne name, whilst knowing he will never be called upon to run the family estates or the many other holdings that make up your family's empire. One day he might find a use for the energy and intellect he was born with, but for now he's an engaging scamp. It doesn't seem to have occurred to him that, if your elder brother is truly lost, he must take over his estates and your late father's business interests in his stead. It must seem one of his best virtues in his family's eyes that he's not in the least bit avaricious.'

'He's not very ambitious, either,' she admitted, astonished his lordship drew such shrewd conclusions about the people around him.

'Born into his shoes, you would feel differently, I suspect.'

'I would want to forge my own path,' she informed him, fairly sure he wasn't listening as he took in every detail of the oak and its surroundings, then jumped off his horse to examine the ground for clues.

'And woe betide anyone who tried to say you nay?' he asked with a quick glance up at her, still seated on her favourite gelding and warily watching him.

'Of course,' she agreed with a regal nod of her head.

'Would you be a warrior or a bandit queen in another time, I wonder?' he mused idly and she felt her temper rise again when he seemed amused by the idea.

'If I had the choices of a gentleman's son, I'd have become a sailor or an army officer. I don't have enough tact or duty for the church or the law.'

'No doubt you would be a general or an admiral before you had left your twenties,' he told her as he bent to examine a piece of dry turf as if it was the crown jewels.

'Now why do I think that wouldn't be a good thing, I wonder?' she asked, intrigued by whatever he found so riveting, but refusing to ask.

'Because I disliked or distrusted most of those I've met.'

'You do have a glowing opinion of me, don't you?' she felt stung into asking.

'Because I don't pander to your reputation as the toast of St James's, it doesn't mean I lost the use of both my eyes in India, Miss Seaborne,' he said to the few blades of dried up grass he found so fascinating.

'Have you any idea how annoying it is to be dismissed as merely decorative, my lord?' she demanded.

When he merely shrugged and continued with his studies, she eyed him furiously. But she wondered if he might understand after all, when she considered what a young Adonis he'd been before he went to India.

'Can you see with your damaged eye?' she heard herself ask with horrified fascination, as if she were a spectator at a carriage accident. 'I beg your pardon, how tactless of me.'

'Not at all, although I hate it when females stare at my wreck of a face, then turn away as if they might turn faint when I gaze back. If you do that,

I might ride away and refuse to let you interfere in my affairs for ever,' he told her with a sardonic smile that threatened to turn her silly and schoolgirlish anyway.

'They aren't your affairs, they're mine,' she made herself say sharply.

'Anything that concerns your eldest brother is related to my missing cousin. This whole business is clearly aimed at flushing Richard Seaborne out of cover, so don't make the mistake of trying to stop me finding out what happened to both your brothers and my ward if I can, Miss Seaborne.'

Swollen-headed beast of a man. Did he really think she would use her looks to fascinate him into forgetting his precious Annabelle?

'I doubt a stampeding herd of wild horses would sidetrack you from a course you were determined to follow, Lord Calvercombe,' she said stiffly.

'Very true, my dear,' he replied with an unrepentant grin.

She reminded herself she found the glint of

laughter lurking in his blue eyes annoying and certainly not attractive in any way.

'Miss Seaborne,' she corrected him shortly.

'Of course. Miss Seaborne the society beauty has dozens, if not scores, of besotted would-be lovers at her feet, has she not?' He looked up from his nature studies to observe, as if she were a prime example of a breed he despised.

'No, she is merely a woman lucky enough to be born into a family who have wealth and position to make them respect instead of try to seduce her,' she was stung into replying.

'So you clearly believe,' he said as if musing on a conundrum he found half-amusing and half-bewildering. 'Have you no idea how truly lovely you are?'

'I'm nothing out of the common way. It's my portion and connections that cause me to be put up on some sort of pedestal. Jessica is far lovelier than I and nobody seemed to notice it until Jack took a second look at her this summer and saw her as she truly is. I really can't make myself take any man seriously who claims to be struck witless by the tilt of a woman's head, the set of her eyebrows, or the turn of her chin or nose—as if she were little more than a well-executed classical sculpture dug up and sold off to a rich English milord with more money than sense.'

'My, my, Miss Seaborne, what extraordinary passion you do feel about a set of silly young gentlemen,' he observed, more absorbed in searching for mysterious marks in the turf than replying sensibly.

'Then you think they contribute to the advancement of their fellow man, my lord?' she asked sweetly, succumbing to curiosity at last and jumping down to peer at his few blades of grass as if they might talk if she listened hard enough. 'I can't see anything extraordinary,' she admitted and turned to peer up at him with a question and a demand in her silver-green eyes.

'I dare say not,' Alex Forthin agreed, with a silent admission that she really didn't know what those clear light-green eyes of hers did to a man.

Nor had she any idea how the rich dark chestnut of her thick and temptingly unruly hair made a man long to see it loose about her shoulders and run his fingers through the heavy softness of it, to find out if it was as silky soft and full of life as it looked. He felt in the acutest danger of doing something reckless whenever he was with her. Luckily, only he knew he'd shamelessly used his quest and the bustle of Jack's wedding to hold himself aloof from her since that heady night in June when Jack Seaborne won himself a wife in a million, and Alex Forthin found himself struggling with a slender yet deliciously rounded young lady at midnight in a moonlit garden full of scent and secrets and impossible promises.

The girl had been out three years, and the toast of St James from the instant the first wolf spotted her. If his life had been different, perhaps he would have been that wolf; perhaps he would have wooed and won such an intriguing innocent as she must have been at eighteen. Or perhaps he would have been vain and careless of such a rare female and idly flirted with her back then, as if she understood he was not and would not be serious. He would have walked away after engaging her interest, piquing her hopes and spoiling her dreams of true love and an enduring Seaborne-type of marriage. The whole family were primed for an unfashionable kind of alliance based on love and enduring closeness he had never aspired to and never would. Three years ago, when the world was very different, he had envisaged marrying one day when bored enough with life and being Alex Forthin: gentleman, beau and wolf in a pleasing pelt.

Now he doubted he would find a tolerant and well-bred female who could look him in the face without flinching and suddenly what he hadn't wanted back then looked infinitely desirable. Persephone Seaborne didn't seem to notice he was marred; her clear-eyed gaze only puzzled that he dwelt on the folly of very young girls so ill at ease with anyone less than perfect. He shook his head to try to clear it of the notion that Persephone Seaborne was the ideal female to soften his hard edges and add purpose and contentment to his austere life. Ridiculous to look too long into her intriguing grey-green eyes, to catalogue the perfection of her features and the delicious promise her maturing body would hold for her lover one day.

'The man who kidnapped your brother carried the hat and ring here from elsewhere,' he made himself tell her and banished all thought of raising her up and kissing her soft mouth to find out if it would yield under his, or repudiate in a rush of revulsion he would find it almost too painful to endure.

'How do you know?' she demanded with a preoccupied frown at his bent blades of grass.

'He wasn't carrying enough weight to flatten the grass right down and there's no sign of a struggle in the vicinity of this tree. It stands alone and even your brother would never be so preoccupied with a lady-love that he wouldn't notice a man standing by it waiting to kidnap him. He was attacked elsewhere and the man walked here to leave his message for your family.'

'So he left Marcus elsewhere while he did so,' Persephone mused. 'Either he left my brother bound and gagged in case he woke and raised an outcry, or he has a confederate.'

'You know the area far better than I do. Would anyone locally want to damage your family by co-operating in your brother's abduction?'

'Every powerful family has enemies, but I don't think any of them bold enough to strike at us here,' she admitted after a pause to run through a mental list of anyone with a grievance against the Seabornes.

'Enemies are unpredictable at the best of times. Can you think of any around here who might be glad to damage you and yours?'

'Jack dismissed a keeper for laying mantraps on the estate a year or so ago, but he was caught poaching himself a few months later and the magistrate gave him the choice between the army and prison. He's probably far too busy worrying about his own skin at the moment to think of avenging himself on us.'

'Does he have family?'

'Yes, and very ashamed of their black sheep they are, too. No, don't look at me like that, they asked to be moved to one of Jack's other estates so he wouldn't find them if he deserted and managed to get home. He was a mean-tempered bully. After he was gone and they were no longer terrified to tell anyone, we found that he beat his wife and terrified his children. Nobody but Belford himself bears ill will towards Jack for banishing him from Ashburton, I can assure you.'

'Jack's no saint, though—are you sure there is nobody who would be happy to see him brought low?'

'You think Jack's been dallying with farmers' daughters, my lord?'

'Can you be certain he has not?' he countered, determined not to let scruples stop him finding anything that might lead him to Marcus, or Rich and Annabelle.

'Because he's Jack, of course. He might have been rackety and wild for a while after he lost his parents and found out how false and toadying the world could be to a young Duke with a vast fortune and large estates, but he would never dishonour his name or himself by tampering with innocents. I challenge you to find one female he ever kept who now regards him as anything other than a generous lover she regrets losing.'

'I agree,' he said ruefully and almost laughed at the look of consternation on her lovely face. 'I spent all my spare moments trying to track a clue that would lead me to your older brother and my cousin these last few months. Sometimes I think I know more about Rich and Jack Seaborne than I do about myself. Despite his rakish reputation, he left all his lovers better off than they were before he found them and he certainly intends to keep no more now he's wed his Duchess. I've heard more mawkish sighs of regret among the muslin company over him these last few months than I would have thought the whole regiment capable of uttering in a lifetime.'

'He's a darling,' Persephone Seaborne said with an indulgent smile for her big cousin. Alex felt a pang of something all the more sharp because he refused to name it as jealousy for an easy affection she would never show him.

'I don't think Jack would thank me for agreeing,' he said with a wry smile and heard her chuckle at Jack's reaction to being thought a darling by his cynical friend.

With laughter in her silvery-green eyes and an affectionate smile kicking up the corners of her lush mouth, she was dangerous. That quirk of connection he'd felt for her earlier might all too easily grow into longing and frustration if he wasn't careful, so he made himself look away from the enchanting picture that Miss Persephone Seaborne made, with all her unselfconscious allure.

Even if he was in the market for a wife, an accredited beauty wasn't the one for him. Maybe in ten years' time when he was near forty and his estates and fortune were restored he might consider it. Something told him he wouldn't dwell very long on the idea of a lady young enough to bear him an heir having to steel herself to become his bride for the sake of his title and position even then. He shook his head at the very idea of a woman deciding she could do no better than a battle-scarred monster with a shriveled-up heart like him. He felt too old and world weary for such a desperate lady now and was well aware the scars he carried made him an object of morbid interest, rather than a desirable *parti*.

'You're a dangerous woman, Miss Persephone Seaborne,' he told her and decided not to look too deeply into what might have been.

'I don't know where you got that idea, my lord,

but it won't help us find Marcus, so what do we do next?'

'I shall search for any sign of him and the rogue who seized him and you will go home to pretend nothing is amiss for the sake of your mother and little sisters,' he told her, hoping she would see sense and not insist in embroiling herself so deeply that he would be distracted from his quest by worrying about her.

'Can I trust you to look to Marcus's safety first and not use him to get to your cousin?' she asked with a very direct look from those clear, cool eyes of hers.

'You can—I am a gentleman,' he said stiffly.

'Can I indeed, my lord? And what does that mean when you're still a man with it? Being both a lord and a man, you might regard your own family as a higher obligation than mine could ever be, might you not?'

'I might, except Annabelle has been gone three years now and your younger brother a few hours. If you are and yours are not to go through what I have done since I arrived home and found her long lost, time is of the essence. You'll just have to trust my word I'll put the recovery of your second brother at the top of my list of things to do today, won't you, Miss Seaborne?'

'I could always make my own enquiries instead,' she muttered mutinously.

'And risk the whole enterprise because you won't accept my word? I happen to like the resty young devil for his own sake, so think what you will of my motives. Do you really believe I would leave a young fool with the delusion the world is his friend to learn how wrong he is at the hands of his enemies as harshly as I had to, madam?'

'No,' she said with a heavy sigh, her gaze meeting his for a long moment. 'You would probably do too much to prevent that happening to another, so promise me not to take any wild risks with your own safety.' she demanded.

'I never take unnecessary risks,' he defended himself gruffly from the notion that she might care one way or the other what became of him.

She gave a significant glance at the scarred side of his face that didn't dwell on the healed web of distorting cuts, but told him he'd put himself in the hands of his enemies precisely by taking unnecessary risks.

'You know nothing of how this happened,' he defended himself with an impatient flick of a long-fingered hand at his half-damaged face.

'Then why not tell me when we have a little leisure from brother-and-cousin hunting?' she said, as if they were going to have time and intimacy to talk of such things when their quest was done.

'It's not a pretty tale.'

'And I'm not an infant to be told sweet fairy tales and kind little lies,' she said flatly, as if he'd disappointed her.

'Whatever either of us might be, we must ride back and I must find an excuse to wander off for a day or two while you pretend all's well. Are you actress enough to carry off such a role, I wonder, or will you fold and let Lady Henry suffer agonies of mind over the welfare of her second son as well as her first one?'

It was harsh, but he could see from the exasperated look she cast him and the queenly lift of her neat chin that he'd managed to goad her into proving him wrong. How long that would last once her temper cooled, he had no idea, but it should give him long enough to evade her and be well on his way before impatience broke through her resolution to prove him wrong.

They rode back in silence, Lord Calvercombe preoccupied with the adventure ahead and Persephone searching for ways to join in the chase but finding he'd left her no way out. If she sent for Jack, he'd keep her out of the search as well. If Alex Forthin was going to creep about the countryside and track her younger brother and his kidnapper, then far safer for them if Jack was oblivious to the danger Marcus might be in, given the hot and headlong temper she knew still existed under the cynical control he used to fool the world he was tamed.

She silently fumed at the conspiracy of gentlemen to keep ladies meek and at home and dearly wished the world was arranged differently. Maybe then she could storm about the place doing as well, rather than sitting about trying not to chew her nails and quietly worrying about Lord Calvercombe and her brothers. Her mother had faced so many blows with unbowed faith in her maker and the basic goodness of the human spirit, which should show her daughter and the rest of the world what a resolute female was capable of, but, no, somehow gentlemen still deluded themselves ladies were fragile and over-sensitive creatures in need of protection.

'Promise me not to ride out alone, even on your cousin's land?' the worst example of them all demanded before they were quite within earshot of the stables.

'Why the devil should I?' she was surprised into protesting crossly.

'I don't know—could it be because your brother was overpowered and taken by a rogue on this very estate or nearby?' he responded sarcastically.

'Surely two Seabornes are enough for any man to try to control at the same time without adding me to the pot?'

'I suspect he has only one at present,' he observed almost to himself, 'and what better lure to bring Richard out of hiding than knowing his precious sister is in the hands of the very man he disappeared in order to avoid? Even a strong, bull-headed and nigh fearless idiot like Rich wouldn't be able to stay away if the brute got hold of you, Miss Seaborne.'

'No,' she conceded on another weary sigh, 'he would not and this man must be a brute indeed for Rich to avoid his own world for so long to steer clear of him. I suppose you're right and I'd best take a groom with me when I ride out.'

'Thank you. It would worry me, too, if this villain had you in his power,' he said gruffly, his eyes on the mellow stable roofs in front of them as if reluctant to concede even that much.

'Then put me out of your mind and find Marcus before whoever has him spirits him further away,' she said, but she had to suppress a shiver at the thought of this aloof man putting himself in danger for the sake of her scapegrace brother.

'Very well, your ladyship,' he replied with a mocking half-bow.

'I'm not a ladyship.'

'No doubt you soon will be,' he muttered darkly as if it was a sin he would find very hard to forgive her.

Chapter Seven

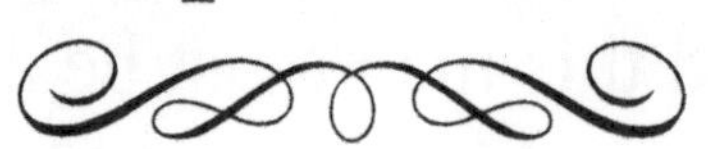

Marcus Seaborne struggled to throw off an odd sense of being lost in dreams and shadows and blinked his eyes tightly shut before forcing them open. He flinched against the dull light in a narrow room he was certain he'd never seen before. Devil take it, but he must have drunk enough to sink a flotilla last night and damnation take the drummer who was beating a tattoo in his ears. He heard himself groan, then felt a terrible urge to retch.

'Drink this,' a very cross virago shouted at him from far too close by.

'Ugrumph,' he remarked.

'Don't argue, do as I say,' she snapped and solved the problem by tipping his head back so she could drown him with the water he'd thought he wanted so badly.

'Glurgh!' he found energy to protest as he began to cough, then retch in earnest as he fought to get the stuff out of his windpipe before she did for him.

Thrusting a chamberpot of mercifully pristine white earthenware under his nose, she held it steady while he rid himself of the water and anything else in his unlucky stomach. Alternately hot and cold and shivering like a sick dog, he passionately wished he was alone and said so as soon as he could string a sentence together.

'You can't want it more fervently than I do,' she muttered gloomily and watched him fumble for the cup of water she'd done her best to choke him with as if she would rather she'd succeeded.

'Then go away,' he ordered gruffly.

'I should like nothing better,' she snapped.

'Then leave me to die alone—I'd vastly prefer it that way.'

'I am locked in here and was ordered to make sure you stay hale and healthy, or it would be the worse for me and my family,' she said obscurely and Marcus decided some cruel joker had locked him up with a madwoman.

'Probably wanted to be rid of your shrewish tongue and unpleasant temper for a few blessed minutes,' he grumbled, then tried to take in his surroundings. He fought a heavy lethargy he couldn't remember experiencing before, even after a night of hard drinking and mischief with his less reputable friends. 'Deuce take it, I feel as if I've been pole-axed,' he mumbled as he tried to stand, felt the room revolve and hastily sat down again.

'Nigh on,' his companion admitted, seeming unimpressed he had found the mighty bruise lurking at the base of his skull.

'You could at least try to sound sorry,' he protested, wincing as he probed a bit too hard and nausea threatened all over again.

'And what good would that do you?'

'It might make me feel better.'

'No, you would probably lie there feeling pathetic and ill, then go into a decline,' she argued and he managed a rueful smile. If he must be knocked out, drugged and imprisoned, the company of a female unlike any he'd ever met in his life before should stave off all traces of boredom for the time being.

Alex Forthin halted his tired horse at last and looked down on the famous prospect of Ashburton New Place glowing richly in the fading light of a late-August sunset. He'd been gone two days and all he had to show for it was acute unease and a rumour that made him feel even wearier. Keeping Persephone safe at home while he routed the Seabornes' enemy was about to grow even harder and somehow he had to make sure she stayed free, safe and annoying as ever.

Doing his best to shake off a tiredness that went deeper than the physical effort of tracking about the English Marches for two days on a wild goose chase, he pressed his knees into the warm flanks of his horse and urged him toward the gracious old mansion, wishing he was bringing better news with him. In this busy, ordered nineteenth century of theirs, it seemed unlikely that three prominent men could come and go as if the gods had wafted them off to an enchanted Aegean island beyond human curiosity, so he knew he had missed some clue to where young Marcus was, even if Rich was cunning enough to hide away as if he'd never been, and their enemy was elusive as ever.

It was logical that their unknown foe would do everything he could to stay invisible, but after weeks of racking his brains he couldn't imagine who the man was and it troubled him deeply. He'd been an effective intelligence officer, which was why he'd been treated to the finest torturer the enemy had at his disposal when he was finally captured. But he'd found no trace of a stranger who had stolen a member of the rich and powerful Seaborne clan from under their noses and gone to earth with his latest quarry.

Even the Romany bands had largely left the area for distant goose fairs and mops and he was sure that those left were as truthful as they ever were outside their own tribe when they shrugged and swore nobody had paid them to kidnap a lord's son lately. As the headman of the tribe he knew from his own holdings told him with the apparently open smile of an expert liar, they would be fools to wear out their welcome for the sake of a stranger who would happily let them hang when the hue and cry was raised after such precious young gentlemen.

'Welcome back, my lord,' Jack's butler greeted him as he did his best to ghost into the Duke of Dettingham's private wing of the house without notice.

'Thank you, Hughes, I should have known better than to try to sneak in and make myself presentable before anyone knew I was back, should I not?'

'Very likely, your lordship. I will send the second footman to attend you, he has some skill in looking after a gentleman and I dare say your own man is enjoying the holiday you were gracious enough to grant him while you are with us.'

'Aye, I dare say he might well be doing so, if I had remembered to employ him in the first place.'

'I beg your pardon, Lord Calvercombe. It is, of course, none of my business, but I must compliment you on such admirable self-sufficiency.'

'Good of you,' Alex said, unable to suppress a

rueful laugh at being gently chided for his lack of state by Jack's major-domo.

'Shall I send Amos up to help you dress for dinner? You appear to have had a long day.'

'Then please send him up along with enough hot water for a bath, if it can be got at such short notice. I'm not fit to get within a hundred yards of a lady's drawing room at the moment and I suppose dinner will be at the usual hour?'

'Indeed, my lord. Lady Henry is still entertaining some of the guests who came for his Grace's wedding,' Hughes observed in a world-weary voice that told Alex that some had worn out their welcome.

'Perhaps it would be better if I had only arrived an hour or two later then,' Alex said ruefully and thought he caught a fleeting glimpse of sympathy in the man's eyes. 'Now I am here, I'd best scurry about,' he said and ran up the graceful cantilevered staircase.

On his way to Jack's ducal apartment, he decided it would take more than the half an hour he had to make himself fit to join the ladies and gentlemen gathered here for dinner tonight. He had a villainous growth of beard and a pressing need to feel properly clean again before he met anyone's critical gaze, let alone finicky Miss Persephone Seaborne's perceptive green-grey eyes and sceptical smile.

'Good evening, Lord Calvercombe, how lovely to be granted this chance to further our acquaintance after all,' Persephone heard her third cousin, Corisande Beddington, murmur in a husky tone that she probably imagined was seductive and mysterious as soon as the Earl of Calvercombe stepped into the smaller drawing room where the family and their few stubborn remaining guests were gathered tonight.

'Good evening, Mrs Beddington,' he responded with a lift of one dark-as-midnight eyebrow that ought to tell Corisande he knew what she was after and wasn't planning to be used or trapped by a harpy.

Persephone managed not to bestow a smug smile and stop-trespassing look on her lovely cousin, but couldn't help keeping an eye on them both. His lordship met it with a challenge, once he had brushed past clinging Corisande with a swiftness that made the family seductress pout and saunter towards one of Jack's middle-aged neighbours with a swing of her hips supposed to make the Earl of Calvercombe regret dismissing an experienced bedmate like her, when he had little prospect of slaking his manly needs with any other member of this very respectable house party. Unfortunately for Corisande, Lord Calvercombe didn't look in the least bit sorry to escape that invitation and concentrated on greeting his hostess and avoiding the *tête-à-tête* both cousins were eager to force, for very different reasons.

'Did you find out anything useful?' Persephone managed to murmur as softly as she could under the polite hum of conversation in the ducal drawing room, once she finally managed to manoeuvre herself a few seconds' privacy with him.

'Nothing but a rumour I can't pin down,' he admitted in a similarly intimate tone, but Persephone doubted Corisande would envy her quite so bitterly if she knew that they were discussing Marcus and not making shady assignations.

She met her distant cousin's hard-eyed glare

with what she hoped was a look of bland indifference, but knew she had finally made an enemy after years of skating round the edges of outright dislike blazing between them. Trying to regret the vague possibility of friendship with a woman with whom she had nothing in common, she turned her back on her cousin and met his lordship's knowing look. Nothing about that silent falling-out had escaped him.

'Would you like me to flirt with her and cast you in the shade? It would be pure pretence, as I disliked the obvious even before I learned to distrust it, but it might make her feel a little better disposed towards you,' he offered and surprised a genuine smile out of her that probably made Corisande all the more determined to hate her for being younger, better dowered and closer to the heart of the powerful Seaborne family than she would ever be.

'No, thank you. Not only would it raise her hopes unnecessarily if you truly feel nothing, but poor Lord Ambleby would feel doubly rejected, since her flattery seems to be going some way to mending his broken heart,' she said, careless of the private affairs of others for once.

She realised what she had done as soon as she saw comprehension dawn in the far-too-intelligent Earl of Calvercombe's eyes and gave him an imploring look.

'It was indiscreet as well as unkind of me to speak of such private matters. I would be grateful if you could forget I ever mentioned it,' she added quietly.

'I will in a while, but I'm not surprised to hear he's put his fortune to the test,' Alex replied with a cynical smile that told her there was no point trying to pretend the genial peer hadn't offered for Lady Henry Seaborne's hand and been sadly but finally rejected.

'My mother loved my father far too much to marry a dear old friend to stave off the loneliness of living without him.'

'They might have been good companions to each other,' he offered with a shrug, as if love between two human beings that endured even after death had parted them was a concept he found distinctly uncomfortable as well as unlikely.

'I'm sure the very idea of living in such a lukewarm marriage would seem far worse to her than carrying on as good friends. Only imagine how the poor man would feel if he knew he was constantly being compared to her lost love. If she had accepted him, I would be far sorrier for him than I am at the moment. Lucky she is too sensible to inflict such a life on an old and valued friend. It's a shame they will lose their ease together now, but I suppose it's better to know.'

'No doubt his lordship will come round to the notion of being her friend again, given enough time to recover his equilibrium,' he replied with a nod towards Corisande, who was hanging on his every word as if it might be sent from heaven to enlighten her.

Persephone frowned at the idea of Corisande wrapping genial Lord Ambleby in her witchy toils, and wondered if she could do anything to save him far worse pain than being gently rejected by Lady Henry Seaborne.

'I believe Lady Clare is at a loose end, now she has both her chicks safely engaged and waiting to join the unseemly scramble to the altar Jack and Jessica managed to launch this summer,' he suggested, with a hard look that admitted he was prepared to assist in matchmaking if it would save a man from the over-eager and self-obsessed Corisande Beddington, so long as she understood he could never endure it himself.

'If she set her heart on Lord Ambleby, they might be very happy together, I suppose. They are both good-natured and principled, if inclined to be self-indulgent. I believe you're right and they would suit each other very well, my lord,' she mused and caught his half-amused, half-horrified expression as he watched her resolve to promote a different match to the one Corisande had in mind.

'Thank heavens you were born a woman, Miss Seaborne,' he said mockingly and she couldn't stop herself asking why, even though she told herself she didn't really want to hear his answer.

'I don't quite see why, when I'm not too sure it was a good thing myself. Being female apparently means I must stay at home and twiddle my thumbs while you males are busy doing things. Why are you particularly glad I'm bound and subdued by convention today more than any other day, my lord?'

'I'm quite relieved about that every day, since you would be far too dangerous if convention allowed you to wander about the countryside at will. But in this case I thank the good Lord you were born a woman because you would be so uncomfortable in the Seaborne nest if you'd been created a man. I can't see you happily embracing an idle life and letting Jack take the lead as Marcus seems perfectly content to do. You would either break out and go your own way, as I suspect Rich has done, or break yourself on the frustration of being born out of the direct line of succession and all the power that goes with it.'

'What a very poor opinion you have of me, my lord. I'll leave you to enjoy it before the matchmakers start speculating about us instead of Corisande and whomever her roving eye settles on next.'

'Don't you want to know what I found out?'

'Of course I do, but you seem disinclined to tell me, and I won't have local society whisper that I have set my cap at you.'

'Meet me later so we can talk properly then,' he said with an impatient look that told her exactly how frustrating he found the conventions that bound them and the onlookers all around.

Considering how public his projected meeting with Jack at the summerhouse by the lake in the outer parkland had turned out to be, Persephone racked her brains for a place that would assure them a great deal more privacy. 'Meet me in the Queen's Apartments then. You know where they are, I suppose?'

He nodded solemnly and somehow she doubted there was a stick or stone of vast and rambling Ashburton he didn't know, since he had obviously failed to leave his role of watcher and sifter of information behind when he left India.

'There's an inner closet that leads off the state bedchamber with no windows to give away a light while we talk privately. That wing is deserted again now Jess is away, so nobody should see either of us come or go and I can't come to Jack's wing myself when you're known to be occupying it.'

'That didn't stop you the other day,' he objected.

'I was so agitated I forgot you were still here,' she said brusquely, and if that really was a glint of hurt pride in his eyes he should review his warrior credentials. 'Midnight,' she mouthed and stalked off as if they'd had a falling-out, which ought to please Cousin Corisande no end.

Alex made himself do his duty and be polite towards Lady Henry's guests while doing his best not to look at them full on, since he'd learnt his damaged eye seemed to bother some people far more than his other scars for some reason. Whilst he was with the lovely Miss Seaborne he seemed to forget he wasn't just one more bemused gentleman, happy to gaze on her beauty and burn. He wondered how many men would envy him his assignation with her and if that meant he should be elated or disappointed she thought he was safe to meet at midnight.

Every single male who still longed for a woman in his bed and wasn't already fathoms deep in love would covet an unchaperoned meeting with her, so he wasn't at all special in that respect. Tonight Persephone Seaborne was even more of a picture of lovely femininity than usual in a gown of cream satin and gauze that showed off her glowing chestnut locks, creamy complexion and graceful figure. He lingered in a quiet corner to revisit an image of her holding court in a London ballroom, which he was glad she had no idea he carried in his memory.

Not long back from India, still tender from wounds of the body and of the mind that had been inflicted on him there, he'd been at the rout in a desperate attempt to find a trace of Annabelle in polite society. He had treasured the vain hope that a whisper might reach him of what had become of her after she'd left his father's dubious protection.

Despite the glitter and fuss and clamour of the *ton* at play during the height of the London Season that made him feel alien and uncomfortable, he had found no sign of his missing cousin. He had been foolish even to hope, since Annabelle was barely seventeen when she ran away. Instead of a trail that might lead to his cousin, he had been fascinated by a beautiful young woman so in command of her world that he realised how ill he fitted in and left as soon as he could tear himself away.

Miss Persephone Seaborne had been almost too perfect that night. He had envied her the security and support of a large and powerful family to scare off fortune hunters and keep the worst of the rakes at bay on Annabelle's behalf. Yet even then he felt ill when he imagined Miss Seaborne wed to some suitable pattern-card gentleman. It was the way of his kind to marry for mutual advantage and he never hated it more passionately than he did in that overcrowded London ballroom.

Alex supposed he had pushed his own failure to protect Annabelle on to Miss Seaborne. Her position as society beauty, toast of St James and close as a sister to the mighty Duke of Dettingham meant that Jack would thrash any man who tried to touch her against her will. Underneath his restless bitterness Alex knew he was to blame for Annabelle's plight and it was doubly unfair to put the blame on Miss Seaborne. He should have sold out and come home as soon as he knew Captain de Morbaraye had been killed and left his daughter in Alex's care, instead of putting it off for fear he and Farrant would murder each other and leave her all alone.

If not for his farcical meeting with Jack one fateful moonlit night, he might have gone on believing Persephone Seaborne was only a pampered beauty who played with men's hearts for amusement. His mouth twisted into a wry smile as he recalled the virago who had launched herself at him to protect her large and formidable cousin from an unknown assailant.

His smile grew into a chuckle as he recalled struggling with the wild-cat while she had done her best to unman him, then scratch his eyes out if that was what it took to save Jack from his evil clutches. Very little of aloof, goddess-like Miss Seaborne had remained in the spitting vixen who managed to land a few blows on him before he could overpower her with an efficiency he should never have had to use on a woman. At least that meeting had opened his eyes to the fiery nature underlying her serene beauty. Maybe next time he met a diamond of the first water he'd be more cautious about dismissing her as a pleasant collection of features and a lushly formed body without a heart to make her human.

The thought of being alone with her in a room designed to be the most intimate heart of a queen's privacy made him squirm with a hot shiver of wanting something he ought to have learnt to live without by now. He was, he assured himself, too cold and aloof to be carried away by an itch he didn't have to scratch these days. The unease he felt at dismissing her as an easily disregarded female, to be desired and taken, then forgotten, told him his feelings for her already ran too deep. No, he truly was aloof—set apart from his kind. As long as he remembered that, they would emerge from this affair as far apart as ever and quite happy to be so.

Chapter Eight

Alex was still reminding himself how little he and Persephone Seaborne had in common, apart from their cousins, when he stole through the sleeping mansion towards the Queen's Apartments that night, feeling like a very amateur cracksman indeed. It was insane to meet her in such a private place and he'd been tempted not to turn up. The thought of her wandering about Ashburton in the middle of the night looking for even more trouble than he was spurred him into keeping this assignation, if only to tell her they could ride out in the morning with far more propriety than they could expect from another eventful midnight meeting.

'There you are at last. Hurry up and close the door so I can light this wretched thing and we can see each other,' he heard her demand impatiently as soon as he crept close enough for her to sense him coming.

At least she murmured so softly he could barely hear her over the normal shifts and settlings of an old house, but he had to swallow his impatience with her for being here in the first place and do as she bid him, because it made sense for them not to be seen or heard. Since they were both still in darkness, he allowed himself one rueful smile for her haste to meet a man most ladies regarded as repulsive, dangerous or even a little of both. He doubted very much she had thought about the consequences if they were to be discovered and found he was grinning at nothing when he concluded she would have come anyway, even if she had.

'How long have you been lurking here, waiting to nag me about this, that and the other?' he said once he had silently shut the sturdy oak door on the world.

For a moment the darkness was stuffy and as black as pitch and he shuddered and recalled too many nights and days shut in a dark hole by his enemies. Alex fought the sense of panic all confined spaces threatened him with nowadays, however hard he had struggled against it after he was freed from captivity on Sir Arthur Wellesley's victory at Assaye and began his long convalescence. He had come a long way since the very thought of being confined to a cabin even to sleep made him rig up a hammock on deck throughout his passage home, once he was finally considered strong enough to stand the journey. He'd slept under the stars of the Southern Hemisphere and the storms of the Northern one during the whole voyage back and suspected the sailors thought he'd run mad.

Forcing himself to breathe slowly and deliberately now, he was still very glad when Persephone finally struck a spark and set the tinder alight. He watched her gently blow on the cloth until the flame was strong enough to light the candle that would illuminate their furtive assignation and did his best to hide this ridiculous affliction from her acute green gaze. Using his own eyes to divert his thoughts from spectres he supposed would probably haunt him for the rest of his life, although he sincerely hoped they would continue to lessen in intensity, he then had to remind himself he wasn't here to admire the way the soft light picked out some of Persephone's finely cut features and made a shadowed mystery of others he wanted to know intimately.

'This is ridiculous,' she informed him, as if it had been his idea and not hers.

'I couldn't agree more,' he countered blandly and eyed her in the half-light the candle cast as if waiting for her to spark like the flint she still held as if not quite sure what to do with it. 'Neither of us should be here and I can't imagine why we are.'

'We couldn't talk anywhere else without risking eavesdroppers. It's your fault for enchanting my cousin Corisande with your dark looks and romantic past until she's jealous of every word you say to another female,' she said severely.

'I've done all I can to avoid her without insulting a member of my host's family.'

'And I can't imagine why you're so delicate with Corisande's feelings when you gave Jack the biggest insult you could possibly think up by accusing him of conniving at your cousin's kidnap,' she argued crossly.

'Jealous?' he asked before thinking what he was implying.

'Never,' she told him with a look of such revulsion that it convinced him she would rather be shut in a room with Hades himself as her namesake had been for half of every year than admit she even liked him.

'I made no attempt to charm your voluptuous cousin Corisande into feeling so aggrieved that you're so much more beautiful than she has ever been and I am very happy to promise you that I never will. Satisfied?'

'No, not since you appear to have intrigued her without trying. Knowing Corisande, I think it might even be *because* you don't try that it worked so well. She's so used to having any man she sets her sights on totally fascinated and at her mercy that finding one indifferent to her charms has her far more fascinated than if you'd fallen flat at her feet and offered her everything you have.'

'If it makes me boring, perhaps I should prostrate myself.'

'Or perhaps she'd pick *you* up if you tumbled under her dainty little feet,' she argued, then seemed impatient with herself and he was too fascinated by now to end this ludicrous encounter and tear himself away from the danger such scandalous solitude offered both of them.

'Not the smallest risk of that, since not even to stop her watching me like a terrier at a mouse-hole could I parade myself as the latest of her legion of lovers,' he said, breaking his own rules not to speak ill of a lady.

The notorious Mrs Beddington was an attractive woman, in her own brash style, but he wouldn't touch her with a ten-foot pole unless she was in peril of her life, and even then he might have to think about it twice.

'You know her?' Persephone asked.

Acute Miss Seaborne must have read contempt for her cousin in his eyes, for all he thought himself so guarded. 'I knew her,' he felt moved to explain, despite the fact every second that passed without a very urgent reason for being here was sheer folly. 'Once upon a time, she decided she wanted my brother and seemed as violently in love with him as Farrant was with her for a few weeks. Then she grew bored with him, since he had little money and was halfway to becoming a drunkard even then. For some reason, she decided to want me instead and made it very obvious, although I was far too young for such a she-wolf at the time and treated it as a joke. At least I did until Farrant and three of his least scrupulous friends waylaid me on my way home from a neighbour's house one night and beat me unconscious, after ordering me to stay away from her if I wanted to live. None of my denials made a ha'pennyworth of difference after she had told my brother I was her lover and a better one than he had ever been, so she was done with him and never wanted to see him again—which was probably the only true part of the whole rigmarole she spun him.'

'So he believed you would behave so to a woman he supposedly loved and attacked his own brother on her say so? How could he put

Corisande and all her lies and whims before his own flesh and blood?' Persephone asked.

Dislike her as she might, common justice made Persephone admit to herself Corisande wouldn't be the first female, or the last, to fantasise over Alex Forthin. Since the younger maids at Ashburton used to hide at the very top of the grand main staircase to gawp at Mr Alexander Forthin when he came to spend a few weeks of the school holidays with his friends, she supposed she could see why her cousin had wanted the youthful Adonis he had been back then so very badly. If she'd been a few years older, she might have crept out of her schoolroom to join in and felt the tingle of excitement he'd provoked in her even then fire into complete infatuation.

'You have too much faith in family loyalty, Miss Seaborne,' he broke into her abstracted thoughts. 'My half-brother was twelve years my senior and my mother had the bad taste to be sole heiress to her father, the Earl of Tregaron. How could poor Farrant *not* hate the only child of a woman he loathed? Our falling-out was about as inevitable as night following day and Forthins have always been very good at despising each other. Your cousin made the situation between us worse, but she certainly didn't create it. Anyway, I decided to leave the country before Farrant could murder me in my sleep, but I truly never thought he would take out his fury on Annabelle as he appears to have done once I was gone.'

'I doubt you were much more than a boy when you joined Sir Arthur Wellesley's army yourself, so how could you anticipate the vile conduct of a rogue like him?' she defended him brusquely and he fought the warm appeal of having such an unlikely champion as Jack's fiery cousin on his side.

'I was seventeen. I joined the first regiment I could find that was about to be posted overseas and Annabelle was only ten when I left. It never occurred to me she might have to run away before she even had a chance to come out in order to avoid his…' He let the words trail off and shrugged, unwilling to name the beast his brother had become to Persephone.

'Did he actually ravish the poor girl?' she asked and did it for him.

'No. I know he tried to, but it's my hope and belief she ran away in time to escape that fate. Although Penbryn was still controlled by first my father, then my brother as my trustees at the time, I really thought she would be safe. I was a fool.'

'Has it ever occurred to you to wonder if your cousin eloped?' she asked gently, as if the notion might hurt him in some obscure way.

Alex asked himself whether she could really think he loved Annabelle as a man rather than as a cousin and supposed guardian, and tried not to spin into a fine Forthin temper at the very idea. It was a notion he'd first seen in Jack's watchful gaze during their initial encounter this summer and then he had found it almost laughable. He'd been home on leave only once during his ultimately ill-fated army career, when Annabelle was fifteen and beginning to blossom from schoolgirl to woman. They still had the same deep affection for each other that made them truly family as the rest of the Forthin clan could never be, but the idea of more had never occurred to either of them.

'I suppose it's possible,' he mused, letting the idea simmer as he wondered why it had never occurred to him before.

'Such a young girl, brought up so secluded on your late grandfather's estate, might find it too terrifying to run from the danger your brother represented alone. You might do well to try to speak to any friends she managed to make, despite their efforts to keep her close, my lord. Young girls have a habit of confiding in each other that makes me glad I chose darling Jess as my bosom bow at a very early age, because I know she will never hold my secret and silly hopes and dreams over me as a less scrupulous person might do.'

'You think one of them might be holding on to her secrets out of a sense of misguided loyalty to Annabelle even though she's been gone so long?'

'Having been a very young girl myself and knowing how passionately silly they can be, yes, I have to say I think it very likely,' she replied. 'Although we could have discussed this problem any time of the day or night, since her disappearance doesn't seem to be a secret, could we not? I thought we risked this highly improper meeting to talk about my brother's disappearance and not your cousin's,' she added, as if once more afraid his quest would override hers.

Alex found himself suffering from a snaky little glimmer of hurt that she could still suspect him of such selfish guile and did his best to squash it flat.

Little did the Earl of Calvercombe know how oddly the intimacy of a queen's private chamber in the middle of a dark August night affected her, Persephone concluded gratefully. She knew from the sense of distance she suddenly felt yawning between them that her clumsy reminder of why they were here had hurt him. It had been meant to remind her they were not close friends and would certainly never be lovers as something in her constantly wondered if they could be, despite her proper upbringing and revulsion at apeing Corisande's wild example. Being closeted here in the middle of the night with him had sparked far too many wanton ideas in her silly head, but that was hardly his noble lordship's fault.

So was it worth losing his friendship, if nothing more, to distance herself from the notorious Mrs Beddington and feel safe from the ultimate temptation he offered elegant but proper Miss Persephone Seaborne to behave very improperly indeed?

The scandal sheets thinly disguised Corisande's identity with initials and made up comic aliases for her lovers, but society laughed at her nearly as often as they gasped at her reckless misdeeds. Persephone had tried to pity her cousin, who had made the mistake of falling for a handsome rogue at a very early age, then eloping with him. Corisande openly rejoiced when her husband drank himself into an early grave and how could anyone pity her after that? Was Persephone guilty of going to the other extreme to prove how unlike her distant relative she was? Probably, she realised, and it felt as if she had stamped on something as delicate and promising as it had been unlikely between her and Alex Forthin and she tried not to mourn it.

Instead she did her best to douse the wisp of heat somewhere deep inside her at being here with him in the middle of the night, while she waited for him to snap back at her deliberate insult. She ordered herself to be grateful to Corisande for an example of all she least wanted to be. So she kept her eyes averted and did her best to close down the rest of her senses. If she really tried, she could refuse to take in the scent of him, the fact of him, the mere whispers of sound his soft breathing made in this luxuriously enclosed space. Somehow she had to keep to her corner of the room and avert disaster. Although disaster would require him to be as sensitive to her every move as she was to his. She could see no sign she meant more to him than a casually met female he had trouble being polite to—and shouldn't that be a good thing?

'I spent two days searching up hill and down dale across this county and half each of the next to try to find some hint of where your brother's abductor has got off to and where he might have hidden him in the meantime. I found nothing but wild-goose chases and one elusive whisper of a rumour,' he told her, frowning as he pondered that rumour and seemed to find it very unsavoury.

'What did the gossips have to say? Was it the story that has Jack disposing of all possible heirs one by one? I thought that piece of nonsense would die a timely death once he married Jess, since he's now in a perfect position to raise heirs of his own without recourse to either of my brothers,' she said wearily.

'No, not that particular piece of spite, although I agree it's idiotic.'

'Which one, then?'

'The one that insists I have spirited Marcus away myself. I'm supposedly incandescent with rage that Rich appears to have run off with my ward and cousin, and I have kidnapped your younger brother in order to flush him from cover, presumably so I can take my petty revenge on one of my oldest friends and cause his family even more anguish than they've suffered already.'

'Well, I suppose it's a plausible enough tale if—'

'You believe it?' he barked, hot fury in his eyes

and a hard look of contempt contorting his face into a bitter mask. Now she certainly had his full attention and it made her shudder that he could misunderstand her so badly.

'I was going to say, "if I didn't know you",' she added with as much cool dignity as she could when she wanted to slap him for believing she was taken in by a spiteful rumour.

'I beg your pardon,' he said stiffly, a flush of colour slashed high across his cheekbones, presumably because he had to admit he was wrong to a mere woman. No, a mere lady, she reminded herself and gave him a cold look that refused to take such a half-hearted apology far.

'I don't know you though, do I? I doubt anyone truly does and I'm sure that's how you like it.'

'What's to know?' he said with an impatient shrug.

It told her he believed he could drop out of the hearts and minds of his friends without more than the odd speculation of 'Whatever became of that reclusive young lord we once thought so fine and promising?' She passionately wanted to disagree.

'I can hardly decide where to begin,' she argued. 'You have to trust someone or you will end up as a recluse. Someone has to know you, my lord, however little you might want them to. You could start with telling Jack what you went through in India, since he's a man and your friend and you need to speak of it to someone. Next you could credit my mother and both my brothers and sisters with genuinely worrying about you when you hide away in that castle of yours as if nobody in the world cares about you. You were Jack and Rich's best friend when you were younger and nothing like as cynical, my lord. That means a lot to a Seaborne, even if it's apparently of very little matter to a Forthin.'

'And what do I mean to you, Miss Persephone Seaborne, since you have left yourself off that list of my well-wishers and friends?' he asked silkily and suddenly the silence in this inward-looking room was alive with questions and answers she dare not explore.

'You're a gentleman of contrary temper and a fathomless mystery to me, my lord,' she made herself joke lightly.

'Much as you are to me, Miss Persephone Seaborne,' he returned grimly.

'Am I?' she squeaked, shocked to find she passionately wanted to be more than a closed book or a bad-tempered virago to the aloof lord impossibly handsome young Alex Forthin had become.

'You are, Persephone,' he replied implacably, his gaze steady on hers.

'I thought you were completely indifferent to me,' she managed lamely.

'Impossible—no adult male with red blood in his veins could be indifferent to the Divine Persephone.'

She flinched, unable to hide her instinctive response to that hated nickname on his lips. 'You have no idea how deeply I wish my parents had named me Jane, or Ann, or Mary, or something equally simple,' she managed to say almost carelessly.

'Then you would have been the Divine Jane, or Ann or Mary, even if I have to admit that it sounds a lot less goddess-like. A name is just a name, sweetheart. No female with your allure and beauty could escape the notice of the opposite sex, even if she wasn't named for spring herself.'

To Persephone, who had grown up surrounded with images of Seaborne women and the women Seaborne men wanted and captivated as their wives, her looks were another version of a common set of family features. It had never occurred to her growing up among them to think herself a spectacular specimen.

'I'm not particularly beautiful and certainly not your sweetheart,' she replied, wishing she didn't care so much how she appeared to this cynical mystery of a man.

It felt as if they were walking on pins round each other in the dimly lit closeness of this intimate space. Hidden from the common rules and regulations of the world, she felt isolated with him by the night and everyone else's slumbers, as if only their thoughts and actions mattered in a sleeping world.

'You are possibly the loveliest woman I ever beheld and any man can dream of until he drives himself nigh mad with longing. Even you can't stop one doing so about you all too often, Miss

Seaborne,' he replied and there was something very serious in his steady look that made her heart thump heavily, then race on.

'Did you do that when you were held and tortured and endured all the other shameful mistreatment they wreaked on you, Alex?' she asked painfully, somehow unable to halt the question on her lips and wondering at herself for wishing he had.

'Not then,' he said with a shake of his head that spoke of honesty and regret. 'Don't forget you were a very cross little schoolgirl when I left for the army, forbidden to play with your brothers, cousin and friend and ordered to attend to her lessons, Persephone. I dreamt of someone very like you are now—a someone who could reach inside my tortured heart and join her clean, bright soul to my bitter one and insist on doing me good, despite all they did to me there to make me hate. I was getting ready to dream of you and only you every night from the moment I finally did lay eyes on you as a grown-up goddess. I've got so into the way of it now that I don't think even your displeasure will stop me doing it any more.'

'Maybe I don't want to stop you,' she murmured and suddenly found it impossible to meet his gaze full on without a host of huge possibilities humming between them like warm lightning after all.

'A man-made monster like me?' he questioned roughly, as if he actually believed he was hideous when he was so far from it she was shocked into meeting his eyes with far too much of her own feelings on show.

'To me you're just a grown-up and infinitely more powerful version of the youthful and arrogant Alex Forthin I first met, my lord,' she assured him, passionate sincerity in her gaze as she dwelt on his slightly imperfect classical perfection and smiled tenderly at his skewed opinion of himself to make him see how wrong he was. 'Wouldn't you have been a little too perfect without that?' she asked him with an airy gesture at the fine scarring he seemed to find so burdensome.

'How can you not find me repugnant and flawed?' he asked huskily.

'Easily enough on a physical level, my lord,

since you always were vexingly handsome. It's only on an everyday basis I find you somewhat trying.'

'Too trying to tolerate?'

'I'm here, aren't I? If I found you intolerable, I should certainly not have come here tonight. Nor would I have suggested a rendezvous where I would be forced to share close proximity to a man who repulsed me in any way.'

'I'm pleased to hear it, as no doubt Jack or one of your brothers would be when it's the height of folly in you to meet me here at any hour, my girl,' he said sternly, reverting to warrior type once more. 'Coming here to be closeted solely with me, in the middle of the night with the house sleeping about us, is madness. You must never risk your virtue and good name in such a reckless fashion again.'

'There you are, you see?' she pointed out indignantly as he went from oddly diffident about himself to a forbidding arbiter of ladylike behaviour between one breath and the next. 'I was right all along; you really are the most trying of men.'

'Because I'm brave enough to point out the

obvious as nobody else seems inclined to?' he asked, as if surprised she might find his condemnation irritating when it was so well founded.

'You have no right to censure my behaviour, my lord. If you think me so very rackety, you should never have come here to risk your reputation in the first place.'

'And leave you wandering about this great barn of a place alone and unprotected in the stilly watches of the night? What sort of a friend would that make me to your cousin and brother?'

'Oh, never mind them,' she rounded on him in a fury even she didn't understand.

Chapter Nine

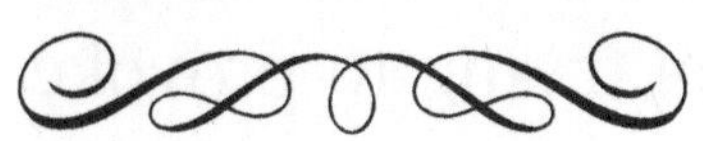

'Stop trying to make yourself behave so impersonally towards me and join the rest of us faulty, living, breathing human beings in the real world for once. However hard you try to make yourself into one, you're not a soulless automaton who doesn't give a damn about anyone else's feelings and never will,' Persephone stormed. 'You're a passionate and driven man, Alexander Forthin. I won't let you pretend otherwise to protect yourself from anyone who tries to get close to you, especially when it's me,' she ended with a smile she knew wobbled perilously on the edge of tears for this sensitive and mighty man who seemed to think he must hide himself from the critical eyes of the world.

'Your wish is my command,' he said with

rather grim humour and grasped the hand she had waved at him in an attempt to get him to take her seriously.

Tugged inexorably closer, she went without a fight. Was this exactly the reaction her inner siren had been trying to provoke from him for weeks now, even if her wicked little secret was unknown to the rest of her? Persephone felt a mass of contradictory hopes and fears churn inside her as he watched her steadily with his blue, blue eyes, both signalling the same message and never mind the silvered blur across one of them. Both wanted her and intended she should know it.

'Don't you know by now that you should take a very long spoon with you if you intend to sup with the devil, Miss Persephone Seaborne?' he murmured as her gaze blurred out of focus at last and his mouth came so close to hers she could feel him not yet quite close enough to kiss her but, oh, so temptingly nearly there.

'You're not a devil,' she heard herself whisper as she struggled with the idea of him as a fallen angel in all his once-perfect beauty and arrogance. 'You're not even half as bad as you want me to believe and you'll never be in the least bit like your father or brother if you live to be a hundred, Alex,' she carried recklessly on, knowing she was tempting him to prove himself right, but unable to believe anything he did would harm her as a hot and feral excitement stirred deep inside her and clamoured for attention.

It felt as if it could do such damage to what was growing between them if he *didn't* kiss her now. Curiosity and frustration banished her instinct to shy away from the unknown, the unimaginable gap between mystery and reality she wanted to plunge into. She longed for any of the real Alex Forthin he would leave unprotected to give, even if it exposed her heart to hurt. Perhaps sometimes you had to take headlong risks with your most vulnerable self to reach out for something wonderful that might never be if you didn't jump.

'For Heaven's sake get on and kiss me, you idiot,' she finally blurted out, afraid this was as close to it as she would get.

'You're the fool to risk me so much as touching you, let alone anything more,' he countered, but he did as she asked as if he couldn't help himself, either.

Astonished at the tight-strung tension in his body, the urgent longing of his firm mouth on hers, Persephone realised she'd underestimated Alexander Forthin. There was fire in his intensely blue eyes and his harsh breathing; his rigidly restrained mouth on hers explored hesitantly, as if he didn't dare unleash his deepest inner need for fear of harming or shocking her with desperation for everything she had to give. Oh, yes, *he wanted her.*

How long had he been fighting against this utter intimacy, the wild heat and desperate longing? Far too long, it seemed, from the faint tremble in his hand when he swept a stray curl behind her ear and smoothed it as if everything depended on its precise arrangement. Suspecting he did it to steady himself, to give them enough time to measure out this sweet seduction of each other and somehow get back to their sensible everyday selves, she countered by reaching up to play with his sooty locks in her turn, feeling the springy softness of them under her hands as he let her distract him, then moved both hands back so they cupped her neck and held her spellbound and open to his ever more urgent kisses.

The first sweet touch of his mouth on hers had been surprisingly gentle and almost supplicating. Now it became ever more hot and certain as she yielded everything she had to give without any caveats of Corisande-like possibilities interfering between them. This was uniquely special and for them alone.

Persephone felt a crucial spot somewhere near her feminine core threaten to melt when he opened his mouth on hers and urged her lips to part and let him in. Nothing could have stopped her doing so short of an earthquake and perhaps not even that. It felt impossibly urgent to open to him in every way she could as his driven eagerness to wind himself into the two of them utterly disarmed her. She moaned at the heady novelty of his tongue probing her mouth, his lips urgent and nigh desperate on hers while he taught her more about kisses than she'd imagined there was to know.

All thought of experimenting with passion for

a few moments then drawing back before too much damage was done melted away. Driven by a compulsion to learn all she could about wondrous and mysterious Alexander Forthin, Earl of Calvercombe, she rose on tiptoes as he shifted his hands so they rested in the small of her back and clasped her as close to him as she'd thought any being could get, until now when a wild instinct and feminine suspicions whispered there was far more for them to know, between lovers.

It felt terribly hot in this enclosed little world she had lured them into. She felt utterly preoccupied with this ardently true self Alex protected from the rest of the world so fiercely, but had finally let her see. She revelled in the intimacy, the trust of it. A conviction she might melt from the inside out after discovering how desperately she wanted the real man under all his armour washed over her at the same time that she knew to step back and learn distance from him again would be a move she'd regret for the rest of her days.

Uncertain where this intense need they had unleashed between them might take them, she stretched against him, greedy for hot, rigidly masculine Alex Forthin's muscular torso hard against her suddenly painful breasts. He felt firm and fit, yet alien against her own hotly aroused body. She drifted exploring hands down his strong and intriguingly sensitive nape to search his wide shoulders and narrow waist, resting there appreciatively before he forestalled her curiosity about his neat buttocks by lifting her a little more off her feet so she was perched on top of some long-dead queen's elaborate Spanish chest and he could control her curiosity better.

Not sure that she wanted it controlled, she pouted her dissatisfaction and saw his mouth quirk into a grin that made her heart jump with urgent delight. Somehow that boyish look had become so dear to her when she wasn't noticing. And that reluctant half-grin of his, the half-grimace that wanted to lock out the world but somehow still had to let her in, despite his self-doubts and fury.

Under her wariness and the anger and distrust she'd felt in him ever since that night by the lake more than two months ago, had this desperation for each other been growing between them all unknowing? It had certainly sprung up like a protected plant now, sheltered from the wild tempest around it by sprouting into unstoppable growth before either of them could kill it, and how glad she was of their ignorance if this was the result.

No wonder she hadn't let herself like him when they met again. And she reminded herself even this physical closeness and intimacy didn't mean he'd ever let her into his locked heart. She yearned to cause such a crack in his defences he'd never be able to shut her out again. Sheer folly, maybe, but somehow the chance and a more basic longing of her for him kept her revelling in his kisses and caresses, wound tight into the web of kissing and exploring each other they were spinning between them with every touch and taste.

He splayed a broad palm over one of her eager breasts and centred it against a shamelessly roused nipple, rubbing an emphatic sensual circle on it through her silk gown with him and her at the centre of it. She moaned on a long gasp of pleasure and felt that fire burn ever higher, feeling frustrated that her eager body gave away everything it wanted from him while setting her away from his masculinity, leaving her to guess his need of her.

Unable to damp down her ardour, curiosity, or feelings as he wanted, she shifted on the centuries' hardened wood he'd seated her on as she felt the ties of her gown give just enough so he could draw her normally demure evening gown down to gape and let the cooling night air excite her heated skin even more. Fascinated by his expression of awed voraciousness in the soft light of that single wax candle, she forgot his sins of omission as he uncovered her eager nipples as if they were the most precious treasure he'd ever laid eyes on.

A faint flash of colour burnt high on his aristocratic cheekbones now, a heat even less unmistakable lit his bluest of eyes to the depthless glow of a high summer sky and his mouth was full and passionate from kissing. He was centred with her, fascinated by every nuance of him and her they were exploring together. Did she look as transformed by this unexpected wonder between them? She promptly forgot her outer image as the incomparable Miss Seaborne as the real, inner

Persephone took over. He flicked a wondering finger over one of those revealed and revealing, tightly urgent nipples of hers and all that mattered now was that her lover had his hands and mouth and even his very breath centred on rousing her already achingly aroused body even more desperately and she wanted even more.

Sure he was the one man on earth she could bear to see her like this, to feel her flame and need so fiercely, she drank in the sight of him. The feel of his touch on one of her most secret places flared and flushed and she was desperate for more and ever more as she watched, fascinated at how deeply he wanted her in return. His pupils flared and contracted as he felt her respond to his touch and to watching him touch. His mouth firmed as he seemed desperate to control himself in the face of that vast and uncharted welcome of hers to do what came next and hang the consequences. She realised he was going to be strong for her in some instinctive feminine fashion, but found it impossible to chide him for it when he was wreaking such endlessly deepening pleasure on her willing body that it soaked her usually acute mind in sensual lethargy and stopped her voice in her throat.

Aghast for just a moment when he dipped his mouth to her breast, she leaned back on her hands on the rather knobbly carved surface under her and let her head hang back with a soundless groan of pleasure she only just managed to silence, in deference to the night. The damp heat of his mouth on her was a glory she wouldn't have even begun to imagine meeting in the marriage bed. Lucky really, she decided hazily, since she might have leapt into it in the wrong company if she'd guessed it could be like this. Not that it would be so uniquely wonderful without him, a wiser Persephone whispered.

She let one hand prop her on the unwelcoming surface of the Spanish chest and raised the other to caress his head where he feasted so tenderly hungry at her eager breasts it made tears threaten behind her half-closed eyes, even as fire shot to the secret heart of her. Moved by the unexpected magic of them together, she flexed her upper body until she could kiss his noble, stubborn head while he nuzzled and drove her nigh crazy with the molten heat rippling like a rip tide between her hard peaked nipples and the hot core of her. The wild rhythm of it all seemed likely to drag her into either agony or ecstasy at any moment.

Raising his head as if he regretted every inch that separated him from her now heavily roused and yet hotly tight breasts, he met her eyes for a long moment of wonder before he put his hands about her slender waist and urged her closer to the edge of her impromptu perch. Unable to deny him anything he wanted of her, even while she was still struggling with her surprise that he was the *one,* her only lover, she let him splay her slender legs a little further apart and hitch up irrelevant skirts before he shocked her with sensuality once more. This time he knelt between her legs and caressed the dark curls at her very centre before giving her a long look as if to tell her all he couldn't say out loud, then he set his mouth to the heated core of her and gently held her still when she would have shied away in an instinctive protest at such an unmapped and undreamt-of intimacy.

His strong hands, hard yet gentle, learned her softest curves, while his tongue caused havoc with the very place she'd vaguely known needed something of him from the start, but probably not this. She was a country girl, after all, and had seen animals mate. Indeed, she had been fascinated by the differences between male and female at one stage in her life, noticing that girls grew into women and boys into men even as her body began to change and her mind strove to catch up. As Alex feasted on her as if he couldn't get enough of the taste and feel and hot need of her, she wondered if even then she had singled him out as a man she might one day want so much it felt as if she might break if she didn't have more of him than this. Perhaps she was making this sensual pleasuring more than it should be, she cautioned herself hazily, but the time for caution was clearly gone, and she couldn't help but long for everything he had to give.

Still he licked and probed and stroked her private heart and flicked his knowing tongue so effectively over parts of her she barely knew she had until tonight. Even as she shifted restlessly on the polished wood beneath her with need of *him,* some unstoppable force was building inside her and outpacing everything else. He was holding her poised on a tightly wound edge with his demanding hands and generous tongue and she felt as if the very bones had melted out of her when she fell back on her lumpy wooden couch to finally let him do whatever would stoke this torturous fire out of control and give her release. Surely such a limitless ride to pleasure couldn't go on for ever? It felt as if it might when it seemed he knew exactly when to withdraw the silky stimulation of tongue and lips to prolong the sweetest, tautest tension she had never dared even imagine before tonight. He murmured something near a moan of desperation, as if he'd driven himself to the far edges of even his control, and he widened her splayed legs yet further so he could grip her hips and concentrate on stroking her into ever-rising waves of pleasure, teaching her to climb some unknown height she risked never reaching as she soared and strove under his driven stimulation.

Then, one last thrust of that wicked tongue into

her secret, heated core and she bowed with ecstasy, urgent pleasure singing and spreading inside her even as she convulsed wildly and longed with all her heart for him to be able to take flight with her. She felt him replace his mouth with a strong and sensitive hand and he lithely rose to prop himself over her supine body, still considering her, wonder-soaked as she was, by bending to seize her mouth with his as his wickedly knowing touch on her core caressed her even further into bliss and she tasted herself on his lips. She soared into a glorious conclusion with his mouth hot and hungry on hers and his long, masculine fingers deep inside her, hinting how it would be when he took her fully. Only a mighty, generous and compelling lover could make this golden warmth more blissful, more wondrous for her.

For endless seconds they kissed and held each other as if it was unbearable to part. His embrace was gentle now, his touch almost soothing as she struggled with her first true experience of sensual pleasure. Despite all he could do not to let her know it, she knew he was hard as iron and desperate for her. He shook with the effort of holding himself back from taking her to full and complete womanhood as his lover. Every inch of her was alive as it had never been before; utterly pleasured and sweetly satiated. Yet she knew that while she had learnt what joy there was between a woman and her lover, he had none of it to linger over with awe and wonder as she did.

'What about you?' she finally whispered when her tongue learned how to speak again, feeling inflexible and unfit for its everyday purpose as she managed to use it for something other than wanting him and telling him so.

'I'll survive,' he muttered, as if not quite sure what words were for, either.

She kissed his wickedly skilful mouth as if to comfort him with the knowledge that though he might not be particularly good with words just now, he was matchless at giving her such pleasure that she'd never even dreamt existed until tonight. She clung to him as if some enemy might be lurking ready to rip him out of her arms. Astonished at herself for becoming such a new-made creature, she felt little echoing jerks of pleasure surprise her now and again as they stayed locked in each other's arms and she wondered how awesomely satiated she might feel after being fully and potently loved by the Earl of Calvercombe.

Overwhelmed with pleasure, she decided, awash with it, marooned by it on some distant shore she might never find the strength to return from. Hardly able to bear the idea of him gallantly holding back and isolated from her as he nobly refrained from taking her maidenhead, she shifted in his arms and met his heat-hazed blue gaze with a question in her own. Still a part of her was amazed at what this private, softly lit little world had made of them. How right it felt to be pleasure-racked and satiated in Alex Forthin's arms, when she had come here tonight with no clue that she wanted this—and yet more!—from him.

'Doesn't it hurt you not to?' she asked a little breathlessly. Hearing a touch of débutante naïvety in her voice, she was a little shocked to find out she wasn't as wise or sophisticated as she'd thought herself until tonight.

'Not enough to kill me, Goddess,' he said with a wry quirk of his mouth that she somehow wanted to watch in complete and besotted fascination until the stars faded and the sun rose every night for the rest of her life.

'But why didn't you?' She finally made herself ask the question lying unsaid between them, feeling sharp reality threatening to creep in once she put it into words.

'Because you are you,' he said dourly and must have felt her flinch.

Refusing to quite meet her eyes, he drew a little apart and pulled her body upright, letting her skirts fall to their proper level and urging her gown to hitch itself up until it at least covered her still-tender nipples from his sight once more. He held her still when she would have hurriedly re-ordered Miss Persephone Seaborne and pushed herself away from him, checking her legs would hold her, then keeping his hands on her slender waist until she had the strength back in them, disarming her attempts to recover her famous aloofness by losing some of his own.

'I won't have you nagged and reproached and bullied into becoming my Countess unless you truly want to be, Persephone,' he told her as if he had been considering his words carefully and the very idea horrified him.

'Doubtless you have a very different one in mind, once you finally rediscover your cousin and re-establish your estates and your fortune to your own satisfaction,' she half-asked, half-concluded in a bitter voice she hated to associate with all that had passed between them since they met here at the witching hour of midnight.

She fought the feeling her whole world was about to contract into a very small space once it was deprived of him in it. She had met this impossible, unknowable man at midnight the night Jack and Jessica finally succumbed to love and pledged the future to each other. She didn't think her latest midnight encounter with Alexander Forthin would result in a similarly happy outcome.

He might still be holding her as if she were precious, but it was only to stop her turning away and avoiding his gaze until they hastily parted. Would that he *were* intent on keeping her here in his arms, so she could feel his heart now beating slow, steady and strong in his chest against her, because he couldn't bear to let her go. She let herself yearn for that unlikely love-struck Alex Forthin as the real one drew in a heavy breath, as if turning his back on what could hurt him as well.

'No,' he said on a long sigh and let it out again, as if the chilling air between them had dealt him some unspoken hurt even as dreams she wouldn't even let herself know died a-borning. 'I doubt I shall ever marry. Sweet little débutantes don't appeal to me any more than I do to them. I can't abide the thought of some hard-headed little widow steeling herself to endure me in her bed for the rest of our natural lives for the title I can give her in exchange for an heir or two, either.'

'You really are an idiot,' she told him seriously.

'No, I'm a realist,' he argued so gravely she could see he believed it.

'Do I seem in any way repulsed by you, Alex?' she asked impatiently. She was sure the enchantment he'd shown her still sparkled in her eyes and flushed her cheeks, whatever they might be doing to kill it off with too much reality.

'You come of a passionate race, Miss Seaborne. I caught you in feminine curiosity and took shameless advantage,' he told her in a clipped voice, his expression closed off as if he was fighting off a dangerous foe.

How dare he diminish the roar and promise that had sprung into life between them, so real and alive only seconds ago? Persephone stamped her foot at his intransigence and the ancient oak boards felt as hard as iron under her lightly shod feet.

'Say I come from a clever race rather, Lord Calvercombe. I can safely promise you I'm far too wary to try out any lord who happens to be handy and might prove passably desirable as a lover,' she reproached him and saw the point of slapping a man for only looking at her the wrong way when he raised one eyebrow and inspected her as if to prove his point. 'I could never let another man take such liberties with me,' she informed him as haughtily as she could, while part of her longed for him to take them again, with added interest.

'He might not do so with your consent,' he said grimly, as if getting ready to flay the hide off any man who dared try to force so much as a kiss she didn't want.

'You think I would risk meeting a man who might take what I won't freely give him as I have you? Please don't be more of a masculine fool about us women than you can help.'

'Arrogant little goddess,' he chided softly. He probably had no idea how she coveted that rueful smile of his and the look in his eyes that told her she was special to him, pretend otherwise as he might.

'Little, my lord?' she asked, offering no protest at the rest.

Knowing the first part of his description was sometimes true, she liked the idea of being unique and shining in his eyes, imperfect as she knew herself to be.

'Arrogant medium-sized goddess lacks the same ring somehow, don't you think?' he asked quietly, apparently as reluctant to release her as she was to go.

Afterwards she couldn't recall what she might have said to persuade him that only he, Alexander Forthin, no matter if he was Earl of Calvercombe or no, could lead her into the liberty of lovers. There wasn't even the sliver of a chance any other man could charm or seduce her into opening herself up to him in so many ways she couldn't bring herself to count them right now. She wasted a few moments of their time out of the real world trying to fill her senses with five indelible stamps of him on her memory, so she might sleep after all and dream of him as totally hers, completely her lover and no other woman's, ever.

Even as she decided it wasn't fair to rest against him and reignite the raging, unsated need she knew was a mere caress away for him, when he was a chivalrous idiot who wouldn't take the last step they both needed and make her his lover in every sense of the word, the heavy oak door burst open and Corisande let the world in with a vengeful, envious glint in her already green eyes.

Chapter Ten

'Now tell me I'm imagining things,' Corisande demanded of her audience of Lady Henry Seaborne and a very sleepy and ruffled-looking Hughes the butler. 'Look at her all rumpled and undone and blushing guiltily if you won't believe me. You wouldn't accept my word when I told you she was meeting a lover, Cousin Melissa, but you can't help but admit it now!' Persephone's not-very-fond cousin exclaimed shrilly, as if she wanted the whole world to hear her. 'And since she's still got the stink of him on her, don't even try to tell me there was anything innocent about their sordid assignation in an unused room, away from sight and sound of the rest of the household and your guests.'

'Stand aside,' Lady Henry Seaborne demanded

curtly, determined to cling to her dignity in the face of Corisande's vengeful accusations, even if her daughter looked to be irretrievably tattered by her night's work. 'Have you two truly been meeting in secret all these weeks?' she asked, as if even the thought they might be carrying on an illicit affair behind her back hurt her terribly.

'No! And why on earth would we feel the need to sneak around so furtively to meet each other in secret, Mama?' Persephone was stung into asking.

Lady Henry surveyed her daughter with a critical eye and Persephone was suddenly conscious they had never got round to re-lacing her bodice and her hair had fallen down. She must look as if she'd been outside in a hurricane, or thoroughly seduced by the Earl of Calvercombe.

'Since you have clearly done so tonight, that's a question I should very much like to have answered at a time when all three of us are a great deal calmer and more rational than we can be now,' her mother said with such quiet dignity that Persephone felt hot colour flame across her cheeks.

'You intend to cover it all up and pretend nothing out of the common way has occurred, your ladyship?' Corisande exclaimed as if horrified such scandal might be swept under Jack's ducal carpet when she'd been flitting about country houses in the middle of the night, intent on far more scandalous encounters than this one, since she was hardly old enough to be out of the schoolroom.

'As we have been politely concealing your wilder misdeeds from the rest of the polite world for years, Cousin Corisande, we Seabornes have had plenty of practice at doing so by now.' Lady Henry turned on the instigator of this scene with such icy self-control Persephone knew how angry she must be under that calm façade. 'I suggest you do public penance for your own sins if you wish to start casting stones at my daughter. That way they will carry a little more weight when you throw them. I'm quite sure your Great-Aunt Augustina will supply you with the name of a suitable convent so we can arrange to have you smuggled across to France or Spain. There you can begin your new career as a pillar of outraged virtue as soon as may be.'

Corisande actually hung her head rather than face more chilly looks from the lady the rest of the Seabornes respected as the true matriarch of the family, despite the Dowager Duchess's apparent claim to the role. Nevertheless, Persephone knew the story would be off and running as soon as the household woke the next morning and Corisande's maid was called to dress her for a day of furtive scandal-mongering. Whatever power was deployed against her, Corisande would never hold her tongue and Persephone resigned herself to becoming a scarlet woman. It seemed all the more of a pity Alex had restrained his manly passions with such a heroic effort and not fully become her lover. If she was to be hung as a sheep, providence might at least have granted her a year's growth of wool to keep warm with.

'I lured Miss Seaborne here at this scandalous hour of the night in order to beg her to marry me,' she heard Alex tell her mother in a gruffly embarrassed voice, and tried her best to believe her ears were deceiving her. 'I thought the setting must be romantic enough to make her relent and say yes at long last,' he carried on as if he'd been begging her to do so for all the weeks he'd been trying to push her away.

'Some sort of yes seems to have been accomplished tonight, whatever the truth behind it,' her mother said with a stern look that made Persephone want to hang her head and shuffle her feet.

Alex managed to look as if he was torn between delight and shame over his extreme methods of persuading his lady to marry him after a long campaign. She wondered numbly at his acting ability as the horror of him being shamed into marrying her ground away any belief she might have left that he truly wanted her as his Countess.

'It is to be hoped you managed to obtain the consent required to restore my beloved daughter's good name, as well as whatever other form you obtained from her tonight by fair means and foul, my lord?' her mother challenged Alex with a straight look for her son-in-law-to-be that might chill the marrow of a lesser man.

'Persephone would never have kissed me back in the first place if she wasn't seriously considering it, my lady,' he said as if he knew her far too well and was longing for his pantomime offer to be accepted.

Lady Henry might be content with that ambiguous answer for now, but Corisande clearly wasn't. 'Are you going to marry him or not?' she demanded sourly, as if she'd thought about doing so herself and begrudged him to anyone else.

Even Persephone knew there was more chance of the Thames freezing over in high summer than his wedding a lady with so little reputation left to lose. If Alex had been caught in carnal congruity with Corisande, she doubted anyone but Corisande would have expected him to marry her. Persephone's racing thoughts stalled when she realised such a lot would fall to her if she refused Alex's *de facto* offer.

Despite her aristocratic status and previously spotless reputation, she would be easy prey to any fortune-hunting schemer who wanted to marry into one of the most powerful families in the land. Her family would be forced to defend her lack of virtue at every turn and poor Jack would be beside himself with fury, even as he fought duel after duel to assert her honour in the face of all the evidence. The idea of him fighting Alex over her blasted reputation made her shudder and rapidly make up her mind to accept his half-hearted offer after all. They had made themselves a marriage bed tonight. However hard it might prove.

'You're right,' she agreed softly, turning to look up at him as if he was the light and centre of her very life and saw a flare of something in his eyes she doubted really was joy and relief. 'I have agreed we will be wed as soon as Jack and Jess are back from their honeymoon, if you will consent to such haste, Mama?'

'Consent, my love? I will dance down the aisle after you two have pledged yourself to one another with the lightest heart a mother ever rejoiced in, if you can promise me you love him as dearly as he clearly loves you,' her mother said, as if she truly believed Alex was as besotted with her as Jack was with his beloved new wife.

'Oh, I do, Mama,' she said with a candour that seemed to resolve all Lady Henry's doubts, since she smiled as if this was a very conventional betrothal rather than a scandalous hand-fasting in the little hours of the night.

Squashing a fleeting sense of guilt, Persephone knew enough about the world to acknowledge Alex Forthin was deeply attracted to her, but certainly didn't love her. He would struggle to make their marriage work because he was a good man and would never walk away from a lady whose good name he had compromised. If Corisande hadn't been stinging from his rejection and determined to bring Persephone down, who knew what they might have built on tonight's conflagration of the senses? Too late for that now, she decided sadly, while she did her best to look like a newly betrothed lady who had just landed a very fine husband indeed.

'If you wish to be invited to the wedding, or any other family gathering at Ashburton or Seaborne House in the future, Cousin Corisande, I suggest you abandon any more schemes you are concocting to damage my daughter's standing in the eyes of the world,' Lady Henry warned with a stern look.

'And as Jack's new Duchess happens to be

related to any of the *ton* he isn't connected to himself, at least *I* shall not need to exert myself unduly to make sure you're very swiftly ruined and expelled from polite society if you move against my future wife in any way, madam,' Alex added with chilling indifference.

Thanks to her intervention, Alex now had to marry Persephone, so perhaps Corisande would believe him. Persephone suspected he was too soft-hearted to let even Corisande sink any lower, but if the annoying harpy believed he would twiddle his thumbs while she was cast out, she might behave long enough for her tale to lack impact when she finally told it.

'It will be a scrambling affair anyway,' Corisande said sulkily, but Persephone knew she would dine out on their wedding for months.

'No, it will be perfect,' Alex argued, taking Persephone's cold hand in his warm one, as if he wanted to make *her* feel better about this scrambled-together wedding of theirs when so much of it was her fault, for suggesting this ill-considered meeting place and possessing a relative like Corisande in the first place.

'But not quite as splendid as Jack and Jessica's wedding was I hope?' she asked with a would-be happy smile that ought to tell anyone watching they could hardly wait to be sanctioned and blessed as a couple.

'So do I, my love, since I don't intend to wait two months to claim my bride as poor Jack was forced to do to wed *his* duchess,' he said huskily and Persephone wondered if he'd ever considered making a living on the stage.

'As mother of the bride, I have dreamt of my eldest daughter's wedding since she was barely out of swaddling bands. Had I known it would be to you, my boy, I might have dreamt of it even more hopefully,' Lady Henry said with a hazy smile that brought tears to Persephone's tired eyes.

If only it were true; if only Mama were right and Alex was indeed the best and most loving bridegroom she could pick out. She would have thrilled to the romance and breathless fascination of being made love to by the dazzling young man she recalled coming here to stay all those years ago. On those days she had longed so desperately to be out of the schoolroom and doing her best to shyly fascinate her elder brother's most enthralling friend, before some other older and more privileged female could capture his wild heart. When he went off to be a soldier she would have given her eye teeth to have him look at her with admiration and longing in his eyes. Now both of them were grown up and all she could expect was driven passion in the bedchamber and cool tolerance elsewhere.

She let herself gaze up at him with everything there could have been in her eyes, then lowered her gaze to meet Corisande's with an unspoken challenge *not* to believe they were deep in love. Glad when her remote cousin let her eyes drop before the cool assurance the Countess of Calvercombe was going to need to get her through her new life, Persephone yawned delicately to imply it was high time they were all safely in their separate beds.

Luckily Hughes had left the moment he realised something untoward was afoot between his fellow conspirators. Corisande was not going to let good manners get in the way of her triumph, though, even if it was a triumph she couldn't trumpet to the world. She waited stubbornly for Persephone and her mother to precede her out of the room with a smug look for Alex, left standing impassive and alone to take up the candle and light the ladies into the great hall, where spare candles could be got and their ways could finally part.

Persephone felt terribly weary by the time they left him to go his way and Corisande hers—Alex to Jack's grand wing, Corisande to the least important guest room Ashburton possessed. Persephone wished vengefully her cousin had the scullery maid's humble bed, close to the vast kitchens so she could light the fires well before dawn. The scullery maid certainly deserved a soft feather bed and an undisturbed night's sleep far more than Corisande ever would.

Lady Henry paused outside her eldest daughter's bedchamber and gave her a look that told her she knew there was far more to this affair than any mother wanted to be told.

'It's high time we were all in bed, my love. We all stand in need of as much sleep as we can get against the frantic day we're sure to have tomorrow, with your betrothal to announce and all the preparations for your wedding to be made in so short a time,' she said softly.

'Indeed, Mama,' Persephone agreed meekly and kissed her mother's cheek, before giving her a weary smile to thank her for understanding she was beyond explaining tonight. Then she stumbled into her deserted bedchamber to fall asleep as soon as her head hit the pillow.

'Shock,' her ladyship muttered to herself before removing her shoes and pulling up the covers. 'At least I managed to get *some* sleep before that wretched female insisted on tracking down our daughter so she could prove to me what a scandal was brewing under dear Jack's roof, Henry my love,' she told the miniature of her late husband she kept on her nightstand. 'Not that you would have objected to the match any more than I do, darling, but I wonder how long it will take those two stubborn children to realise they could have been put on this good earth to love one another, they're so well suited?'

Eyeing the irrepressible humour obvious in

Lord Henry Seaborne's finely painted image, she nodded as if he'd spoken and smiled a wry smile. 'Aye, it did take us two far too long to discover the same thing, did it not?' she asked the soft pre-dawn air and fell into a reverie about bridesmaids and flowers and music that inevitably drifted into memories of her own wedding day.

It had been a wonderful spring wedding, the airy romance of it all almost wasted on Miss Melissa Caroline Malvan and the very suitable Lord Henry Seaborne, neither of whom had had the sense to know at the time that they were wedding the love of their life one fine May morning at Ashburton Church nearly thirty years ago.

'I have high hopes for this hastily arranged marriage, Hal, despite a distinctly raffish start to it I cannot help but wonder at,' she muttered as her eyelids grew heavy and her breathing began to slow after all.

As she drifted into sleep it was almost as if she could feel her love next to her and see his knowing smile as if he sleepily answered, 'Sometimes they turn into true love matches all unknowing, my love', then turn over and went back to sleep as he might have done if only he was still alive and real in her bed, instead of a certainty out of sight and touch that she hoped her darling daughter would never have to miss so savagely in her own marriage bed.

Marcus Seaborne stirred on his hard bed and listened intently for any sounds in the corridor outside his cell. He had come to the conclusion this had to be a gentleman's residence of some sort, although it had clearly fallen on hard times. The occasional rumble of heavy hooves on cobbles or the light sound of a pony cart said there was no elegant hurry of leisured families calling on each other at polite hours of the day. When he stood on a rickety chair to look out, all he could see was an inner courtyard, long abandoned and rank with weeds.

He'd begun to dig mortar out from round the base of the bars on that high window. Not that an inside court with walls all round looked the best place in the world to escape into, but if he didn't do something he might run mad. It was a slow and perilous job, since his chair wasn't much better than the rest of the rotting lumber in his improvised cell, but it occupied a few weary hours. There was nothing else to do but struggle with the ancient prayer book he'd found in a chest of motheaten blankets or read endless volumes of Richardson's *Clarissa* his occasional cellmate kept here against the boredom of his conversation.

Marcus preferred action to the stalwart suffering of a tragic heroine and had wondered out loud last time she bustled into the room what such a practical lady had in common with lovely, doomed Clarissa Harlowe. He smiled as he recalled her salty answer that beggars couldn't be choosers and to thank his lucky stars it was at least in English and not some barbarous tongue. Wondering what she thought boys did at their lessons besides learn to decipher barbarous tongues, he smiled into the gloom of his subterranean cell and pondered his captivity.

His nurse and wardress hadn't been locked in with him for long since that first day when he was almost delirious. She had a silent companion who locked the door behind her, then opened it when she shouted to leave. He had learnt to listen for them while he scraped at the mortar grain by frustrating grain and wondered if someone would question the girl's disappearance if she came at set times of day. He couldn't think of anyone he had offended so vilely they might take such a revenge on him and had the impression she was uneasy and at odds with the person who silently escorted her here. Shaking his head, he gave up on his excavations for the day and lay back on the makeshift bed with his tousled head resting on clasped hands.

He grinned as he thought of his fair gaoler passing the pot from the ancient commode they had at least allowed him to the unseen presence outside, as if he deserved it, and wondered if the man remained whilst she shaved the prisoner, then solemnly passed razor and whiskery water out of the door for her confederate to dispose of as well. This odd business had removed him from the frenetic round his life in town had become. How astonished a younger Marcus Seaborne might be, he decided from the vantage point of three and twenty, at how the amusements of a leisured gentleman could pall once he'd sampled most of the pleasures high society had to offer him.

Of course, his ladybird could always be relied on to relieve the tedium and he frowned at the thought of Clary waiting in vain for him at the neat house he'd installed her in while he was out of town. He wondered if she'd gone back to her native city to find a more reliable keeper and realised he wouldn't mind that much if she had. She was a sweet little armful, but he was struggling by now to recall if she was a blonde or a brunette. He was jolted out of his reverie by the sound of the key in the door and jumped to his feet, determined not to be discovered lying abed.

'What hold does he have over you?' he asked softly, in case the man was still close enough to hear him speak and might come back to eavesdrop.

'I've brought you dinner,' she told him, as if he hadn't spoken.

'And are you intending to dispose of me horribly if some demand is not met?' he made himself ask lightly.

'I have no idea,' she responded as if bored by

the whole unsavoury affair, but he saw unease in her dark eyes before she turned away.

'Then at least have the kindness to tell me what day it is?'

'Friday,' she replied shortly, setting the covered plate down.

'And my family have still not found me? How remiss of them,' he said as if it was only a matter of time.

'Indeed,' she said coolly.

'I wager local society flock to listen to your eloquent banter.'

'They hardly know I exist.'

'Their loss,' he told her as if under some obligation to make her feel better.

'And my gain,' she snapped back.

'Undoubtedly,' he agreed genially.

'You have all the choices of how to spend your time a gentleman of your privileged birth can rejoice in, do you not?'

'I don't aspire to be part of Prinny's inner circle or take up politicking.'

'You could take any path through life, but you do nothing?'

'I have a formidably capable cousin and a restless elder brother. They did and, on the part of my cousin Jack, still do, all the putting the world to rights one family will ever need,' he told her with a would-be lightness he no longer quite felt.

'So while they work, you worry about the pattern on your waistcoats, the cut of your coat and the polish on your topboots? How profligate.'

'At least I do no harm to anyone else. You kidnap gentlemen who never did you harm and flower unseen in the social wilderness, then twit *me* on a wasted life, Miss Morality?'

'Who says I'm a miss?'

'This does,' he replied with a careless flick of his index finger across her generous mouth. 'And as such, you should never be left alone with a rake like me,' he warned in a voice even he could hear had dropped an octave at the thought of her lips under his. He held her fathomless gaze for a moment, but something more than curiosity in her eyes made her seem too vulnerable.

'I know,' she agreed absently.

'Yet still you keep coming back,' he made himself almost accuse her.

'Eat your dinner,' she ordered abruptly and shouted for release.

Marcus leant against the rough-hewn wall nearest to him and made himself look indifferent. Truth was, he realised, he spent every hour in this dreary hole dreaming of the next time she would enliven his life for a few moments.

Chapter Eleven

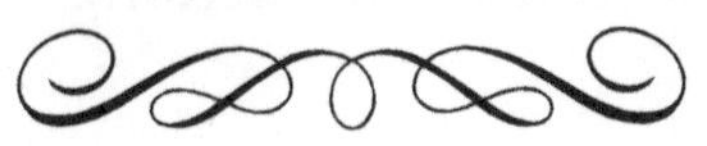

'There's no news, is there?' Persephone asked Alex as soon as they could escape Corisande and the more conventional chaperons and talk privately once the fuss and furor over their sudden engagement had died down and their guests had resorted to their rooms to frantically write letters to all their friends.

'No more than there was yesterday,' he returned grimly and she still found it almost impossible to meet his eyes and see how trapped he felt by the marriage about to be forced on him because he'd tried to find Marcus for her.

'I'm sorry,' she said with a feeble attempt at a smile.

'So am I, but how is it your fault he is missing?'

'You know very well that's not what I meant.'

'Then so am I, but if wed I must, better if I wed you than any other female I ever came across,' he told her with that crooked smile she had learned to look for so attentively over the last few weeks and months without even noticing she did so until today.

'Well, that's something at least,' she said as lightly as she could manage after a sleepless night and too many hours of self-recrimination.

'No doubt you can think of many more worthy gentlemen than I to call husband, but you seem to have yourself promised to an unworthy one without ever saying yea or nay to the idea. It is I who must be sorry for that, Persephone.'

'Then don't be, I'm well content,' she said, meeting his eyes at last and finding them quizzical and impossible to read, as if he'd somehow closed himself off to her again after the scorching intimacy of last night, and she did her best not to feel bitterly disappointed.

'Then it will be both my job as your husband and my pleasure as your lover to keep you so once we are wed, my dear,' he told her with the sort of wolfish look she felt he expected her prospective bridegroom to send her.

She supposed he must have learnt to conceal his deepest feelings long before he left for the army, then India, after a childhood such as the one he must have endured without a mother and with an indifferent father and a jealous half-brother to blight it. After he was captured, he seemed to have turned that self-sufficiency into a steely barrier to conceal his emotions from the world, however hard his captors tried to force them out of him, and it felt as formidable between them now as a seven-foot wall.

'What do you expect of your wife in return then, Alex?'

'Whatever you want to give me, Persephone. I expect you to let our marriage lie lightly on you, so it doesn't become the trap so many ladies of breeding and expectation seem to find their marriages, once they finally achieve the end they have spent their whole lives preparing for. Although nobody could accuse you of being a husband hunter, I hate the idea of my lady feeling she's been caught and catalogued under the label "wife" and must endure my husbandly attentions until the requisite heir and a spare inhabit the nurseries in all sorts of antiquated old houses we will have to try to bring up to date somehow. It is to be hoped you have more talent for making ancient old barns into homes for us than I do, by the way, for you will have a fair few of them to civilise if you and our future family are ever to be comfortable.'

'We shall soon find out, shall we not?' she said, thinking that her future accommodation seemed like the least of her problems at the moment.

'I suppose you must be more worried about your brother's whereabouts than you are about enduring the discomforts of my more ancient possessions?'

'Of course,' she said on a weary sigh, for he seemed to read her as easily as a chap book while his deepest thoughts and fears were unknown to his future wife.

'Then I'm ready to admit we are going to need help in tracking him down. I can hardly keep disappearing from your life as I did last week now I'm openly declared to be your deeply besotted fiancé. Mrs Beddington will watch us like a hawk from now on, in the hope of seeing estrangement where we assured her there was only the most irresistible of passions.'

'And how she would love to spread scandal about us, so I dare say you're right,' she agreed as if she was already a meek little spouse and saw from his frown how little he liked the idea. 'I'm very tired,' she said with a shrug as if that might explain her unusual docility.

'Your mother proposes we meet her by the lake after you have had luncheon, and house guests like Mrs Beddington, who simply refuse to be tactful and finally leave us to plan our wedding in peace, can look after themselves for once. Apparently she knows a way there they are all ignorant of and hinted you would show it to me if I asked nicely. An afternoon spent resting or doing nothing in particular in Lady Henry's good company sounds an ideal antidote to intense passion and drama to me. I'm told I can fish whilst you and your mama doze or plan the best ways of making a September wedding memorable, if still a little hasty.'

'She doesn't mean to be bossy,' Persephone explained feebly.

'It's more a sort of motherly inevitability so far as I can see,' he said with an affectionate smile she dearly wished she could win from him herself, instead of the guarded one he had greeted her with this morning, as if she had been added to the list of people he had to hold at a distance from his inner aristocrat.

'That's Mama exactly,' she agreed, wishing her mother could soothe away all her troubles as easily as she had when Persephone was a little girl.

'Your cousin's new wife promises to have the trick of it herself before long. I suppose it comes from being a great lady with large responsibilities.'

'Probably,' she agreed with a hollow feeling in her belly that being compared to Jess and found wanting might teach her new depths of human frailty.

'So you and your best friend will be able to compare notes on how it can most graciously be done, without either of your husbands becoming aware they live under an iron hand in a very velvety glove.'

'Then you think I am about to become a great lady?'

'I know you're about to be my Countess and I could not have chosen a finer one if I searched the length and breadth of the British Isles for her. As to the great lady part of the equation, I would argue you are one of those already, my Persephone,' he told her with a whimsical smile that let her a little closer and affirmed their marriage could lie lightly on both of them, if she would only let it and not yearn for anything more.

'Then I shall be content to wed a great gentleman. We can congratulate ourselves on our mutual splendour and greatness every morning at breakfast, to make sure our households realise how lucky they are to have us ruling over them.'

'That should do it,' he said as if already practising the art.

'Persephone!' her little sister Penelope interrupted and any chance to discuss the intimacies and traps their marriage promised to throw at them was lost as both her sisters came to exclaim over her news and reproach her for not telling them about it herself a lot sooner.

'Happy, my love?' Lady Henry asked her eldest daughter as they watched Alex strip off his splendid waistcoat so he could fish in his shirtsleeves and teach Penelope to cast a line more fluidly.

'I will be,' Persephone replied with a weary smile.

'If only Corisande had not chosen to interfere, I suspect you would have worked your way towards it in your own time. She always was searingly jealous of you, love, so I suppose a chance at putting you on the wrong side of the line for once instead of being there on her own seemed irresistible to her. I doubt she knows how hard Jack and Marcus and your Alex will watch her from now on after that particular piece of spite. She wouldn't look half as smug about the prospect of you having to wed at her instigation if she had the intelligence to see what she has done to herself by interfering.'

'There's no point taking petty revenge on her,' Persephone said and found she genuinely meant it, although she would never have chosen such a way to find her husband—the one she was going to marry could hardly suit her better. 'Lord Calvercombe and I will rub along perfectly well together and that will be revenge enough on Corisande, who never contrived to live in contentment with any man for more than a week as far as I can see.'

'I would have you aim for a little more than contentment in your married life, my love,' her mother said gently and Persephone found Alex's powerful figure was blurring in front of her as her tired eyes threatened to fill with tears.

Blinking them back firmly and telling herself not to be such a widgeon, she let herself remember how it felt to be almost loved by him last night. It had been wondrous and she couldn't wait to be completely and totally his in every way there was between lovers. That would be quite enough urgency to get her to the wedding and beyond it into the marriage bed with him and, if Alexander was content to take her as his wife, she was very happy to be so taken and not think any deeper until she had to.

'More will be up to us when we get there,' she said with her gaze steady on her future as she made up her mind to put every effort she had into it once they were wed, so they both had to be happy or waste so much promise of it as would seem criminal. 'It could be wonderful to be Lady Calvercombe, once Alexander gets used to sharing his life and at least some of his thoughts with me. I can't imagine how his family set him so low that they didn't value the fine, honourable and happy man he has it in him to be, Mama. How could his father and brother have been so heartless and careless of his feelings that he went off to India to get away from them until he was of an age to take possession of his inheritance from his grandfather?'

'It's in the nature of heartless, careless and shallow men to hate their opposite when it is in front of them every day. Little Alex Forthin was forever before Walter and Farrant Forthin as an example of all they were not. He gets that fine integrity and absolute determination from his grandfather, as well as a passionate nature and what he would probably hate me for calling the soul of a poet from his mother—even if she did leave him for an actual one and betray it. There is very little of the Forthins in the lad, for all he takes his height and those blue eyes from his father's line. Only think how galling it must have been for Farrant to watch his much younger brother grow into someone far more like a young god than any Forthin before him.'

They watched the fishing party, at ease as Persephone would have thought her little sisters incapable of being with a virtual stranger and realised they had accepted their brother-in-law-to-be as part of the family. Unforgivably envious that her family might prove a greater attraction than she was herself, she took her eyes off them long enough to look to her mother for more information about her fiancé.

'Mr Farrant Forthin was not blessed with good looks, then?' she prompted.

'No, and little wonder Farrant hated the boy, I suppose, considering he was mean-minded by nature and always ready to blame Alex for his own sins and omissions. I can see why old Lord Tregaron had the boy visit as often as he could until he died, but once he was gone that only made Alexander's life more difficult. He had to live with a father who was jealous of his future possessions and a brother determined to strip him of as many of them as possible by fair means or foul. I often wondered what Lady Elyssine Llyn saw in the husband she insisted on marrying, despite her father's opposition and every scrap of common sense her friends tried to talk into her. Walter Forthin turned out to be every bit as bad as they said and I wonder if she ran away because he beat her and perhaps worse.'

'How could she leave her son with such a father?'

'I doubt he touched the boy with his own stamp so plain to see, despite the lad's good looks. But how could she make him live a poor and precarious life?'

'Poor Alex,' Persephone observed as she continued to watch his every move as if there was no keeping her eyes off him. 'Having an indifferent father and jealous brother was bad enough, but it seems his mother was spineless as well.'

'They certainly produced a far finer character in your future husband than any of them deserved, my love, especially since the world seems a little too ready to believe him a rogue because he carries a few scars,' her mother said, watching her future son-in-law gently guide her youngest daughter's ham-fisted attempts at fishing at the same time as keeping an eye on Helen, who was now out of her mama's direct sight, sketching the scene with her usual sharply observed fluidity.

'He's not a rogue at all,' Persephone heard herself fly to Alexander's defence as if she was totally besotted with the man and blushed under Lady Henry's knowing look and secretive smile.

'Oh, I rather think he is a little bit of a one, my dear,' Lady Henry replied sweetly, chuckling at her eldest daughter's confounded look when Persephone eyed the man in front of her once more and duly noted her wolf in wolf's clothing had little of the perfect gentle knight about him and a lot of dangerous predator.

'You could be right,' she said with a secretive smile.

'Of course I am, I'm your mother,' Lady Henry replied complacently.

Having established her omnipotence, Melissa Seaborne was content to let her younger daughters go their own way while she sat and planned the perfect autumn wedding in her head. Persephone finally succumbed to tiredness on the softly cushioned day bed and her other daughters forgot to be in awe of Alex's spectacular, if slightly battered, good looks or the past experiences he carried on him for all to see. *Yes*, Melissa decided as she reviewed her day, *it's all going so much better than I dared to hope back in June, when Alexander and Persephone were forever glaring at each other as if they hated what they saw.* Now she only needed her eldest son to come home and her younger one to stop chasing ladybirds and carousing with his more disreputable friends and settle to the sort of life that would make him happy.

'These rumours of your involvement in Mr Seaborne's kidnap are impossible to pin down to a particular source, my lord,' the agent Jack employed informed the Earl of Calvercombe a week or so after the announcement of his lordship's engagement to Marcus's sister.

'Gossip needs no evidence to flourish,' Alex said with a resigned shrug.

'It's an oddly persistent piece of tittle-tattle, don't you think?' Mr Frederick Peters asked his latest employer impassively.

'This whole business is devilish odd.'

'And carried out with a very definite purpose in mind, my lord.'

'Obviously to make me redouble my efforts to find Rich Seaborne and my cousin,' Alex said, distaste at the idea of betraying one brother to recover the other bitter on his tongue.

'The Duke believes his eldest cousin disappeared deliberately, so his staying lost could be his way of avoiding some great trouble for him and his, my lord,' the clever young lawyer suggested.

'Very likely, but it won't bring his little brother back. Marcus's disappearance argues someone wants Mr Richard Seaborne back out in the wide world very badly indeed, Peters. Buying up that ring, if he didn't steal it from Rich some time during the last three years, must have cost a small fortune, even if he got it from a fence.'

'Which argues he must have left a clue behind him somewhere; perhaps a minor detail he forgot to cover up that will lead us to the man behind all this in time.'

'But maybe not soon enough for Marcus. Anyway, I've been trained to pick out the smallest clue to a man's true allegiance, even when he's proclaiming his loyalty to the heavens. I've seen no sign of such double-dealing since young Marcus Seaborne disappeared.'

'But have you applied such tactics to all your acquaintance, my lord?'

'What acquaintance would that be, Peters?' Alex asked, to remind the man he wasn't exactly a social animal.

'Inside knowledge or close observation led to this kidnap, my lord. It was a shrewd as well as a cruel move to take the gentleman shortly to become your brother-in-law. It's an open secret you were a hunter after the hidden and intangible in service of your country, so what better man is there to chase his quarry down if he could find a way to make you dance to his tune?'

'Jack told me you were a shrewd devil, but I wonder if even he knows how clever you really are, Peters.'

'Praise indeed, but the answer to this puzzle may well lie with you, however clever or stupid I happen to be to think so, Lord Calvercombe.'

'You honestly believe someone I know is party to this scheme, if not actually behind it?'

'You were out of the country and attached to Sir Arthur Wellesley's army for several years and have kept yourself very private since your return. Few outsiders can know much about you other than by rumour, my lord.'

'I never thought being a recluse might help me find my future wife's brother one day, or I might have embraced solitude with a gladder heart,' Alex observed with a smile that softened his guarded expression more than he probably knew when Persephone entered the room.

'No doubt, my lord,' the acutely observant Mr Peters agreed blandly.

'What have you been discussing whilst I was busy struggling with our enormous guest list, my lord?' Persephone asked as she slipped her hand into Alex's as if that was where it belonged.

'Your brother,' he replied with a grim look she wished she could soothe away.

'Which one?' she asked bleakly.

'The one who disappeared against his will, rather than the one Peters here believes lost himself and my cousin quite deliberately.'

'Which is only what you had come to believe of your own accord, is it not? Have you two come to any conclusions about Marcus's disappearance though?'

'Only that someone I know might be involved, if I could only find him among my slender acquaintance,' he answered with a preoccupied frown.

'Why don't we make a list of anyone who might be even remotely connected to you and the kidnapper? Since I seem to have been given the role of list maker today, you can recite whilst I record,' she invited him with as intimate a smile as she dared unleash on them with this thread of waiting tension strung so tight under all their dealings nowadays.

Chapter Twelve

'An excellent idea, Miss Seaborne,' Mr Peters approved with a brief smile that made her like him far more than she'd been inclined to on first meeting.

'Thank you, Mr Peters,' she said meekly and eyed Alex expectantly.

'I have few enough relations for us to concern ourselves with,' he admitted as he seemed ready to take seriously the possibility someone he knew might be at the heart of all this. 'Apart from Annabelle, who we know too well has not been seen or heard of for three years, I only have one or two living relatives. My Great-Uncle Mortlake Forthin is nearly ninety and probably incapable of carrying out such a complex scheme, even if he had a reason to move against such a powerful family and risk dangling on the end of a hempen rope.'

He paused while Persephone wrote the name down anyway, on the supposition nobody could yet be ruled out, however unlikely they might sound.

'Then there is my father's scandalous cousin Corinthia, who married a part-time horse-dealer and circus acrobat rejoicing in the name of Luciano Clevedon. She was banished to one of the remoter of my predecessor's estates with him to contemplate her sins in obscurity and bring up the only child they produced who survived birth.'

Persephone wrote both those unlikely names on her list. 'So what was the poor child's name? I must say your family seems as addicted to thinking up unlikely names for their children as my own sometimes allows itself to be,' she said while he brooded over the dilemma of naming anyone else who might want to harm him and subjecting them to Peters's rather merciless scrutiny of their every word and action when they could be totally innocent.

'Electra!' he finally recalled. 'I knew it was

something outlandish, but neither she nor her parents were often discussed by the family, even when my father and brother were speaking to me long enough to talk about them.'

Persephone wondered how unlucky Electra felt about being rated neither fish, fowl, nor good red herring and deemed unfit company for even such a rackety family as the Forthins.

'And which of the remoter family estates were they sent to?' she prompted.

'How I wish my steward was here to remind me, since he was my late grandfather's man and seems to have acquainted himself with the finer details of my new estates far better than I have managed to myself up to now,' Alex mused, then shook his head as she shot a questioning look at him. 'I refuse to believe Griffiths has any hand in this murky business. He looked after my interests whilst I was out of the country and nobody else bothered to try to check my father's depredations. He's a sincere churchman who could never square it with his conscience to put Marcus at risk. He's also a genuinely good man and

I'm not such a fool I haven't learnt to recognise one of those rarities when I meet one.'

'I shall put him in the least likely column, then,' Persephone conceded, exchanging a quick look with Mr Peters to silently agree he would look at the Penbryn steward anyway, despite his employer's scruples. 'Did this Electra of yours have any children herself?'

'I recall my father laughing about Electra wedding the son of a local vicar, but I wasn't particularly interested in my father's idea of a good story at the time. He and Farrant thought it a great joke that the daughter of a circus acrobat and possibly the proudest and least well-favoured lady they had ever met had to content herself with such a humble, if respectable, mate. I believe they still live on the estate my cousin allowed them to occupy as an act of not particularly splendid generosity.'

'So she and her husband live in this obscure manor and you can't recall the name or location of it?' she asked, sharing Peters's frustration that Alex couldn't recall the name of an estate he now owned. If ever a group of people had reason to resent the senior branch of their family tree, it was this particular one.

'I doubt if old Octavius gave them a second thought once he had ordered his cousin to retire to it and live there quietly without bothering him. It was probably falling down round their ears even when they went there and I hate to think what kind of dereliction they have had to put up with since.'

'I dare say this Electra, and any children she might have, must resent you and yours for treating her so callously, don't you think?'

'Why, what did I ever do to them?'

'Nothing, but they might fear you will remember them one day and evict them from the ramshackle home your late cousin grudgingly allowed them, so that it can be sold. I wonder how it must feel to be allowed to stay in your home on sufferance, and fear losing even that shabby and unkempt shelter at the whim of a man they don't know.'

'Desperate, I should think,' he conceded, frustrated by his inability to recall more. 'My father and brother had no time for family and Cousin

Octavius probably left them to scratch a living as best they could from the home farm and whatever else they could use to their advantage. He probably thought he'd been very generous to them, when he thought about them at all,' he said on a pass down the room he was pacing as if action might release the name he sought.

'My mother might be able to help, as she seems to know all sorts of unexpected details about families I've never even heard of,' Persephone offered as she sat and waited for this remote memory to fall into place and sympathised silently over his own spartan childhood, spent with two such selfish and preoccupied men.

She couldn't recall ever meeting Farrant Forthin or his disreputable father, but had never thought she could hate a pair of dead strangers as she hated those two. Every detail Alex let fall about his lonely and loveless childhood made her loathe more fervently a father and brother who could treat a sensitive young boy so harshly. It explained why he was so devoted to his little cousin, she supposed, when the one spark of warmth in their young lives had been their affection for one another. She felt her former jealousy fall away and was actually grateful to Annabelle and hoped she and Rich were happily lost in some safe place together.

'Kingslake Moot Castle! That's the name of the place and a ramshackle old barn of a house it is as well, if only half what I've heard of it is true,' Alex said at last, breaking off his pacing to give her one of those rare, un-self-conscious smiles she secretly treasured more than gold. 'Remnants of the castle and the manor house built within its walls in Tudor times are more than half-ruined, according to the report Griffiths commissioned from an architect who worked on Penbryn for my grandfather. The two tumbledown old farms that make up the so-called estate are not a lot better, although Griffiths put works on the farmhouses and cottages attached to them at the top of our list of urgent repairs. I dare say my cousin's family were too proud to beg for work on the castle to take precedence when the surveyor was making his report, or perhaps they were too bitter at being marooned there in the first place.'

'Can you recall the precise location of this castle, my lord?' Peters asked.

Persephone thought it sounded the ideal place to hide Marcus and would neatly account for the oddly persistent whispers that Alex was behind it all, as well.

'I have never heard of it and doubt many others have, either,' she said, and the thought of Marcus incarcerated in a decrepit old fortress made her shudder.

'West Shropshire, but I dare say it's pinpointed on the estate maps, or maybe we could ask Lady Henry? Considering I'm trying to put my houses in some sort of order before becoming a married man, she might not think it out of the ordinary if I want to know where one of them actually is,' Alex suggested and she wondered for a moment if it might save him a ride into Wales to consult the estate maps and that survey.

'Mama is far too acute. She's already concerned at the lack of any word from Marcus since Jack's wedding, without dropping clues she might seize on when she thinks about it later,' she argued after a few moments' thought.

'I agree it would be too much of a risk, my lord,' Peters added.

'Then I dare say you're both right, but we need details about the place and my relatives before we march up to the front door and accuse them of abduction and possible extortion. Can you find all we need to know in time for us to rescue Miss Seaborne's brother before our wedding, whilst doing your best not to alert anyone else we may be on his tail at long last, Peters? You will be a very remarkable man if you can pull all that off under their very noses, if you ask me,' Alex observed sardonically.

'It's my job to discover such things without anyone knowing I've done so, my lord,' the man replied with such quiet confidence that Persephone believed him, although Alex looked a little less convinced.

'I'm glad you're on my side then, Peters,' Alex only half-joked.

'Whilst I'm thankful not to face you in any sort of battle, my lord,' the man said solemnly, 'I wouldn't work for a kidnapper, or anyone who forced a gentleman like Mr Richard Seaborne into hiding to protect his family from harm.'

'And the wretched man will be suspicious if Lord Calvercombe leaves Ashburton before our wedding to wander about Shropshire looking for ancient castles,' Persephone concluded. 'If we put it about Mr Peters is acting for your steward, he might come and go easily enough.'

'The thought of a younger man on his way to inspect the castle might scare them into doing something foolish,' Alex argued.

'Then let me find out all I can in my own way, my lord. I can don a good enough disguise to deceive the acutest of watchers and come and go without being seen by most ordinary people going about their business,' Mr Peters said immodestly, but Persephone believed him. Alex would have to put his faith in the man until they knew they were on the right track and could get on with rescuing Marcus at last.

'My cousin has various maps and geographical guides in his library you can consult if you need to, Mr Peters,' Persephone offered, but he shook his head.

'My thanks, Miss Seaborne, but you never know what spies your enemy has recruited even here. Some observant soul might note which books have been moved and pass the information on. With only half a county to explore, I should be back before a week's out.'

'If you can do all that and not alert our quarry we're on his tail, I'll pay you twice the fee we agreed, man, and the Duke will double it as soon as he gets back.'

'Best perhaps if we discuss such things after we free Mr Marcus Seaborne, my lord. My rates are high enough to cover my needs amply,' Peters announced and left with his usual quiet and economical movements.

'Supposing our foe to be awake on every suit, I can't help but wonder if he might already be aware of Mr Peters's profession,' Alex mused.

'If we credit him with superhuman powers, we'll never make a move against him. I want Marcus at my wedding, Alex, even if he did declare he's had his fill of them before he rode away from Jack's and got himself kidnapped. I need one of my brothers to give me away. Jack can be your groomsman as you were his, and it's not that Jack isn't as dear as a brother to me, but Mama will be heartbroken not to see one of her sons give me away as Papa cannot. Not that she won't be heartbroken anyway if we have to tell her Marcus is being held until we somehow manage to find Richard.'

'It's intolerable!' Alex barked as he marched up and down the room again as if he wished it was the ramparts of a defeated enemy's stronghold. 'Damnable to do this to you when you've lost one brother already for fear of this rogue. I wish I could have the crook at my mercy for half an hour and teach him to suffer for once.'

'You don't have it in you to torture another being. At least this wicked man doesn't know where he is and has had to think up this fanciful scheme to use Marcus as bait to make us find him,' she said philosophically.

'I'd love to know why he thinks he has the right to hound you all; there just can't be a good enough reason to cause such suffering to Rich's family.'

'One day we'll know it, Alexander,' she assured him.

'What if that day isn't soon enough?' he asked, stopping to stare down at her with unaskable questions in his eyes.

'It will be,' she told him fiercely. 'Rich would never give up fighting for what he loved and neither would your cousin Annabelle from the sound of her. Marcus might be young and untested in comparison to the rest of you, but he'll do all a man can to confound this enemy of ours somehow.'

'But will he still be your light-hearted young brother at the end of it all?' Alex asked painfully and Persephone had to fight to keep her gaze steady on his and not let it veer towards his visible scars, because she knew they were talking of his captivity and not Marcus's now.

'Maybe he will be someone better,' she told him softly.

'Aye, and maybe he'll be nigh as big a monster as the man who put him wherever he is now against his will.'

'Nothing could make him as ruthless and unfeeling as that, my lord. It's no more in my brother's nature to become such a cold-hearted beast than it was in yours in a far worse situation than any Marcus is likely to encounter.'

'And you think I wasn't such a beast?' he asked grimly.

She could see such painful shadows in his eyes that it was tempting to change the subject and laugh him into the here and now instead of there and then. Pain that he'd had to face so much absolutely alone and stripped of everything that made life bearable gnawed at her, but she couldn't let it show in case he mistook it for pity and she didn't need him to tell her how much he would hate that.

'You would be an unlikely saint and not the man I want to marry if you simply shrugged and walked away from your ordeal as if it hardly mattered. No doubt whoever did that to you, when they finally had the wild and beautiful young man I first remember you as in their clutches, had a dark and dangerous mind that needed stopping from causing any more harm. I'm sure you did whatever you had to do to make sure he couldn't do it to anyone else. Whatever you had to do to track him down and rob him of his power to hurt others has only made you suffer more.'

'You really thought I was wild and beautiful? How admirably you young ladies do conceal your emotions from silly young men, my dear, for I swear I was convinced you scarcely knew I existed when I used to come here for holidays my ever-loving family couldn't be bothered to offer me when I was a callow youth.'

'I knew,' she said shortly, with a steady gaze into his slightly bewildered blue eyes as she let him know how acutely she'd noticed him and would never find him insignificant if they both lived to be ninety. 'And, yes, I thought you the most breathtakingly handsome youth I ever laid eyes on.' She saw warmth and laughter leap in his bluest of blue gazes and held up a hand to prevent either of them getting carried away. 'I also thought you knew it a little too well and would become even vainer and sillier if you launched into polite society as such a gilded youth. They would have flattered you into thinking yourself a demi-god, sent from heaven to dazzle silly little débutantes out of the few wits they had in the first place.'

'I would have had to wait a few years for you to come along and humble me then, I suppose,' he said, quirking a dark eyebrow and inviting her to smile with him at the two spoilt and much-flattered socialites they could have been.

'Considering I risked having my head turned when I first came out, perhaps it's just as well we never did meet on the dance floors and promenades of the *ton*.'

'Afraid we wouldn't have liked each other?'

'Certain of it. We hated each other on sight when we met again this summer and I was far less bearable at seventeen than I have learnt to be now,' she told him, still refusing to let him know how hard her silly heart had fluttered and her skin tingled the instant she realised whose arms she was struggling to escape that fateful night in June.

'Which leaves me with the question of what made you lose your goddess-like certainty you were put on this earth to rule it, Persephone mine,' he teased, yet he waited for her answer as if it was important to him.

'I broke a young man's heart,' she told him shortly and winced at the memory. 'With four years more experience of the world, I can see being a Seaborne and first cousin to the Duke made me irresistible to a youth with a title and fortune to hand on.'

'Then why blame yourself?' he asked and the frown was back in his eyes and it was wrong to hope it was caused by jealousy.

'Because I didn't notice him, I suppose, then he insisted I'd ruined him for anyone else and I must marry him, although he has since wed.'

'You clearly didn't break his heart then.'

'Since he and his doting mama and sisters proclaimed to the world I did, some of it still thinks me hard-hearted, proud and vain.'

'Then they're wrong—you might be headstrong and loyal to a fault, but you're neither heartless nor obsessed with your own reflection in the mirror. The idiot would have found himself with a tigress by the tail if he'd managed to badger you into accepting his proposals and you would have been bored half to death.'

'True, and we could find out if I'm truly unlike the tame little kitten he married instead if you like, my lord,' she suggested with a bold invitation in her eyes she hoped he found very hard to resist.

'Not yet, you witch,' he protested huskily, as if the idea appealed very strongly, but he didn't dare come near enough to test his will power any further. 'We have a wedding to accomplish first.'

'You *could* just kiss me then, I suppose,' she offered in a martyred tone.

'No, I couldn't,' he said, the need he finally let her see urgent in his heated blue gaze. Clearly he thought even a kiss would burn away his formidable self-control and wasn't that exactly what she wanted?

'Since we will be wed in a month anyway, why don't we risk it all?'

'Because we're going to be wed for life, Persephone Seaborne, and need some mystery and magic to get through it without you becoming as bored with me as you would have been with your fine young lord. I can't offer you anything less than the rest of my life and don't you dare expect a marriage of convenience from me, woman. If you're thinking to take lovers once we've made the first two or three of our boys together, then you'd better cry off now and we'll face down the scandal somehow. We can have girls by the dozen, of course, since I never wanted to hand this bedevilled title on in the first place, but if you will insist on boys, we'll somehow manage to endure making our marriage renowned for faithfulness rather than disloyalty between us.'

'I suppose we might as well, then,' she answered, preoccupied with the hugeness of the whole enterprise he'd outlined for them to take on and live by. 'I want to start now,' she admitted, the need to feel his child grow in her belly so strong it seemed wrong not to get on with making their first as soon as possible.

'You always were impatient, from the first moment I met you dancing up and down on the Ashburton steps haranguing your brothers and cousin to hurry up and join your latest misadventure before your governess caught you. Even back then you seemed to me a whirlwind in miniature to be avoided as often as possible, so I knew you were trouble at first sight. It's high time you learnt you see more of a country by the long route, Persephone,' he said huskily, as if the need to risk making those unruly babes right now goaded him as harshly as it did her, despite his fine words.

So why would he hold back from her when it was what they both wanted? She ran the idea through her head of who he might be considering if not her. Her mother? She doubted Lady Henry would be deeply upset by the idea her headstrong eldest daughter had anticipated her marriage vows by the distance of a few weeks. Indeed, she thought her mama might be more shaken to know Persephone was still a maid when she had a wildly handsome and passionately wolfish nobleman as her promised husband.

Lady Henry would very likely expect a dangerous gentleman like Alexander to bind his chosen mate to him by every available tie there was between man and woman. Knowing her mama, she would then congratulate herself that her Persephone had found the ideal man to provoke, then enjoy, her wilder impulses and deepest passions. Mama had never wanted the sort of milk-and-water arranged marriage for her daughters many aristocratic mothers seemed to expect for their offspring, as if they were merely goods to be traded in exchange for wealth and position.

It couldn't be the thought of Jack's protective wrath that held him back, because Jack had proved himself a very faulty Galahad indeed when it came to adoring *his* love from afar. Persephone doubted Jack and Jessica had spent a night apart from some time before the day their betrothal was announced until they were legally wed and entitled to spend them together. So, as she was almost shamefully willing to abandon her maidenly modesty and learn the next heady stage of her life in his powerful arms, that left the only person who could hold them back from blissful fulfilment—Alexander Forthin himself, who looked as if he was on the rack with wanting her and not being able to take her at her very willing word.

Chapter Thirteen

'Did you make Jack some sort of ridiculous masculine promise?' Persephone asked incredulously and saw a faint flush of colour burn across Alex's high cheekbones before he avoided her eyes by pacing back to the windows to gaze out.

'How could I have done? I haven't seen or heard from him since the day of his wedding and neither of us are given to prophecy,' he growled at the view from the finely leaded casements most commentators on the ducal pile raved about, but then, they were actually looking at it and not glaring into the middle distance.

'Because you're both men, and Jack very recently found out how hotly masculine need of the most unexpected of women can burn and rage until neither are strong enough to resist it. So, did you or did you not promise him you would not make love to me if you stayed here to guard his empire from his enemies during his absence, Lord Calvercombe?' she demanded furiously, the very fact they could have discussed her so intimately threatening to stoke her temper white hot and reckless.

'He brought up the subject, not me,' Alex Forthin told her with an infuriating manly shrug, as if that disclaimer made the whole topic safe, and she totally disagreed.

'Why? What did you say to make him suspect you might even try to seduce me? I hadn't the slightest inkling you'd noticed me as anything other than Rich's annoying little sister until the night we met in the Queen's Apartments. Was that mere proximity? Would any female not actually repulsive to look on and receptive to your oh-so-flattering attentions have done just as well, my lord? Was I nothing more than another grey cat in the dark to you, Alexander Forthin?' she demanded, hearing some of the pain and fury at the very idea in her voice and wishing she had his ability to cut himself off from his fellow beings as she stood here glaring at his broad back.

'Never,' he told her as if it was the only word he could get past clenched teeth.

'Then what was it?'

'Nigh uncontrollable need,' he snapped as if she was torturing him when all the time it felt as if she was the one under almost unbearable pressure at the idea she would only ever be his accidental wife.

'Then you did promise Jack not to seduce me, didn't you?' she said on a heavy sigh that sounded weary and a little lost even to her.

'Yes, damn it! I laughed it off when he cornered me the day of his wedding and asked me to stay on here after he left, so he wouldn't have to have nightmares about what might be happening at Ashburton while he was gone every night of his honeymoon. Of course, I knew he would fret and fume about what might happen here if I didn't agree to stay because he's Jack and that's what he does. Perhaps his instincts for trouble are better than mine—he had already set Peters on Rich's trail by then. He must have wondered what sort of trouble that might stir up along the way, but your cousin loves his Duchess so deeply, how could he not take her away from the bustle and burdens of the Duchess of Dettingham's new life and make love to her until she was a lot more certain she can carry them? I didn't have it in me to let him ruin his new wife's bridal tour of the Lakes when she was looking forward to it and to having him to herself after all the fuss and palaver of the wedding.'

'I can see why you stayed and you're right, Jessica does need to know she matters to Jack more than Ashburton does if their marriage is to be the happy one they both deserve. It's the conversation you two must have had about me that still concerns me so deeply,' she informed him coldly. The idea of them discussing her fiery responses to a certain annoying Earl made her clench her fists in humiliated fury.

'He claimed he'd had his eyes opened to fools like himself, who went about blundering into ladies of beauty and character such as his bride as if they were just another attractive example of young womanhood. He'd discovered how desperately he wanted his Jessica before the reasons why had the slightest chance to catch up with his instincts to hunt and capture, apparently. He even had the audacity to warn me I already felt far more strongly about you than I knew and told me to avoid meeting you in the stilly watches of the night, now he knew how potent moonlight could be for a Seaborne, male or female.'

'Drat him for an interfering idiot, then,' she condemned, some of her fury with this particularly annoying man transferring to her utterly infuriating cousin instead.

'Curse him for being right, Persephone. Damn him for dragging that promise out of me, despite my scepticism at the time, but I can't call him an idiot when we proved every word he said was true as soon as his back was turned and we were alone together,' he told her gruffly, turning to face her with the same mix of frustration, puzzlement and burning desire that was eating away at her.

'We weren't alone, though, were we? He was there with us every moment you held off from me and honoured your promises to my cousin more than you did any you could make me. Jack was with us that night as surely as if he was standing by glowering at us like the most unlikely chaperon I could imagine in my wildest nightmares. How can you let him dictate our lives from afar, Alexander? He's keeping us apart when he certainly didn't keep away from Jessica before their wedding and that makes him a hypocrite of the worst sort. I doubt they spent a single night apart during the weeks it took Mama and Lady Pendle to organise their wedding. The poor darlings had to deploy every social skill they possess to stop the two of them making it very obvious to the rest of the world the Duke of Dettingham spent all his nights, and much of his days, making love to his bride-to-be well before the wedding took place. Now Jack is insisting we do the exact opposite and act like polite strangers until *our* wedding night.'

'He wasn't to know we would be so desperate for each other it was nigh unendurable not to love one another to the finest degree of desperation,' he excused his friend rather lamely while he avoided her eyes again, as if that might make it easier on both of them that they had weeks more of frustration to endure before they were properly wed and, finally, bedded.

'I could learn to hate him for being only half a soothsayer, then. He must have known you would make me an honourable offer if you ever let yourself get carried away by that proximity with me we're doing our best not to talk about,' she said flatly, wondering why it seemed so fascinatingly urgent to lose herself in his arms when she still wasn't sure exactly how she felt about him even now.

'I wonder if he might not have thought of that as well. Perhaps we do need to know each other better before we fall headlong into a fever for one another that we still don't really understand,' he muttered as if he was half-heartedly trying to find the bright side of a thundercloud.

'I thought you were a rake, at least once upon a time, if not since you came home and learnt to hold yourself aloof from your fellow beings, Lord Calvercombe,' she said severely, surprised to find herself chiding her future husband for not being as wild as rumour once credited him with being.

'I was,' he told her with a pantomime leer that made her shiver at the heat and wicked intent one pair of masculine eyes could convey, as if he'd been holding that rake on a very tight leash ever since the night by the lake back in June. The beast looked as if it was straining hard against its collar now as it snapped and snarled and wanted her so badly it took a mighty effort to keep the curb Jack and his own honour had put on it firmly in place.

'Then passion certainly isn't a closed book to you,' she said, jealousy of all the other loves strewing his path to now lending an edge to her voice.

'It is with you, and I can assure you I know now, even if I didn't before I met you again, that there are very different kinds of passion that plague the human heart and mind until I scarce know where one begins and another ends with you, Persephone. I know a vigorous young man like Marcus has the fiery need for female company biting and roaring at him until he has to find out more about the passion that burns between man and woman than soirées in Mayfair or polite dances at country balls will ever teach him. So, yes, Miss Seaborne, I know what mere passion is and what it can do to a man, unless he learns some measure of wisdom and control over its wilder excesses. Which doesn't explain why I feel so raw and driven by my physical need of you that it's like a finer torture than even this—' he waved dismissively at his scars '—to play the honourable idiot with you as I am now,' he told her.

'There's something more than mere wanting between us and I don't understand it any more than you do,' he barked as he went back to his pacing, as if it was the only outlet for suppressed feelings he dared allow himself.

'How do you know I don't?' she asked defensively, wishing Jack hadn't blundered in and had left the finding out a little easier on both of them.

'Don't be more foolish than you can help,' he snapped, as if the mere thought of her experiencing even a tithe of the desire she'd felt for him with another man might drive him to madness.

'Not that I ever experienced passion with another man, you idiot, but I might understand what this is better than you do. I might know what it is by feminine instinct,' she defended herself, wishing she really did know what she felt for him so fiercely it was distracting her from everything else in her life that should be important, such as finding both her brothers.

'If you did, you would probably be handing out an ultimatum like the one your friend gave Jack when they unleashed all that fire and fury between them and she refused to wed him unless he loved her. Am I fated to get to the altar and discover you won't turn up until I swear undying love for you, Miss Seaborne?' he almost mocked.

'No, Jessica is a romantic and I'm not so deluded that I expect you to love me,' she said with as much offended dignity as she could cram in without shouting at him.

'You were deluded enough to meet me at dead of night in as compromising a place as a lady could without actually inviting me to join you in your bed.'

'I was, although I can't help wondering why you came to risk your freedom and your rakish reputation when you must have known how silly it was of me to suggest such a meeting. I'm no longer quite so innocent of what we're both capable of after that night, but surely *you* were taking a foolish risk, my lord?' she said with a shrug that invited him to be philosophical about their stupidity as well.

'Especially when you're not foolish enough to actually love me?' he asked as if it was a possibility that had haunted him.

He'd made it clear from the first time he laid eyes on her this summer that he only reluctantly admired her. Now he seemed to want reassurance she would try to love him, with no indication in return that his feelings towards her had changed. Pride and an aching heart meant she couldn't look too deeply at her feelings for this painfully aloof, damaged man while he wouldn't, or couldn't, do the same for her.

'What would you have me do, my lord?'

'I'd have you give as much or as little of yourself to me as you dare trust me with,' he replied harshly and she let out her waiting breath with a sigh.

'To me it looks more a question of your trusting

me than the other way about,' she said and shook her head sadly when he went back to studying the view as if it fascinated him far more than she did.

'What sort of woman could love me, Miss Persephone Seaborne?' he asked as if at least half his attention was on the distant hills.

'Only the deluded kind,' she said with a wobbly apology for a smile at his averted dark head it was as well he couldn't see while she counted on her fingers the reasons why she would be a fool to love him. 'I would need to be patient and forbearing if I was going to put up with your morose silences and your aloofness, gracious to cover up your gruffness with strangers and make you almost human to your friends. I would have to be strong enough to take some of the burdens off your shoulders as well. Fiery enough to blast my way through your ridiculous belief that a few scars and the actions of a ruthless enemy somehow set you apart from your fellow man. It seems to me you need to marry a harem full of women to accomplish all that, my lord, not just one faulty individual like me,' she finished as lightly as she could.

Even if she knew she would ache intolerably if he ever so much as looked at another woman with haunted longing in his eyes, there was no need to give him too many advantages by letting him know it.

'Or maybe the one very special she who would put up with all that and still do her best to love me,' he said softly to the vista outside.

Persephone felt as if a void had opened inside her as she wondered if he'd loved his little cousin like that and only been waiting for her to grow up to come home and marry her. The idea froze her in place and she felt silence stretch between them like tensioned wire. She had fallen into his arms like some overripe plum, so he couldn't help being splattered with sugary sweetness, and he'd responded as any healthy young male would to her shameless encouragement when she'd thrown herself into kissing him as if it might be the last thing she did on earth.

A flush of colour surged all over as she realised how responsible she was for the pickle they found themselves in. He had gallantly saved her good name at the expense of his cherished freedom and a dream perhaps he wouldn't let himself realise he had ever dreamt now. Apparently Persephone Seaborne had made the mighty mistake of feeling something powerful for a man whose true feelings lay with the girl who had run off with Persephone's eldest brother while his back was turned.

'I suppose there might be such a brave woman alive, if you're prepared to look hard enough for her,' she heard herself say limply and felt her heart thud in panic as he turned from that fascinating view as if steeling himself to meet her eyes instead of his precious Annabelle's limpid gaze.

'To win a female so special, I would have to be a lot more godlike than I actually am, Miss Seaborne,' he said solemnly, as if she ought to understand such things only happened in myth and legend.

'This mythical lady of yours would probably prefer you to be yourself, not some beau ideal she might find impossible to live with every day for the rest of your lives together,' she told him numbly.

Whatever he might have said in reply was lost as her mother sailed into the room, somehow managing to look as if the atmosphere between her daughter and the man she had committed herself to marry was as light and joyous as a fine May morning, when Persephone felt she could cut the tension in the room with a knife.

'There you are, my dear ones,' she said brightly, as if they might not have noticed each other. 'I fear you've been closeted alone quite long enough and I had to come and play bodkin before the gossips got busy with both your reputations. Luckily Corisande will have to trip you two up through a third party now you have that promise of hers to stop her making a scandal herself, but your engagement doesn't mean she has lost any of her jealousy of you, my love. More the opposite, I fear,' she said with a nod at Persephone that Alex seemed to understand better than she did.

'A fair warning, my lady,' Alex said as he exchanged a long look with Persephone's mother and she wondered what they were telling each other about her.

The temptation raged to stamp her feet and

shout at them for protecting her from Corisande's envy in some way she didn't quite understand, but she curbed it. 'I'm glad Cousin Corisande has been persuaded to return home for a week or two in order to visit her modiste, since she seems to think no gown can be properly made unless she can have it altered every time her mood changes with the direction of the wind,' she suggested carelessly.

'She might, if she could afford to,' Alex said shortly and she could tell he wanted the topic of her spiteful cousin over with as soon as possible.

'And it's far better to keep your enemies close where you can see what they're up to, is it not?' Persephone challenged them to exclude her from any scheme to contain Corisande's malice.

'Much better,' her mother agreed blithely as if she had no idea what her daughter was so angry about. 'And luncheon was nearly ready when I came in, my dears, so we might as well get on with it, since the vicar is calling this afternoon to discuss the wedding. At least nobody can make anything out of you two being closeted in Jack's study with him as your chaperon and I can consult cook and dear Mrs Maybury about arrangements for the wedding breakfast.'

'Will you not be joining us when Mr Wootton calls?' Persephone asked a little desperately, wondering what innocently uncomfortable questions the saintly vicar of Ashburton villages might ask if she and Alex were alone with him.

'Of course not, it would be ridiculous of me to chaperon you so closely that the good Reverend felt unable to give you his favourite talk on the love and duty a husband and wife owe to each other within marriage. Your father and I received it much as you two will do this afternoon, my love. Would that we had known then how happy we would be together, so we could have taken better note of what he had to say. Do listen—Mr Wootton will be so happy to know the daughter of a couple he married so long ago will be nigh as happy in her marriage as her mama and papa were before her that it seems a shame not to indulge his romantic side and enjoy it.'

'Then of course we will pay close attention, Lady Henry,' Alex insisted before Persephone could think of an excuse to avoid that speech.

'Of course we will,' she echoed meekly and hoped it wasn't a rehearsal of their marriage for her to echo whatever Alex said and for him to expect such meekness.

Her heart somewhere around the level of her elegant indoor shoes, Persephone took her fiancé's offered arm and followed her mother from the mellow old room. At least preparing a look of contented amusement would give her something to do while she came to terms with the idea of wanting a man who could never love her. Jessica had been so right to hold out for love, and how desperately she longed to be strong-minded enough to forge her own path in the world without him. Well, her bridges were already burnt as far as that went and she didn't have it in her to be so resolute as to go through her life without him. She shuddered at the idea of skipping off towards social damnation and knew she would agree again, even now, rather than bring scandal and disgrace on her family and Alexander Forthin, Earl of Calvercombe.

'Cold, my dear?' he asked as if he'd felt the chill that shot through her at the idea of a possible fifty years of marital indifference yawning between them.

'Of course not, it's a lovely day,' she murmured and tried not to let him see how truly disturbed she was while he snatched a shawl one of her sisters had left lying about the hall and tenderly draped it over her shoulders. 'How kind of you, my lord,' she managed to thank him limply.

'What a gallant Earl I'm in danger of becoming,' he replied with an ironic smile and she dropped her gaze so he couldn't see how hard she was having to fight not to cry about marrying a very gallant Earl indeed.

Marcus lay in the stuffy little chamber he knew better than he wanted to. Weary of captivity and impatient with the sticky heat, he needed a bath and his freedom, then maybe his temper wouldn't be so raw. He was frustrated and bored and there was nothing to do or see. After spending so many hours picking at the mortar round the bars of his cell, he found they were built into the walls and steady as rock. Unable to find a bright side to look on for once, he intended to sleep away the heat of the day, but he felt something had changed here and wished he knew what it was.

He made himself breathe slowly and wondered if he was being watched, managed a sleepy sigh and turned his back on the stout oak door. It was mid-afternoon, he decided, fifteen days into his captivity, and how he wished he'd listened harder when Jack and Calvercombe were discussing their enemies back at Ashburton.

An average-sized man in average clothes was all he recalled of his attacker and the drug the man forced into him had made even that picture confused. Wigs, cheek pads and paint could disguise a man if he was good at what he did and the cold glint in his kidnapper's eyes told Marcus that his abductor got what he wanted from life. Either the man was a lunatic, or he had a motive beyond a fat ransom. Marcus didn't think that cold-eyed man was deranged, so he'd probably done this to control Jack or Rich in some way. Jack was long gone by the time Marcus had left Ashburton, so that left Rich and Marcus squirmed at the idea of being used to make Rich reappear. With luck his brother was in another country and had no idea his little brother had let himself be kidnapped while too preoccupied with luscious little Clary to notice his attacker until it was too late.

Marcus had never resented the fact Jack and Rich were brothers in all but name and his sister Persephone was always happy to join in any mischief going. Now for *her* all the Seaborne men would run their head into a noose. The villain he had met that night certainly wouldn't hesitate to attack a female, and, if Rich was truly in hiding to protect Alex Forthin's young cousin Annabelle, that proved *she* was at the heart of this conundrum and not his brother. To lose himself so completely for her sake, Rich must feel something deep and important for the girl. Marcus concluded his brother thought her enemy dangerous and forced himself not to shudder.

If the man who had taken him with such cool daring on Seaborne land was using him to bait a trap, he wouldn't care if Marcus knew he was here or not. The rascal had left others to take any risks that came with his abduction and Marcus could only identify the dark-haired lady with any certainty. The self-serving cruelty of leaving his lady gaoler to take the risks whilst the true villain waited for whatever he wanted to happen struck him as intolerable and Marcus was tempted to leap to his feet and stride about his cell in frustration.

It dawned on him this was the first time he'd thought urgently about his situation since he woke and found himself locked in her lumber room. His wardress was definitely a lady, but now the promise and intrigue of her finally hit him, he wondered why he hadn't seen through his own eagerness for her company sooner. Not that she'd have him if he came gilded, he decided, with a wry smile.

If only she would trust him, they could seek sanctuary at Ashburton or Seaborne House. Then he could make sure she was dressed and chaperoned as a lady should be and he tried to picture his fiery lady guard in pale muslins and demure white silk and failed. Her masses of dark curls and darkest of brown eyes called for strong, pure colours and extravagant jewels to highlight the silken fineness of her creamy skin. It was no good—he couldn't lie here in a stew of urgent need at the thought of his nameless lady as his lover, or maybe even his wife, only in her lovely bare skin and never mind the colour of her discarded gown.

Chapter Fourteen

Alexander felt about as much use as a three-legged horse staying in Jack's house, impatiently waiting to marry Persephone while another man searched for her brother. He'd thought he was beyond caring what the world thought of him when he came back from India, so it came as a surprise he was furious the villain had taken Marcus Seaborne then tried to push the blame for it on to him.

The very idea he'd harm a hair on the thoughtless young idiot's head made him want to stamp about the room and rave at his fellow men for being so gullible. He longed to challenge the gossips to explain how they thought abducting one of their own would help his relations with the powerful family he was about to marry into. Refuting ill-informed gossip would only make the story stronger, but the goad of the malicious tale still tore at him.

'Mr Peters has come to call again, my lord. Now isn't it lucky I saw him creep round the corner of the stable-block and head towards this obscure corner of my cousin's mansion and decided to let him in myself?' Persephone informed him after she preceded that gentleman into the room and dared either of them to send her away.

'As well nobody else is aware you're here, I suppose, man, but couldn't you contrive to get here without Miss Seaborne seeing you?' Alex greeted him irritably. 'I thought you told me you could ghost in and out without a sign you'd ever been here.'

'I can, my lord. Miss Seaborne seems to have a remarkable talent for finding out whatever she wants to know, don't you find?'

'Aye,' he agreed, with a look for his fiancée that should have told her he found it one of her least attractive traits, but she stared serenely back at him as if he was in the wrong for trying to exclude her in the first place. 'Miss Seaborne is undoubtedly very talented indeed,' he added grimly.

'Why, thank you, gentlemen,' she replied as if they were heaping high praise on her modest head.

'She clearly doesn't possess a morsel of tact, though,' Alex challenged.

'Being a Seaborne, I have no need of it. Ask my grandmother.'

'Now why should I do anything as foolish as that, my dear?'

'True,' Persephone said with a rueful grin and couldn't have chosen a finer way to disarm him if she'd tried for a week. 'Then let me stay because it's sure to be Marcus you're discussing and I need to know if he's been found, and whether we did the right thing by not telling Mama of his disappearance,' she said with a look that told him how heavy all this had weighed on her.

'Stay, then, but first promise me you won't race off on some wild scheme to rescue him on your own. I couldn't even begin to find a way to tell your mother you'd been kidnapped as well as your second brother and I'd miss you rather badly myself when it came down to it.'

'How flattering,' she said flatly. How could he tell her the very thought of her at the mercy of an enemy who obviously had very little of that quality tore at his heart and soul?

He had rashly promised her a marriage of not exactly convenience, but one that offered equality of passion and their deep commitment to a shared future. Yet now he'd come to realise Persephone was essential to him in some crucial way that was beyond all that and he couldn't risk telling her so and having all idea of a marriage between them rejected, out of some gallant notion she couldn't accept his increasingly passionate need for only her without being able to offer something similar in return. Half a loaf being better than no bread, he was content to let her drift towards their on-coming marriage without realising she was wedding a wolf who would guard his mate as fiercely as he would if they were wandering some wild and hostile steppe on their own.

All of which meant he wanted to keep her as happy as she could be while her brother was missing and content to go on with their coming marriage without feeling the bonds he sometimes wished he could bind her with, so she would be unharmed by all this. As if anyone could be so sheltered from life—or that his secretly rather wild and headlong Persephone would even want to be guarded from reality. It would be the challenge of a lifetime for him to try to make himself civilised enough not to let her feel trapped by his warrior instincts once they actually were married, but that was for then. For now he had to make sure she was safe before he went after Rich's would-be nemesis.

'Promise?' he said implacably, knowing this was a line he couldn't let her blithely tear across if he was to stay sane.

'I promise,' she agreed with a long-suffering sigh, after a long moment of meeting his eyes as if trying to understand all he was doing his best to conceal.

'Unfortunately I'm not dim or naïvely trusting enough to take that as a blanket undertaking to behave like a delicately bred lady from now on, Miss Seaborne. You'll have to promise me you won't storm off to rescue your brother alone as soon as my back's turned before either of us breathe a word of where your scallywag of a brother has got off to this time.'

'Not unless you take me with you when you finally decide to get on with it,' she challenged with the lift to her determined chin that made him itch to take up the call to battle in her stormy green gaze and kiss her in front of Frederick Peters.

'What a shame your grandmother's not here, or she could come as well,' he offered as an almost acceptable alternative to embarrassing poor Peters for life.

'My promise in return for yours, my lord,' she replied, as if the notion of the Dowager Duchess storming impatiently into Marcus's prison and demanding all this nonsense stop immediately weren't niggling at her sense of the ridiculous.

Alex weighed up the idea against some wild sisterly crusade to grab her brother from the hands of his enemies and decided his wife-to-be was rapidly teaching him the art of compromise. 'Aye,' he agreed grimly, hoping his eyes looked steely and uncompromising even as she was wringing a promise out of him he would have given much not to make.

'Aye to what?' she prompted as unmercifully as he would have done in her shoes and even as he felt the sting of it he admired every regal inch of her.

'Aye, I will take you with me when we manage to work out the best way to rescue your brother from Rich's enemy, as long as you stay any wrongheaded impulses you're brewing to storm in where angels fear to tread and demand your brother back just because you happen to want it so.'

'It might work,' she offered, as if she thought there was a strong possibility the generations of ruthless piratical Seaborne blood in her veins could awe Marcus's captors into meekly handing him over.

'Maybe, but a rational plan would probably serve far better.'

'Very well, I promise to save it as a last resort,' she said and still her willow-green eyes challenged him to pledge his word in return.

'Then behold me reluctantly part of a council of three,' he said with a bow that genuinely honoured a formidable opponent.

'That will do for now, then,' she replied with another of those queenly nods that gave him permission to proceed with their meeting.

This time his elegant bow carried more than a hint of irony, but she managed to signal that they remove themselves from the proximity of the door and any potential listeners as if she was chatelaine of this vast mansion. She led the way to the wide windows where they could make sure the private courtyard garden beyond stayed neat and empty. Reluctantly admiring the instincts of a true conspirator, Alex and Fred Peters went like good sheep under the guidance of their shepherdess and he marvelled at the power his future lady exerted.

'You shouldn't be here,' Alex whispered into the riot of escaped curls about Persephone's ears and decided only a fool would ever be deceived by her breeches.

'We have a bargain,' she muttered so low he

had to get even closer to hear her and he wondered if she knew exactly why he was finding her presence so distracting and was taking some sort of devious feminine revenge on him for trying to exclude her in the first place.

'Your brothers and your cousin would have my hide to tan and bind books with if they knew I'd brought you with me.'

'Now I thought I had brought *you*, my lord, but I'm beginning to wish I hadn't since you're making so much noise.'

Stung by her criticism, Alex stood silent with her in the deepest shadows he'd been able to find on the tree-lined slopes above Kingslake Moot Castle and gloomily reflected that the woods were full of brash and brambles and as much in need of attention as the rest of this ramshackle estate. He hoped young Givage and Joe Brandt had found a path clear enough to give chase if only they managed to find this wily rogue who was intent on plaguing the Seabornes tonight. Alex didn't know if he wanted to meet the ruthless villain now that Persephone was dogging his every step as if she knew he would try to leave her behind if the man so much as put his toe inside Kingslake Woods tonight.

'He's arrived,' she breathed into his ear, and he was so busy controlling his instinctive response to her closeness he nearly stumbled over her words.

'How can you know that?'

'From the same sense of evil I felt on Jack's wedding day and I'm not fool enough to shrug it off this time,' she informed him as militantly as a woman could when trying not to leave even a murmur on the wind to reveal their presence.

Brooding on the likelihood of her being denounced as a witch in less enlightened times, he shrugged in what he hoped she would read as agreement and charged his senses to confirm her instincts. He hoped Peters was as good at creeping about the countryside as he had boasted and that Joe wouldn't take some reckless risk when this man had already proved himself a cold and ruthless foe. He was the one with the most experience of furtive night work and he was bound to his lady's side as surely as if they were tied together by his fear of what she might do if he parted from her for even a second. It occurred to him he must actually love her to let her trample all over his plans and prejudices in the first place and filed that revelation away to be looked at later, when he had leisure to be horrified.

As close to Alex as she could be without actually being in his arms, Persephone knew half of him longed to be off and away on the chase. She felt the instincts of a born hunter in the quiver of his powerful body when she told him the man who took Marcus was near and the curb he clamped on them as soon as he reminded himself he had her by his side.

If she was a truly noble woman, she would slip off back to the distant hollow where they had left the horses, or make herself stay at home in the first place, but not even Alex's gruff frustration at her presence could have made her stop away tonight. She was right; she felt it as if she could see through the darkness and the heavy undergrowth and untidy canopy of trees to the black-hearted villain stalking all their lives at the moment. Holding her breath, she listened intently and had to acknowledge there was hardly a brush of leaves or the stir of a woodland creature protesting to give the man away.

Still her heart thumped in her chest and the finest hairs on her nape stood on end and at least she knew this time she wasn't wrong about the presence of evil. A petty kind of malice and the soul of a scavenger perhaps, but evil all the same, she decided, as she struggled yet again with a reason why his mean gaze had fallen on them in the first place. Rich was behind it all somehow, whether through his fugitive lady, Annabelle de Morbaraye, or after his disreputable adventures had uncovered some secret others wanted hidden.

Her eldest brother's restless wanderings and rakish reputation never deceived her and she knew from the start he was up to something dark and dangerous under cover of a more than usually wild young gentleman about town. If he hadn't been far away in India, the man at her side would probably have joined in and she didn't know which acute peril she preferred him to have survived when she thought how he had suffered at the hands of a different enemy. Glad now she was here to hold him back by her presence from running his handsome head into the first trouble that came along, she stepped even closer to remind him he couldn't dash off to risk everything she now held precious on a wild dash into danger.

Deeply thoughtful at the notion he meant everything to her, she supposed she might have to thank this invisible enemy she sensed, pausing and sniffing the air like cautious quarry scenting a predator. The hot negative that sprang into her mind stopped that thought in its tracks, but still the terror that lingered in her fast-beating heart and desperately controlled breathing was for Alex and not herself.

Better to die herself than live without him, and now she had another conundrum to struggle with—how not to let him know she loved him so dearly she'd fallen into the trap she warned herself about on Jack's wedding day. She'd given her heart away so completely there was no hope of ever getting it back and was now at the mercy of The Fates. If he lived and prospered, so would she—if not, then her life would become dark and diminished. Persephone Seaborne had failed to learn from Lady Henry's example of what it cost a woman to love her husband so completely.

A breath of sound had her thoughts sharp on the present, instead of on some mournful and terrible future that might not happen. Ears pricked for any hint who had moved, it seemed as if the whole of nature was holding its breath and the stillness of the September night itself seemed alert and edgy. A pheasant called out its harsh chiding cry of protest at being disturbed and this time Persephone thought it was the man trying to insinuate himself into these woods unseen to watch Kingslake Castle for potential rescuers who stopped to strain every sense.

Evidently he didn't dare put himself into the power of too many others, since he seemed to be alone here. That gave him something of an advantage over Alex's party who had each other to look out for. Given the choice, she was certain her own particular lord would have come alone as well, so she was very glad she hadn't allowed him that luxury.

This was no simple rogue then, he must have a name and a position that would suffer if he was revealed as Rich Seaborne's enemy. As they stood here like a very serious version of children playing statues, Persephone marvelled any man would risk his freedom and reputation to draw two powerful families into his web. A very daring one, she decided with a shudder, and hoped they were as well hidden in this shadowy corner of Kingslake Woods as Alex thought they were.

The man shifted and came on and she did her best to excuse Alex for inexorably pushing her behind him as they could almost feel the tread of softest leather soles through the summer, dry earth of the path under their feet. She dare not struggle against his determination to take any blow that came before it could get to her, but frustration bit against that earlier revelation she'd suffered that her life would be only shadows without him. To save Alex from hurt, she would sacrifice this whole operation to seize Rich's bitter enemy and the taste of acid in her throat threatened to overwhelm her as she was sickened by her own dilemmas.

It was cowardice not to take the man if he could be stopped before any more harm was done and she had to fight the battle all women of power had fought for centuries. The one where their men went out to lay their lives on the line for some cause they believed in and they had to let them. Again she shivered as she pictured some unlucky Cavalier wife or mother forced to split her loyalties between husband, son, brother or father as one fought the other. She silently thanked God she was living in a better age and concentrated on not giving in to the temptation to make one of those choices even so and alert their foe before he could do any damage.

Alex tensed for the fight that would come if the man took another step and Persephone made herself relax her frantic grip on his black coat and not wrap her arms about his narrow flanks to hold him back. At least he didn't know she had in her pocket the deadly little pistol Jack had taught her to shoot, and, if only she could see her target, she wouldn't hesitate to use it. Fumbling it out to use as a much-less effective club instead, she got ready to race into action, despite all Alex's efforts to keep her dithering on the sidelines.

At last that step came and Alex launched at his

quarry with a feral snarl that made the hairs on Persephone's neck lift again with primitive excitement, at the fight this time instead of in fear, and she got ready to add her slender force to her lover's might. The impact of body on body made a soft thud that had her forcing her fist into her mouth so she didn't cry out and distract Alexander at the worst possible moment. She heard the whoosh of a winded man as the rogue staggered under the impact of over six feet of hard-packed muscle and bone, and she heartily wished for a little daylight so she could at least be sure of hitting an enemy if she struck out instead of the man she loved. Now there was the noise of a savage struggle without rules or boundaries.

The sound attracted the other watchers' attention after what seemed an interminable wait and Persephone heard running footsteps as they fought their way through overgrown paths. A desperate struggle for life was going on while she stood here, helpless as any Mayfair maiden about to faint because no other alternative was on offer. Two men engaged in that brutal battle heard them, too, for the thickset one she could just pick out under Alex's longer-limbed body by the faintest of starlight began to fight a different battle.

Instead of trying to overcome his opponent, the man was now struggling to escape with every street-fighter's trick he could come up with. Persephone winced as she heard the scrape of boots on flesh when he kicked Alex on the shin, then seemed to gather impossible strength and spin upright in a desperate surge. Alex sprang after him with impressive speed, but the stranger had found time enough to whip a glinting weapon out of his boot top as his enemy came at him and Persephone screamed a warning.

'He's got a knife!' She bellowed her caution at Fred Peters, as well, as he emerged from the deep tangle of briars that would make her wince for him at any other time.

Spinning on his heel with what could be classed as admirable agility if you didn't care about the outcome, the desperate rogue threw his weapon at Mr Peters with a deadly accuracy that spoke of a very villainous youth indeed and simply seemed to vanish into thin air while they were still horrified at the sound of fine steel thudding into flesh.

Alex plunged towards the quiet little lawyer without another thought for the desperate man fleeing the scene as fast as his legs could carry him. Persephone hoped Brandt and Givage wouldn't try to stop him if he had more than one concealed weapon about him and hurried after Alex.

'Is he mortally wounded?' she asked as she caught up with her impulsive love and resisted the urge to examine him for damage first.

'Not much more than a scratch, Miss Seaborne,' Mr Peters said manfully, although she thought his voice sounded weak and shocked as he did his best to stand with Alex's assistance. 'Be sure to bring the knife so I can examine it by daylight,' he instructed and she meekly picked up the bloody thing between thumb and forefinger and held it at arm's length.

'It won't bite,' Alex told her with amusement in his deep voice that she somehow found almost unforgivable after what he'd put her through tonight.

'Be quiet, you,' she ordered between clenched teeth and led the way back in what she hoped was a dignified silence.

By the time they reached the carriage and horses waiting for them over a mile the other side of Kingslake village, Alex and Brandt were nearly carrying Mr Peters between them with young Givage lurking behind them, casting suspicious glances at the trees behind them through the ever-lightening dawn. Persephone stalked ahead with her pistol openly on show and the abhorrent stiletto in her other hand and felt she would cheerfully use them on the wretch if he was rash enough to step in front of her now. Certain the man had flown like a hare from a hound, she wondered what on earth Rich had on the wretch to scare him into coming after his kin so ruthlessly.

'Now what?' she demanded crossly once they were back with Brandt and the stable-boy he had brought with him to keep the horses quiet.

'We go and get Marcus before that jackal can move him,' Alex said calmly and helped Peters into the carriage before inviting her to follow him to the nearest stand of trees where she could resume her proper raiment in peace.

Casting him a dark look, she collected the neat bundle Brandt Senior handed to her with silent encouragement to do as she was bid for once and dared Alex to follow.

'Hurry up,' he ordered brusquely as he did so without a pause and she tightened her fist until the pistol was in danger of going off on its own.

'Arrogant great bear,' she muttered as she donned her habit over her breeches, since she didn't intend to be shuffled into the carriage like an unwanted package and they would make riding more comfortable.

'Stubborn little witch,' he greeted her placidly when she emerged and she wondered if a single thing she said or did ever escaped his notice.

'Too much to expect you to ride inside and minister to poor Peters like a quiet and seemly maiden, I suppose?' he said when she went to stand by her spirited mount and looked at him expectantly for a leg up.

'Far too much and he wouldn't like it if I did,'

she said with a sympathetic smile for the young man who looked as if he would very much prefer to be riding with them in the fresh air.

'It's only a scratch,' Peters insisted, but she could see how pale he was and left him to enjoy a brief respite from being peered at like a prize exhibit as Alex finally gave in to the inevitable and threw her into the saddle.

Having a gallant if rather gruff gentleman about to tuck her boot in the stirrup and fuss over the proper arrangement of her habit so no other man could glimpse her shapely legs in their breeches wasn't a necessity, she decided, but it felt like a luxury. She looked forward to enjoying a lifetime of being ruthlessly guarded from wolves, considering she was very happy to have her own particular one and keep his eyes solely on her in return.

With very few doubts they would be compatible in the marriage bed after that scandalous encounter in the Queen's Apartments. At least that was one aspect of their marriage she was certain would be mutually and spectacularly successful. For the rest, she couldn't ever dream of marrying another man now she had met her match, and if he didn't love her as she loved him, no doubt she could learn to live with even that rather than live without him.

Chapter Fifteen

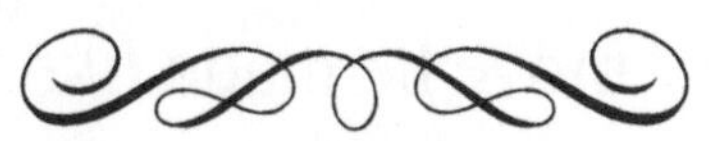

The sound of soft-soled shoes scurrying on worn stone steps interrupted Marcus's early morning reverie. He glanced out of the high grille and saw the distant rising sun was flushing the ancient stone with rose. How he longed to feel it on his skin again, with a need for good daylight he couldn't even have comprehended a few short weeks ago. He'd spent so much of his youth expecting adventures to fall out of the sky on him that he wondered why he'd been content to live the life of an idle buck rather than following in his elder brother's footsteps. Fear, he supposed, as the old Marcus seemed a stranger to the one who had been forced to learn the true meaning of idleness.

There was the vague excuse of his mother's

sad eyes whenever someone unwarily mentioned her absent son and Cousin Jack's determination to make sure he didn't do as Rich had and disappear for months at a time. The task of finding a wild life to live, with the Duke of Dettingham watching every move he made like the proverbial hawk, had simply been beyond him. Even with weeks to think out alternatives, he didn't know if he could escape the iron grip Jack kept on him even when pretending to hold the reins in a velvet glove. Now he wasn't sure he even wanted that wild life any more and was fairly certain the cause of that change was hurrying along the stone corridor outside his cell at this very moment.

'I hope you've brought something better than an ancient novel or a third helping of yesterday's pease pottage with you,' he greeted his wardress disagreeably.

'Hush!' the girl ordered in a panicked semi-whisper a deaf dowager might have missed, but nobody else within a hundred yards could fail to hear.

'Why should I? I'm the one in captivity,' he allowed himself to mutter and he watched her turn the key in the stout lock and rush in so she was firmly on the inside with him.

'Just be quiet for once and we might both come out of this safely,' she ordered in an impatient undertone as she watched the door as if it might bite her.

'Why?'

'He's sent someone to get you,' she whispered impatiently.

'Who has?'

'Lord Calvercombe, of course,' she said with only half her attention on him.

'What the devil?' he bellowed and she turned on him as if he'd given the whole game away and ought to be ashamed of himself.

'Idiot, can't you be silent for five minutes? He'll know for certain Papa and I lied when we told the men you overpowered us and escaped if you don't.'

'You're talking in riddles,' Marcus said in his normal voice.

'His lordship told us to house you on pain of being evicted when he brought you here unconscious. He wanted you kept safe while he tracked down a witness against you for the rape and murder of his young ward and cousin.'

'If he's been pretending to be Jack's friend all these weeks I'll kill him, but why did you ever risk being locked up with a monster like that when I was brought here drugged and nigh out of my mind?'

'Papa and I were certain he had the wrong man as soon as we set eyes on you, but we thought if we held you here, the true villain might relax his guard. And we really don't have anywhere else to go,' she excused them with a shrug that told him she wasn't very convinced of her own arguments.

'Tell me what his lordship looks like?' he insisted, thinking none of that sounded like the Alex Forthin the Seabornes all thought they knew.

She looked puzzled, as if he might as well ask her why the sun rose in the morning and set at night. 'He's darkish, I suppose. He hid his face and I've heard he has terrible scars and shuns company, so I didn't get a really good look at his face.'

'How tall is he, then?'

'About middling height, I suppose. I didn't take much notice of his appearance, since I was so busy being horrified by what he had to say at the time.'

'You were deceived,' Marcus said grimly. 'Calvercombe is over six feet tall and a powerful and dangerous-looking devil you'd remember after one glimpse.'

'Then it wasn't him?' she said blankly.

'He was my cousin Jack's groomsman the day I was beaten senseless, then drugged and brought here, so I can assure you I know the man. I certainly never set eyes on the one who overcame me before that night, and Alex Forthin has far more interesting quarry in his sights than me.'

'Then could that man have been acting for him?'

'If he was, I'm the man in the moon. Now open the door so I can challenge your latest visitor for the rogue he surely is.'

Alex wanted to pace again, but made himself stand still and did his best to look forbidding and far too dangerous to argue with instead. The room didn't lend itself to pacing anyway and he cast an impatient look round it. This one was so stuffed with ancient treasures that he doubted there was a piece of good furniture left anywhere else in the entire castle. How typical of the magpie at the centre of it to gather every comfort there was to be had here and keep it to herself.

'If Mr Seaborne is imprisoned here, madam, why is it taking your daughter so long to fetch him?' he demanded brusquely.

'I should never have permitted Warrender to keep him, Lord Calvercombe,' she said as if her husband had brought a dog into the house, instead of stowing the first cousin of a Duke somewhere in the castle's vast undercroft.

'If you took the trouble to meet the young man, you might have realised who he was yourself,' he pointed out, unwilling to let her get away with this 'it was nothing to do with me, blame my family' attitude of hers.

'It would be unladylike to trouble myself with such unpleasantness.'

'Yet it doesn't seem to trouble you unduly that

Miss Warrender was exposed to this conspiracy?' he said sternly, not that he had any intention of prosecuting his own relatives, but this harpy didn't know it.

'Dear Antigone and her father have a coarser nature than mine. They are lucky enough to be able to undertake the most repellent of tasks without flinching.'

'Or perhaps they prefer to get on and do whatever needs doing, rather than starving to death or being forced to go barefoot,' Alex said impatiently.

Clearly Electra Warrender made sure every available penny the family had was lavished on her, while her husband and daughter endured her greedy self-interest with a stoicism he struggled to find admirable. A little healthy argument and outright rebellion would have done the whole Warrender family a great deal of good, in his opinion, and he was surprised stormy-looking Antigone Warrender had put up with her unreasonable dam for so long. Necessity, he decided grimly, considering the very few avenues open to young ladies of breeding and no fortune whatsoever.

'A lady does not toil nor does she spin,' Electra explained and Alex thought of busy Lady Henry and his Persephone's active lifestyle and wondered if he could dislike his new relative any more than he did already.

'Miss Warrender certainly does,' he said, glancing at highly polished cabinets and neatly mended tapestries this woman certainly did nothing to maintain.

'Her father is not a gentleman. Antigone lacks the breeding to feel the shame of our position as deeply as I do.'

'Yet you don't feel it enough to be moved to help her?'

'I am your cousin, Calvercombe, how can you even ask such a thing of me?' she said, seeming genuinely bewildered.

'You are my predecessor's cousin three times removed, madam. Your relationship to me is so remote I doubt even the College of Heralds could unravel the fine detail of it without months of careful research I don't suppose you'll welcome.'

'Since your name was used by the thug who brought a Seaborne under my roof, I doubt I need to worry about such remoteness if you refuse to do anything for us, my lord. Rumour can do so much to damage a reputation, even that of an Earl who has so very little regard for his family.'

'I am engaged to marry the sister of the gentleman who has been held under your roof for nigh on three weeks now. You should be very careful indeed what further gossip you spread, Mrs Warrender, since you are one of the most culpable of the parties to this story,' he told her impatiently. 'No doubt you have a wide acquaintance,' he said with irony so broad even she might detect it, 'but I don't believe circulating tall stories that reflect so badly on you and yours will add to it.'

'Neither my mother, Lady Henry Seaborne, nor I would receive you if you do any such thing, Mrs Warrender,' Persephone added as she finally gave up waiting impatiently and entered the room to find out what had happened to her fiancé. 'We have known Lord Calvercombe since he was at school with my elder brother and my cousin, the Duke,' she said, the possibility of social exclusion cold in her voice and Alex realised she knew how to humble this chilling social mushroom of a woman far better than he did.

'Miss Seaborne, may I introduce Mrs Warrender?' he asked formally, glad she had disobeyed his request to wait until he was certain it was safe to enter Electra's lair, but determined not to show it.

'Mrs Warrender,' Persephone said with the weary air of a very high-born lady and Alex hid a grin by kissing her finely gloved hand in more personal greeting.

'Miss Seaborne, how delightful,' Electra twittered as if all her social ambitions had come true and of *course* she wouldn't dream of spreading spiteful gossip about the head of her own family as soon as his back was turned.

Alex was gloomily convinced she might be right about those ambitions when Persephone welcomed Mr Warrender with a genuine smile. Clearly his love approved of her host as much as she disliked his wife. Alex foresaw a ruthless Seaborne campaign to do Electra as little good as possible, whilst rescuing her husband

and daughter from her clutches, and looked forward to watching that sleight of hand from the sidelines.

'Where is Miss Seaborne's brother?' he cut through Electra's effusions to demand of henpecked Mr Warrender.

'My daughter has locked herself in the cellar with him and won't come out until you prove you're who you say, my lord,' Mr Warrender said with a shrug that told them he didn't exert much authority in this household.

'How admirable,' Persephone approved warmly and Alex resigned himself to having control of this farce wrested from him.

'She has my horse pistols and threatens to shoot the first person who tries to break in,' Antigone's fond parent said with a gloomy shake of his greying head.

'I'm sure dear Marcus won't let her do anything so drastic,' Persephone said with a stern look to tell Alex she could read his suppressed mirth far too easily.

'He said he was damned sure it was the real Lord Calvercombe this time since he'd risked coming here in daylight and she should let him meet you and confirm it,' the lady's father told them.

'What did Miss Warrender say to that?' Alex asked, only just managing not to laugh at the picture his imagination was painting.

'That she would shoot him if he tried to get the key off her and they were staying exactly where they were until Lord Calvercombe appeared in person, or realised the game was up and went away again.'

Electra's mouth opened and closed a few times and her eyes went frantically from one to the other as if looking for a clue as to their mood. When she failed to find one, she fell back on the standby of fainting artistically on to the nearest soft surface. Alex and Persephone left her there to wonder how long she should take to recover and followed Mr Warrender downstairs to the cellar.

'My wife suffers with her nerves,' he claimed loyally.

'It looks as if everyone else suffers from them more than she does,' Alex observed drily.

'Perhaps,' Warrender replied with a sad shake of his head and Alex couldn't help thinking some resolution would have improved his marriage a great deal, even if he shuddered at the very idea of being leg-shackled to a harridan like the one upstairs. 'My late mother-in-law brought Electra up to think herself neglected by the family she was so proud to belong to,' Warrender went on. 'Corinthia Clevedon was a very difficult woman who married a feckless fool who wasted what money they ever had. She spoilt her only child as if she was heiress to a fine estate, rather than tenant of a near-ruinous pile of stones. My wife lacks the character to see it was all a sham, I fear, and thinks the world owes her something for all those disappointed hopes,' he explained and Alex silently conceded it sounded a very unhealthy upbringing.

'Your own daughter can hardly have grown up with that delusion,' he said grimly, taking in the neglect and ruin outside Electra's genteel cocoon.

'Antigone has had a little too much reality in her young life.'

'Then we must conspire to improve her lot, Mr

Warrender,' Persephone said and Alex smothered a groan as he wondered how many poor relations and assorted waifs he'd be expected to house when he finally had a Countess in his bed.

'You haven't met my daughter,' her host informed her dolefully and shook his head as if he didn't know which was worse to live with, a stubbornly deluded wife or a resolutely realistic daughter.

'Maybe not, but Marcus seems to have survived the encounter,' Alex murmured as they descended a steep stone stairway and could soon hear a heated argument echoing along the vaulted stone passageway below.

'A redoubtable young gentleman,' Mr Warrender agreed and Alex wondered if he'd underestimated reckless and flighty Marcus Seaborne after all.

If the unladylike curse that preceded the sound of a large key being turned hastily in the door at the end of the passageway was anything to go by, Miss Warrender had misjudged him as well. Signalling the others to keep silent, and astonished when they obeyed, Alex waited to see what his young friend would do next. He was pleased to see Marcus take a look out to assess what lay ahead instead of barging headlong into trouble, even as he somehow managed to control the wriggling and furious lady trying her best to push him aside so she could go first.

'They don't want me, you tenfold idiot. Any sensible man might want to shoot you, but they won't put a bullet in a woman,' she argued furiously.

'Fool yourself. Their lives might hang on silencing you and keeping me in their power. Blackmail and extortion are capital crimes, my dear.'

'I know,' the girl told Marcus with an undercurrent of anguish in her husky voice and Alex sympathised with Antigone Warrender and decided his love was right to start a campaign for a better life for her latest protégée before she had even met her.

'Any trial would need a witness to prosecute,' Marcus told her with what sounded suspiciously like tenderness to Alex.

'And if you catch the man behind all this, won't you need us to tell our tale in order to punish him?' she asked as if ready to do whatever honesty demanded, whatever the cost.

Alex was astonished how different from her dam Miss Warrender obviously was. A conundrum Marcus would have to struggle with if he truly had tender feelings for his unusual keeper.

'There won't be anything left to say *when* we catch him,' Marcus said grimly.

'I should imagine the man I saw just now has plenty to say, whoever he might truly be,' Miss Warrender insisted doggedly.

'Good afternoon, Marcus,' Alex intervened to prove it.

'Forthin, you can't know how glad I am to hear your voice,' Marcus exclaimed and managed to thrust the door fully open as if he didn't have several stone of resisting woman fighting him every inch of the way.

'Believe me, Seaborne, I can,' Alex drawled and Marcus grinned broadly.

'Dare say you can,' he said. 'Since I've found out the hard way that losing your freedom is almost as bad as losing yourself, you have my most profound admiration for coming out of it as sane as you have,' he added, with a severe look for the lady who now appeared to be trying to hide behind him.

'Thank you. Once I might have disagreed I was anything of the sort,' he said, even as Persephone pushed past him to hug her brother fiercely.

'Marcus,' Persephone crooned contentedly and Miss Warrender stiffened, then flinched away from Marcus as if she'd been stung.

'Per-se-phon-ee,' he greeted in what Alex guessed was a childhood joke at their unwieldy names. 'Don't you dare get my shirt damp now it's been so tenderly washed and mended by my fair hostess,' he joked.

'Miss Warrender?' Persephone asked the girl. 'Who are you?'

'At last, a name,' Marcus said with a hard look for his hostess.

'Better you didn't know who we were, and I refused to lie.'

'I can imagine. Am I allowed to know the rest, or is that a secret as well?'

'I am called Antigone, Mr Seaborne,' the girl

said with her chin in the air and Alex couldn't help admiring her for admitting it so defiantly.

'Never mind,' Marcus replied with a complicit grin. 'My sister Persephone sympathises as well, don't you, love?'

'Deeply,' his spectacularly lovely Miss Seaborne agreed with a shake of her head that set her glowing chestnut curls dancing and probably made Antigone long for even a pinch of her elegance, although she did seem to relax a little once she realised the beauty in Marcus's arms was actually his sister.

'We have great deal to answer for,' Mr Warrender put in mournfully from the back of the procession. 'My mother-in-law considered it almost as fine a name as the one she gave her own daughter and neither of us felt able to argue for something more usable at the time, my dear,' he told his daughter apologetically.

'Never mind, Papa, since Miss Seaborne and her brother seem to live with their names, I dare say mine will not trouble me overmuch in future.'

'I'm sure something can be done with it,' Marcus informed her as if he would be using some form of it a great deal in future and she shook her head emphatically.

'No, I shall go out as a housekeeper, so it will not be used at all.'

'No sane household would employ you,' Marcus told her brusquely and Persephone and Alex exchanged knowing looks at his obvious displeasure.

'I know enough about managing on next to nothing to fill a book. Any sensible householder would be delighted to give me a job.'

'No woman would employ you and I doubt any man would take you on with anything approaching a pure motive in his heart.'

'Don't be ridiculous, I'm a plain spinster with no prospects,' she insisted gruffly and Marcus kissed her in front of her father, his sister and the openly amused Earl of Calvercombe.

'You're not plain,' he informed when he raised his head. 'Nor are you going to be a spinster for much longer. Say you'll marry me, so I don't have to take you back into that cell and lock you in with me until you're well and truly ravished.'

'You don't really want to ravish me, or marry me,' she argued bitterly.

'Want to bet on it?' he asked with a rakish leer and, since he had obviously liked it the first time, kissed her again and she kissed him ardently back, despite her doubts.

'Shall we leave them to it?' Alex asked Persephone as Mr Warrender allowed himself a smile of fatherly satisfaction.

'Better if we get them both away from here, don't you think, my lord?' Mr Warrender asked when the young lovers looked up as if they barely understood their own language.

'Aye, while that cunning villain is free none of us is totally safe.'

'And Mr Peters *was* able to flit in and out of the castle without being seen,' Persephone pointed out.

'I dare say one cannon-ball lobbed into the midst of the keep would set the whole lot tumbling about our ears as well,' Alex agreed ruefully. 'I'm surprised you found a safe place to hold a prisoner here,' he told Mr Warrender.

'The keep is sound enough, my lord, as I'm

sure your surveyor reported. He seemed a truthful man of forthright opinions. My wife disliked him intensely.'

'This is her home,' Persephone allowed and Alex sighed, knowing rebuilding and refurbishing Kingslake Moot Castle had leapt to the top of his list of things to do.

'She will have to leave until the place is sound and you will need staff to keep it so even then,' Alex said, wondering where he could safely place the Warrenders so they weren't constantly under his feet.

'They will come to Westerhowe with me,' Marcus declared.

'You should wait until you've met her mother before you decide anything so rashly,' Alex warned with an apologetic glance at the Warrenders.

'It doesn't matter, although I hope you'll be a good brother-in-law and restore the place, so I can have my bride to myself before the end of the next decade.'

'I haven't agreed to marry you yet,' Antigone protested.

'Yes, you have—don't you dare have second thoughts now.'

'I never said I would marry you.'

'You didn't need to; your enthusiasm for the idea said it for you.'

'Nevertheless, a lady likes to be asked.'

Marcus Seaborne amazed himself and everyone else by hastily kneeling on the stony floor and taking Antigone Warrender's work-worn hand in his. 'Will you marry me and make my life worth living, Antigone?' he asked earnestly and she looked down into his for once very serious green Seaborne eyes.

'Are you sure?' she finally managed.

'My life will be no fun without you in it. Be my big adventure, love?'

'Yes,' she breathed and flushed with joy until she looked exotically lovely, even in her washed-out grey gown and austere hairstyle.

Just wait until he sees her in a gown of dusky rose-pink silk with her hair dressed to make the most of those midnight-dark curls, Persephone promised them both silently. This summer would be a very lucrative one indeed for Madame

Elphine and what luck the exclusive modiste had already agreed to leave her beloved London for the wilds of Herefordshire to fit Persephone with her latest triumph.

Chapter Sixteen

'Your brother seems to have grown,' Alex remarked quietly when he handed Persephone down from the carriage at the side door of Ashburton New Place the family used to come and go informally.

'And he'll need every ounce of maturity he can call on,' Persephone murmured wearily. 'I can't tell you how I wish you and Marcus had listened and let me ride back with you.'

She massaged her temple to ward off a headache from a thirty-mile journey over bumpy roads, listening to Electra Warrender prattle endlessly about herself. Antigone had endured the monologue as if so used to the endless sound of her mother's voice she hardly heard it any more, and Mr Warrender had cunningly insisted on sitting on the box with Brandt Senior and playing guard to their wary cavalcade.

'I had to know you were safe inside the coach, not giving that vile rogue a chance to hurt me mortally by targeting you out of frustration. You're going to be my wife, Persephone. How could I endanger you so when he's been robbed of his quarry and is still intent on hunting down your eldest brother?'

'Don't,' she argued huskily. 'If you're even thinking of keeping me chained to your side for our whole married life we might as well part now, whatever the cost.'

'It's too high for me,' he said after a tense pause when she could see all sorts of possible terrors running through his vivid imagination. 'Promise you won't take wild risks for the thrill of it, Persephone. It will drive me insane if my wife is out running her head into any danger on offer to prove how brave she is every hour God sends us from now onwards.'

'I'll make sure you're included in any I take on, then,' she promised lightly.

'Probably the best bargain I'll get from you, but

don't be surprised if I'm grey as a badger before I'm thirty.'

'I doubt it, my love,' she told him and raised her hand to smooth windswept raven hair, oblivious to the fuss and greeting taking place behind them once Lady Henry and her daughters realised Marcus was finally home and had brought a very odd assortment of guests along with him.

'Mama says you can adjust his lordship's hairstyle when we're not so busy, Persephone,' Miss Helen Seaborne informed her as if she had no idea her elder sister and once awe-inspiring Lord Calvercombe wanted to be alone.

'Does she indeed?' Persephone said as she emerged from the cocoon she and Alex seemed to have wrapped themselves up in against the world without the spark of anger her sister was probably hoping for. 'I rather doubt it.'

'Well, we do have three unexpected guests and Marcus to accommodate at very short notice,' Helen said, as if that excused passing on the message with her own unique slant on it.

'Lucky the guest wing has been so very well aired in the last few weeks then, is it not, little sister?' Persephone pointed out and met her sister's inquisitive gaze with a bland smile.

Helen would just have to find out about love and marriage for herself, as her cousin and elder sister had in their turn, however impatient Helen was to start adult life and find her own hero. A woman needed maturity to take on the weight and depth and sheer feeling of such life-changing emotions, Persephone reflected. She had been too awed to accept the possibility for herself even in June. Her best friend Jessica had been struggling to come to terms with the fire and need that had flared into life between her and Jack so fiercely even they couldn't ignore it, so the reality of passionate love was there in front of her and she couldn't pretend it didn't exist.

Then Alex had come like a thief in the night, thinking he was too scarred for fine young ladies to look on, and shaken *her* world without trying. He was so harsh and changed and wounded by life, he'd made her temper snap into action to cover up her contrary feelings when he met her eyes with a challenge in them and fear she would turn away with revulsion. All she had really wanted even then was to wander off into the night with him and comfort them both for what war had done to him, she realised now. But it wasn't their night. Thanks to her interfering cousin a joyous consummation between them would have to wait another four weeks, and every day felt endless as a prison sentence.

'Thank heavens the guest wing is as far away from the rest of us as we can get,' he muttered wickedly now and made her splutter with unexpected laughter.

'I don't think your distant cousin drew breath the entire time we were shut up in that wretched carriage together,' she replied, in danger of forgetting her sister and the rest of the human race once more and trying hard to snap herself back to reality. 'My brother will need all the patience he can muster, and a large supply of cotton wool to stop his ears with, until he has his new family settled, I fear,' she told him.

'Aye,' Alex agreed with a rueful smile. 'I should try to persuade him they must come and live at Penbryn, instead of staying here to plague your family.'

'You *are* my family now, Alex. You can't isolate yourself from the Seabornes again when you're about to marry me, unless you're prepared to disown me after all.'

'Never, but are you truly willing to endure weeks of that silly and selfish female's company, after the hours you just spent with her?'

'Don't joke about our marriage, Alexander.'

'I wish I knew what you two were talking about,' Helen said acerbically, 'and it's getting darker with every minute. Why on earth won't you come inside and argue about nothing to your heart's content in comfort?'

'Where you can hear and see us, I suppose? Are you really prepared to marry into relatives like mine, Alex? Some of them are a sad challenge to their family's patience at the best of times.'

'I should certainly like a couple of ready-made little sisters to plague,' he replied with one of his self-deprecating smiles for Helen.

'As if we need another over-protective male in our lives,' Helen said and rolled her eyes, but Persephone knew her love had made yet another conquest.

Persephone decided Marcus could tell the rest of the family it would be getting a closer alliance with the Warrender family than they were aware of, while she went upstairs and enjoyed the luxury of a hot bath after such an appalling journey. After their interminable carriage ride, she began to wonder if a nice quiet dungeon might not have its attractions compared to any space that contained Electra Warrender for more than five minutes at a stretch.

'I have one more errand to run today, my dear,' Alex whispered after he had shepherded Persephone inside and Helen could think of no more excuses to linger.

'Does it concern him?' she asked, knowing he could understand she meant the lurking enemy she had been terrified might attack either Alex or Marcus all the way home, despite that ugly fracas in the woods that might be expected to send him scurrying back to his lair with his tail between his legs.

'Not this time,' he said uninformatively.

'You will be careful though, won't you?' she said with the flutter of terror in her heart at exactly what that enemy could do to them, now they needed each other so profoundly. Alex shrugged and gave her a long look that told her he hadn't quite come to terms with her own insistence on living a normal life, despite that enemy.

'What's sauce for the goose is sauce for the gander,' he told her with a look that reminded her a little too well of the wild and unrepentant young buck he'd been when she was a wild and equally shameless romp of a schoolgirl.

'Lady Henry has ordered supper to be served in an hour, Miss Persephone,' Hughes informed her sympathetically when he ghosted back into the hall to find her staring out into the shadows after Alex, as if she might be able to send her love and protection after him somehow.

'I suppose I'd best go upstairs and change then,' she said with a weary sigh and trudged upstairs to remove what felt like the dust of ages and one or two of Kingslake Moot Castle's ancient cobwebs that she hadn't been able to brush off the skirts of her travelling gown.

Luckily Electra decided she wasn't the centre of attention and sought her bed as soon as the informal meal was over. The wedding guests had finally departed and even Corisande had taken herself off to London to order that outrageous gown to outshine the next bride. So there was nobody left to tattle the story abroad when Marcus finally told his mother and sisters the story of his kidnap. Persephone's thoughts drifted from the comical narrative Marcus made out of his ordeal as she wondered why her fiancé had slipped away again as soon as dinner was over, until Alex returned and gave her an even better reason to be distracted from a tale she already knew.

'Is all well?' she whispered as he joined her on a sofa apart from the others so stealthily she doubted they noticed he'd returned, or perhaps that he'd ever been absent to start with.

For her the air fizzed with energy and life the moment he came into the room, but the rest of her family weren't in love with the man and could hardly be expected to feel acutely conscious of his every move as she was.

'Very well,' he murmured with a smug look and refused to say why his errand had been so urgent he couldn't have stayed to share the telling of Marcus's tale.

'Hush!' Helen urged sternly when her eldest sister tried to quiz Alex more closely. 'Marcus has got to the best bit.'

'He should go on the stage,' Persephone replied with a frown that should say she only believed about one word in five out of his colourful narrative.

'Anyway, I can't tell you much about how I was brought to Alex's Gothic horror of a castle. I was unconscious throughout and have no real idea who left me there or how I was received by my host and his family,' Marcus said.

'Can't you make something up?' Persephone asked with a sceptical look that told him she knew part of his tale had been trumped up between him and Alex on that long ride back to Ashburton.

'Not when Mr Warrender is sure to know more about this bit than I do,' he said with a deference his future father-in-law clearly found as unlikely as the rest of Marcus's tall tale.

'Which is little more than nothing at all,' the

unassuming gentleman said with a baffled shrug Persephone refused to take at face value as well.

'Yet you must have seen this man who claimed to be Calvercombe before that day, or surely you would not have believed his story and done as he bid you by locking Marcus up until the man had firm proof of his evil deeds?' Lady Henry pointed out, proving to her eldest daughter she saw through all the holes in the story they were spinning as easily as she could.

'Aye, he arrived one day about a month ago, announced he was in two minds about letting us stay in his lordly wreck of a house and convinced my wife he would find us a neat house in some minor watering place where we would be much more comfortable, if we did exactly what he asked us to from now on without questioning the whys and wherefores.'

'But why did you believe he was Alex?' Persephone couldn't help asking.

'Because he told us he was, I suppose, my dear,' Mr Warrender replied with a shrug.

'And that was all it took to convince you, sir?

Anyone could go about the countryside claiming to be the Earl of Calvercombe by that reckoning.'

'Indeed, but my wife assured me the man was her cousin, although he insisted on keeping the collar of his coat pulled high about his face and his hat low on his brow, so I was amazed she could discern anything.'

'We heard that you had suffered disfigurement whilst serving in India, you see, my lord,' Antigone admitted bravely. 'So the fact the man did his best to hide his face convinced us he was you and, as we have never set eyes on you in our lives, why would we question his identity when he claimed to be you?'

'Which was very astute of him, don't you think?' Alex said cheerfully and Persephone gave a quiet sigh of relief that he'd got over caring what the world thought of his scars, as long as the bit of it he cared about valued him for the unique person he was, with or without them.

'He thought he could use Marcus to pressure the rest of the family to find my eldest son and Miss de Morbaraye for him, did he not?' Lady Henry cut in, refusing to be diverted from the cold and heartless core of Marcus's abduction by his inference it was done for every other reason he could come up with but that one. 'And he clearly thought that, by blackening dear Alexander's good name with his lies, he could throw any pursuit off himself, which was a despicable trick even for a villain.'

'What a truly wicked man he must be,' Helen said with a shiver of unease.

'Certainly he's a clever, as well as a desperate, one to come up with such a wild scheme to draw Rich and my cousin Annabelle out of hiding,' Alex added into the quiet as they all realised how close evil had come to the Seabornes this time. 'If he wants to find them so badly, he'll be even more dangerous now we have contrived to get Marcus back without paying the devil's bargain he offered us.'

'But we are all on our guard now,' Mr Warrender said with a quiet resolution Persephone hadn't thought he had in him, but she supposed his beloved daughter's fate was now wrapped up with a Seaborne, so their cause had become much more important as far as he was concerned.

'Then you and Marcus must be sure to stay especially so, Mr Warrender, considering you are the only ones who have actually set eyes on the villain. Although we are all assuming he has acted alone, somehow I don't think this scoundrel would trust anyone else to hold such power over him, do you, Alexander?' Lady Henry said with a shrewdness Persephone knew should not surprise her, after twenty-one years of living with her clever mother.

'No,' he replied with a thoughtful frown, 'but it was a clumsy move brought about by frustration that Rich didn't do as he probably expected and turn up for Jack's wedding. I suspect the man knew it was a strategy that was unlikely to bring him the results he wanted, but he had to know if we are secretly in contact with Rich. If your eldest son came out of hiding to protect his brother all the better, ma'am, but at least the man now knows as much as we do about Rich and my cousin's whereabouts, which is nothing at all. He's learnt where not to waste effort in future and we know why Rich is so determinedly absent, so both of us have learnt a little from the fiasco.'

'It didn't feel trivial at the time,' Marcus protested indignantly.

'You need a keeper,' his fond fiancée told him gruffly.

'Then isn't it lucky I stumbled across you, my love?' he said with such genial obnoxiousness nobody would have been surprised if Antigone smacked him.

'I don't think that was luck,' his beloved said with a long cool look for her father, which he returned with cherubic innocence.

Persephone decided she'd been wrong to write him off as an amiable, if somewhat doleful, non-entity. Marcus would enjoy a challenging life with his fiery Antigone and she was far better suited to his stubborn Seaborne nature than some meek little débutante he could slot into his life and hardly even notice she was there as he went on his merry way. How satisfying that in doing evil, the villain of the piece had done her younger brother so much good all unknowing, and even brought about her own marriage to a man she couldn't envisage living without.

'Come, my dears,' Lady Henry said with a motherly look at her eldest daughter and younger son as weariness finally caught up with them both, 'there will be plenty of time for talking in the morning, after we all have a good night's sleep.'

'Meet me on the terrace at dawn,' Alex murmured in Persephone's ear when Lady Henry discreetly averted her eyes so they could say goodnight.

'Why?' she asked sleepily, surprised into meeting his dark gaze and seeing devilment and far more complex emotions deep within them as he silently asked her to trust him. 'Oh, very well,' she said as she took the candle he offered and smiled up at him as she fought off wave upon wave of weariness.

'Come on, my love. I think I'd best come and help you out of your gown so you don't wake up face down on the pillow come morning fully clothed,' her mother said and put an arm round her elder daughter's waist to tow her off to bed as she had when Persephone was a little girl and far too stubborn to give in to the night.

'Why?' Persephone repeated to her betrothed almost as sleepily as she had last night after she unlocked the side door of the family wing of the house several hours later and stepped out into the waiting dawn to meet her love.

'I'll answer all your questions when we're further from the house,' Alex told her mysteriously and she let him lead her through the September dew, despite the fact it got her soft-soled shoes unromantically wet and she still felt dazed with sleep, even after the shock of cold dew against her once-warm feet.

'Are we walking all the way to Ashburton village?' she demanded once they were far enough away for the sharpest-eared chambermaid not to hear them if she spoke softly enough.

'We're not,' he said uninformatively.

Seeing her mama's landaulet waiting for them at the first stand of trees where it was hidden from the house, with Scrooby and his grooms doing their best to stop the team protesting at leaving their nice comfortable stable so early, she finally dug in her heels and refused to move until he told her what he was up to.

Alex eyed her cautiously as if she might erupt into a fury if he didn't handle this very carefully indeed, but she saw vulnerability in his eyes as well as the sheer masculine arrogance of him and bit her tongue, for now.

'Will you marry me?' he asked with a gravelly harshness in his deep voice that told her how serious he was and how much her answer mattered to him.

'I have already said I will, Alexander Forthin. Why are we out here when all respectable folk are in bed asleep, rehashing a matter I thought we'd well and truly settled several weeks ago?'

'No, we scrambled into it more or less by accident, love. So it's high time I asked properly and you gave me a yea or nay in reply.'

Chapter Seventeen

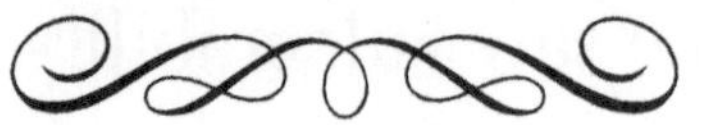

Persephone decided she must have been wearier than she thought last night. She was probably wandering in a hazy dream right now, not really taking care not to crunch the finely raked gravel drive underfoot in the pearly light before sunrise. Now this handsome apparition was asking her impossible questions and Alex had certainly never named her his love whilst she was awake to appreciate it.

'Why now?' she asked, her eyes wide and heavy with those dreams as she did her best to wake up properly and dispel this unlikely fantasy.

'Because it's the right time to ask. An answer one way or the other would be good,' he insisted, as if it was the most urgently longed-for answer he'd ever waited for. 'Will you marry me, Persephone Seaborne?' he asked very seriously indeed once again and sank to one knee on the damp ground, despite her horrified attempts to make him stand up again and the dawning realisation this really was happening and she wasn't dreaming, after all. 'Not until you say yes,' he argued stubbornly, all the hopes and dreams she had never dared look for until now open and desperate in his dear blue eyes.

She finally awoke to the glorious reality of her love on his knees to half-beg and half-demand her hand in marriage—and wasn't that so typical of him that this had to be real? 'Yes,' she whispered with a mischievous, triumphant smile that risked making the sun stay at home this morning for fear of being outshone by Alex's besotted gaze. 'Yes, I will marry you. Yes, I love you, Alexander Forthin, Earl of Calvercombe, and suspect I always will, despite everything you will surely do to infuriate me by treating me like some meek and feeble female in the years to come.'

'I already know you'll never be so if you live out your century. Now I'm almost used to your stubborn independence, I wouldn't have you otherwise,' he said with the wry grin she'd come to love and got to his feet to kiss her breathless.

It took a series of ever louder coughs to remind them they were not alone out here as the birds stirred into action all around and discovered at least a small part of humanity didn't need reminding it was time to get up.

'So will you marry me now, my one and only love?' Alex asked with heat and joy and laughter in his eyes and a broad smile on his lips that told her it was possible.

'Now, this minute?' she asked as the whole business seemed in danger of drifting off into dreamland again, just when she had her love warm and masculine and very definitely wanting her in his arms.

'Well, in five minutes if we hurry,' he said as he scurried her up into the carriage and Scrooby gave in to the romance of the occasion by snicking his whip just short of the leaders' ears to spring them into action.

'Yes,' she said on a long and blissful sigh as she realised her love had finally found a way round Jack's wretched embargo on her joining Alex in the former ducal bed, now Jack had declared it his intention of sharing the Queen's Apartments with his Duchess for the rest of their days at Ashburton.

'I love you, Persephone,' he assured her as if she might not have heard the first, second or third time.

'I know, isn't it wonderful?' she said brightly as she watched the first rosy streak of sunrise tint the sky over the east of Ashburton Church where she was about to marry the man she hadn't dared dream of spending her life with all these years.

He laughed as if sheer joy made him forget they were supposed to be quiet and held her close in contented silence on the way to church where they could become man and wife in the sight of God as soon as Scrooby got them there.

Luckily the peace that always seemed to permeate Ashburton Church quieted the urge to shout her commitment to this man to the rooftops, and the freshness and birdsong of very early morning for their music made their promises seem all the more heartfelt and binding. Every moment of her unexpected wedding would live in her memory for evermore, Persephone decided with a dreamy sigh. So Alexander Matthias Geraint Forthin, Earl of Calvercombe, married Persephone Ann Seaborne for the first time with an unusually solemn Marcus waiting to give her away and Mr Warrender proudly standing in for Jack as Alex's groomsman and witness. She could not have felt more truly wed to her husband and lover than if the Archbishop of Canterbury had performed the service and the King was there to watch him do it.

'Congratulations, my Lady Calvercombe,' Marcus said as he kissed his sister shortly after the vicar had pronounced them man and wife in a triumphantly ringing tone that seemed to fill the whole church. Antigone Warrender in her old grey gown as Persephone's sole attendant and Scrooby and as many grooms as he could spare from keeping his horses from rousing the whole village echoed his words as quietly as they could when they too wanted to shout their good wishes to the rafters.

'Lord Calvercombe is the one who needs most

congratulation,' Mr Warrender observed with the spark of mischief Penelope had learnt to look for in his eyes. 'But I don't think he'd be any too pleased if *I* kissed him.'

'Don't encourage them, we'll be here all day and then the cat will be well and truly out of the bag,' Marcus argued, and the very idea of what his mother would have to say about all this made them all want to hasten back to their beds, before anyone even suspected they'd ever been out of them.

'Here's a guinea for each of you to celebrate our nuptials with,' Alex told Scrooby and his most trusted lads when he and his bride stepped down from the landaulet and Marcus, Mr Warrender and Antigone were already on their way to their beds. 'And another if you manage to keep a still tongue in your heads as to why you're making merry, at least until the next time we do this all again in daylight,' he added and Scrooby grinned and wished him joy of a fine morning's work, before returning the rig to the stableyard with a very cold eye on anyone who dared question his reasons for exercising the team very nearly in the middle of the night.

'What next, my lord?' Persephone asked with apparent innocence as they stole back into the house and crept upstairs hand in hand.

'Shush!' he admonished softly and dragged her into the nearest unused room as a sleepy housemaid sped downstairs to her breakfast and never mind if she did take the front stairs at this time of day.

'Now what?' Persephone whispered.

'Well, since we've paid over our penny, now we get to eat the bun,' Alex murmured very close to her ear and she felt a delightful shiver run down her back, as the fact they were legally wed and about to bed each other sank in after all the weeks of longing for the magic and mystery of him in her bed.

She looked at him expectantly and marvelled he had the will-power not to fall on her right here, but her lover had exquisite self-control. How could she doubt he would insist on making this wonderful for both of them to look back on when they were old and grey? Impossible, she decided with a joyous smile that seemed to dazzle him with its trusting brilliance. He blinked as if she outdid the autumn sun so merrily rising outside for him and she wanted to dance through its mellow brilliance with him, but couldn't spare time from the delicious promise of so much eager loving to come.

'I'm not having you stealing about the place at risk of being caught creeping back to your room, so it will be my pleasure to come to you, my love,' he told her in a husky whisper that told her he was nearly at the end of his tether.

She considered the idea for a long moment, decided she would risk anything to have her husband in her bed this fine September morning and smiled in agreement as seductively as she knew how, before tugging him out of the side room and slipping through the sleeping household with her hand so firmly in his that an earthquake was unlikely to part them. It was her turn to hush him as she pointed out a board that creaked, but at last they were outside her bedchamber and nobody had seen or heard. How on earth he would get out of here without everyone knowing where he'd been and why was beyond her, but that was for later. All that mattered now was beginning the Countess of Calvercombe's married life in her husband's arms.

'Hurry,' she muttered as she urged him inside and he closed the door on the world with a sigh of relief.

'What if your sisters are awake?' he whispered back.

'They will need to hear like bats even if they are, as they still sleep in the nursery wing on the other side of the building. Now will you please hurry up and get us both into bed and doing what a newly married couple should be doing now we're finally alone together?'

'What about your mama?'

'She sleeps in the other wing, away from the bedchamber she and Papa shared when he was alive. Anything else? Would you like me to list where and how everyone in the entire household sleeps and wakes, so we can be sure they won't burst in on us? I suggest we simply lock the door and pull the curtains round my bed so Corisande couldn't see us, even if she was still here to peer through keyholes. Or have you gone cold on the whole notion of bedding your wife, Lord Calvercombe?'

'Does it feel as if I have?' he asked as he obliged her at last by setting about her sleepily fastened gown with fingers that shook with need, but finally got on and did the job he set them.

'Alex-ander,' she said on a long drawn-out sigh as he hastily pushed the soft muslin off her shoulders and let gravity do its work with a little help from him when her curves got in the way of that fine force of nature.

'Per-seph-one,' he sounded out with infinite satisfaction as she stood before him impatiently in her short shift and no corset, since she had lacked the patience to don one in the little hours when she woke and stole out to meet him.

'Why do you have so many confounded buttons and manly reasons for me not to get at you as easily as you seem able to get at me?' she asked crossly and he grinned unrepentantly as he began to strip for her as if they were illicit lovers going back on a solemn promise to her cousin, rather than man and wife with vows made between them that trumped all others.

'Will that do?' he asked with a wicked grin as he stood before her in a white linen shirt and cream breeches that clung lovingly to every lean muscle and manly inch of his long, long legs. He stood straight-backed and superbly at ease with his powerful body as any arrogant potentate about to take another harem favourite.

'You need to ask *me* that? My goodness, Alexander, we're in trouble,' she observed with a flirtatious look designed to get him to strip bare for her delight without her actually having to give in and do it for him.

'Personally, *I* was in trouble the first night I finally set eyes on you again across that fanciful Grecian temple one of your ancestors built out in the midst of nowhere in particular, probably for the express purpose of giving men like me ideas about goddesses like you,' he said, but she noticed he was ridding himself of his pristine neckcloth and immaculate white shirt with so much haste his valet would probably give his notice as soon as he saw what his master had done to them.

'Do you think I have never seen a man before, when I have two brothers and a cousin who always insisted on swimming in the lake in a state of nature, Alex?' she asked with a tender smile for his consideration of her supposedly maidenly nerves.

'I can guarantee you never saw one like this before,' he said in a voice thick with need and yet oddly diffident about the effect his fully roused manhood might have on the love of his life.

'Ooh,' she allowed herself to say appreciatively as he finally did as she wanted and stripped himself as naked as the day he was born. 'You could be right,' she added as her gaze lingered on his rigidly eager member and wondered.

'I sincerely hope I am,' he teased her gruffly and flicked the straps of her shift aside so it would go the way of her gown and he could gaze on her tightly betraying nipples and every last inch of silky naked skin as if he was starving for the sight, sound, scent and touch of her. 'I want you so much, Persephone,' he said shakily and she found it more seductive than if he told her poetry, or seduced nearly every inch of her slowly and worshipfully as he had that night in the Queen's Apartments.

'Then have me, husband. Take me to wherever we went last time and a lot further as well.'

She felt his shuddering response to her wanton invitation and realised he'd been on fire with need for her ever since that memorable night. Awed by his physical need for her, at the same time she knew that need was only a symptom of his deep and abiding passion for her as herself, Persephone Forthin, his wife and only lover from this moment on. A wide and lovely symptom it was as well, she decided hazily as he took her at her word and seized her in his arms and kissed her breathless at the same time as he was expertly caressing her into a wild woman again, seducing and enchanting her at the same time.

'Alexander,' she whispered as soon as he let her mouth take a brief rest, 'I want you,' she encouraged huskily and felt the fire he'd shown her that night leap fully back to life.

'Persephone, you are about to have your wish

fulfilled,' he half-boasted and half-moaned with need of her. 'Are you quite sure?' he asked as he paused, his manhood taut and craving at the centre of her womanhood.

He waited for her final permission with a patience she found so touching that tears threatened to fall and mislead him into thinking she wasn't as ready for him as she and her body were telling him she was. So urgently indeed that she wanted to scissor her legs together with the pleasure-pain at the heart of her greatest need for him.

'Never more sure of anything in my life, darling Alex. Hurry up and seduce me completely before my maid comes knocking on the door, there's a good Earl.'

'Dear scold,' he said on a mighty laugh he had to lose in the tender skin between her neck and shoulder as he did exactly as she bid him and took his wife in a great surge of love that bore them both to some new wonderland she was breathlessly eager to explore.

Feeling him fight himself for control again once he was deep inside her and she came to terms with her maidenhead being a thing of the past, she concluded the brief moment of sharp pain as he breached it had been worth every second to feel as if he was somehow taking up her whole world now, within and without. The sense of fullness and a seductive completeness, as he tried to hold himself still inside her and allow her to get used to so much breathtaking novelty all at once, held her for the briefest of moments on an edge that needed exploring fully some other time, just not this one, when there wasn't time to spare for such luxuries. Now he was inside her and the wildest of needs and passions was drawing her to shift and long under his formidable control and want to break them out of anything tamed and held back into a fury of driven loving.

'I won't shatter, Alex,' she whispered as she let internal muscles she hadn't even dreamt she had before flex around his mighty manhood and find it as perfectly designed to pleasure her as the rest of him, as he stretched her to the most exquisite fullness to take his mighty shaft in so tight and sweet a fit.

'I might,' he informed her shakily, as if this

was everything he'd ever needed and never dared hope for.

'Try,' she encouraged him shamefully, riding a wild euphoria now she finally had her lover between her legs and he was about to plunge them both into infinity, together this time.

She began to move experimentally in the rhythm he'd taught her last time and found it sent surges of delight right through her when he gave in to the drive and infinite sweetness of it all and took over, to pace them with strong, deep thrusts that sent those surges growing and gathering ever more power with each rise and fall inside her, with him. His mouth was on hers, his hands braced and his eyes open under sensually heavy lids as he gazed into hers, as if neither of them could bear to shut themselves off from so much when they could share it instead. She did her best to tell him with every sense and thought she loved him and loved fully making love to him. However, he'd already taught her greed and infinite need, so could he please get on with taking them both to the ecstasy she learnt last time, plus so much more satisfaction now they could ride it together.

Then his pupils dilated and his densely blue gaze seemed to go almost black as he changed the drive of his body to a new depth and slowness. The deeply sensual pace now took her with him, to feel first that contortion of delight he'd already shown her, then a full-bellied contraction of utter pleasure as he convulsed with her and they soared into some sort of heaven together and melted utterly into each other. It was the most sensual and spiritual experience of her life all at the same time and the joy of it made her heart sing with delight, but the best part of all was sharing this exquisite ecstasy with him. Knowing everything with him, feeling every pore and beat of him centred on her and giving all of herself back in return.

For long, lovely moments they lost themselves in each other, his eyes looking deep into hers, his breath short and harsh as he gasped in air and she felt him suck life down into his lungs, heard and felt his heartbeat as he let his arms take most of his weight, but couldn't seem to deprive them of Alexander joined intimately with Persephone, Earl in his Countess, lover within lover.

'There, we're still whole,' she murmured as if she somehow needed to offer him comfort, and after all that ecstasy of wild pleasure as well.

'You might be, my love, I'm not so sure I am,' he told her as an echo of his old self-doubts and uncertainty he could be lovable surfaced.

Chapter Eighteen

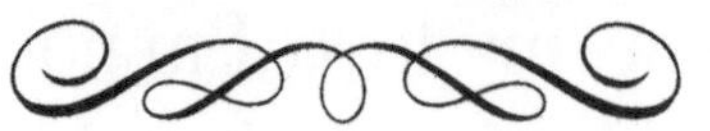

'You are everything to me, Alexander Forthin, and don't you ever dare doubt it again. I won't let your father and your wretched brother go on convincing you from beyond their graves that you're less than worthy of being loved. If it takes me the rest of our lives together, I'll make you see our love for what it is—you deserve love, my darling. You have love and you do love, whether you want to or not.

'My family love and value you for yourself and not your pretty face, and we are going to adore any children we bless each other with so immoderately you're going to see for yourself how different a family ought to be from the one you grew up with. Moreover, you have me to nag and worry you into knowing yourself better, Alexander Matthias Geraint, and, if you don't realise how much of a wonder that is for both of us very soon, I shall make myself kick you out of bed until you've learnt to know yourself as deeply loved as my beloved Lord Calvercombe should.'

Grinning like the sultan she'd likened him to earlier, he hugged her close and rolled her over so she rested against his powerful chest and couldn't escape the fact he was already more than ready to show her a lot more about herself, at least if his increasing state of arousal was anything to go by.

'Unfortunately it's about time I kicked myself out of it, unless you really want the whole of Ashburton to know what we've been at this morning, my loved and lovely Lady Calvercombe?' he told her with the very cocky knowledge he could set her crooning with delight if she even tried to make him go back to his lonely bed against his inclination, and hers.

'Best if we don't,' she said after a long moment of consideration. 'My mother would never forgive us if we cheated her of her eldest daughter's wedding, especially now Marcus is back to give me away, and it looks as if he and Antigone will be following us up the aisle as soon as their banns have been read.'

'They can wait, they're young enough. Since we went through our few weeks of hell waiting to wed and bed each other, they might as well learn what it's like to burn as well,' he said unsympathetically, as if someone else ought to suffer after he'd spent so long tortured by needing his woman in his bed and not having her, because of an unwary and unknowing promise he'd made to her sly devil of a cousin.

'What makes you think Marcus has the slightest intention of burning for his love all that time, Alex?' Persephone asked, and he looked grim for a moment when he realised Marcus hadn't given any spur-of-the-moment vows not to lay a hand on a lady Jack had never met and couldn't guard, as he himself had done.

'I pity the poor idiots who fall head over ears with Helen and Penelope,' he said unwarily.

'If you think only idiots fall in love with Seaborne women, you are in the wrong bed, my lord,' she informed him as haughtily as any woman could when the movement of a certain Alex

Forthin laughing under her prone body was tickling her all-too-responsive nipples with the abrasion of the swirls of midnight dark hair finely spaced over his wide chest.

'On the contrary, only the most deserving and dashing of gentlemen will ever be good enough for a single one of them,' he said solemnly.

'I told you to believe in yourself, not become a swollen-headed turkey,' she chided as she fought an attack of the giggles and risked not caring if they tumbled over one another and straight into another loving.

'I will try to become your perfect lord, if only you will practise to be as aloof and lovely as the Northern Lights to all other men but me, my love. If you smile at a single one as you just did at me, I might have to go mad with jealousy or ferociously call him out to eat grass for breakfast.'

'Don't you dare. I will only ever look at you, Alex, and there will never be another man for me. We Seabornes love for life, or don't love at all—there are no half-measures so far as we are concerned.'

'And us Forthin men would as soon imagine

the sky falling on our heads as we would love any other woman but the one and only, my Persephone,' he assured her very seriously indeed.

'Easy for you to say when you're the only one left, but we'll rewrite the sad history of your wretched family between us, my darling. You can start a tradition of strong and faithful men who show that the ones who went before them were the exception to the rule and not you, lover.'

'I suspect my cousin intends to start one for the female line, as well, so perhaps there are some wild and romantic Forthin traits in me to go with the Welsh ones my mother bequeathed me, after all,' he said half-seriously.

'I'm glad you found them, Alex, even if your cousin Electra does seem likely to drive anyone forced to spend more than half an hour with her halfway to insanity. They are family and you sadly lacked much of that once your grandfather died,' she said, finally giving up on coaxing another loving out of this over-gallant husband of hers as he reluctantly rose from her bed to dress with a heavy sigh.

'I did when Annabelle left home anyway. I

wish we had managed to find her as well as Antigone,' he said with a frown for the gap his first cousin had left in his life.

'We will find her one day, my love,' she reassured him, her faith in her eldest brother probably even greater than his own in Annabelle, since she knew Rich had so much of their father in him, even if he didn't as yet realise it himself.

'I hope so. Although I don't know how much more joy one man can take in his life, it would be pleasant to have the chance to try.'

'And perhaps I will have both my brothers back one day as well,' she said wistfully and he hugged her close, risking all the clothes he'd hastily scrambled back in place as the urge to offer and take comfort nearly got burnt up in his endless need for his wife.

'Until then, we'll just have to make do with loving one another,' he told her solemnly and grinned at her when she batted him with a half-hearted smack on his noble chin.

'As a consolation prize?' she suggested with a roguish look she wished would make him have second thoughts about leaving her.

'As an Olympic triumph, my Persephone,' he argued and there was sincerity in his dear eyes, as well as teasing, as he knotted his mangled cravat about his neck and shrugged into his coat and waistcoat in a fashion that would horrify the men who made them so lovingly. They fitted him with a perfection of muscular power she admired almost as much as his mighty form without a stitch of clothing on it, but only almost.

'I don't think my namesake was as lucky as I am with my prize,' Persephone said gently, all her love and admiration for this once-wounded warrior of hers in her own willow-green gaze as she let him see into her very heart and soul now she could look at him openly with the eyes of love.

'Or her prize with her. But I must go, love, or all that creeping about in the dawn will be wasted and my mama-in-law will hate me from the outset of our overhasty marriage.'

'Go, then,' she said grumpily and gave up on testing his will-power by shrugging into her dressing gown and accompanying him to her door.

'Until later, Wife,' he whispered, after one last

kiss to make her long for him even more bitterly until they could do it all again.

'Do you want me to hate you, as well?' she asked grumpily and pushed him out of the door before she could drag him back in and devil take the rest of the world.

She closed the door on him, leaving him to make his way somehow from her room to his in Jack's wing of the house, as if that was what Earls always did at this time of day. If he could talk his way out of the disgraceful state of his usually immaculate linen and the almost-dressed look of a rake well satisfied, he surely deserved his one-time reputation.

He did deserve that anyway, she decided as she lay back in her feather bed with a foolish grin on her face; he deserved it so richly she would have to make sure he was thoroughly occupied satisfying his wife for the next fifty years or so. She stretched sensuously against the satin bedcover and felt the odd twinge and ache in the deepest secret places of her body whose fullest potential he'd shown her so thrillingly, and sighed with contentment.

Who would have thought on that heady moonlit night in June she had met her love as surely as Jessica had finally found hers in Jack? Thank heavens Alex had come here looking for his cousin, she decided, as the terrible deprivation of not having him in her life bit into her state of lazy contentment like some terrible nightmare. She finally understood the absolute risk of loving as she thought of her mother deprived of her father when they should have had so many years left ahead of them. It would be sheerest agony to lose Alex and she flinched away from the very idea, but decided in the end it would be worth even that pain rather than never meeting him again in the first place.

Somehow luck turned out to be on his side, Alex concluded when he reached the splendour of his borrowed bedchamber in the Duke of Dettingham's private wing of the great house. It had been turning his way ever since he had met a spitting virago in the dark last June, he decided with a reminiscent smile. He considered the bitter, scarred and disillusioned man he'd been back then and met his own eyes in his shaving mirror to see if love had expunged the physical marks of his ordeal at the hands of a zealot.

No, they were still there, but somehow lesser than they had once seemed. He wondered if time had faded the marks of hatred left on his skin, or if the eyes of a loving wife made him see they never had been as bad as he thought they were to start with. Whichever it was, he accepted they were part of him now and he might as well live with them as best he could.

He contemplated the fuss and flutter his second wedding to his beautiful wife would generate and wondered where the reclusive Earl of Calvercombe had gone off to when it only seemed a welcome second chance to vow to love and share everything he was with her for life, rather than a hideous ordeal. Sparing a thought for his cousin Annabelle and Rich Seaborne, he hoped they were even half as happy together as he was with his newly made wife, and decided to trust them to each other, wherever they might be. He'd come here earlier this summer to find the only member of his family he had ever felt close to, and found a whole new one instead. Annabelle would be sure to regard that as a blessing and wish him happy.

'Be happy yourself, little cousin,' he whispered into the mellow warmth of the late-summer air. 'And, if you are, may your Rich be so as well,' he added, as if prompted by Annabelle that she wouldn't be so if her chosen rogue wasn't as well.

'I never would have thought it,' Jack Seaborne, Duke of Dettingham, told the Earl of Calvercombe as Alex sat with his arm shamelessly about his wife's waist the evening after the very public wedding of Miss Persephone Seaborne to the notoriously private Earl.

'Which particular part do you find so hard to believe?' Alex asked lazily.

'All of it,' Jack replied comprehensively.

'I knew,' Jessica said with a smug smile as if she'd foreseen the whole complex business and decided to go off on her honeymoon anyway, so they could get on with working the details out in peace.

'You're in danger of becoming as awesomely

omnipotent as my grandmother, Duchess Jessica,' Marcus chided from the sofa where he sat with Antigone and pretended he didn't mind she had insisted he kept his arm by his side, instead of where he would so much have preferred it to be, until they were married as well.

'What a dreadful thought,' Jess said with a shudder and leant back against her own husband's arm far enough to look up at him with a question in her eyes, as if she truly believed she would ever be like that formidable old woman.

'Banish it from your mind, love, I can't think of anyone less like the Dowager than you are. I should never have married you if I thought otherwise.'

'You would have when my vast tribe of brothers and brother-in-laws and my father had descended on you and demanded you did so, unless you really did want to be dismembered limb by limb as they no doubt informed you they could still do if you fail to make me blissfully happy,' she chided her own particular Duke.

'And how am I doing at that so far?' he asked.

'It's under consideration,' she told him solemnly.

'Is it indeed?' he said, as if considering a whole lot more before the night was over, then he appeared to recall where he was and turned a half-serious frown on Alex.

'Did I remember to have that particular conversation with you concerning my cousin before you married her, Calvercombe?' he asked with a return of the furiously protective cousin Alex had almost had to face down this morning.

'If you didn't, then I did it for both of us, Jack,' Marcus intervened with lazy menace in his voice, as he glared at his new brother-in-law as if he thought he might suddenly turn from besotted bridegroom into Bluebeard, now he had his wedding ring safely on Persephone's finger for all to see.

'Odd that you needed to, since I seem to recall sharing my feelings about anyone stupid enough to lay a finger on Persephone the day I left here on our honeymoon, Calvercombe,' Jack informed his new relative by marriage.

'Idiot man,' his wife told him sharply, and

Persephone contented herself with a bitter glare at her over-protective cousin while she decided to leave punishing him for his interference to Jess, who could do it so much better.

'Alex behaved with the strictest of propriety as far as I was concerned,' Persephone rashly came to her lover's defence all the same.

'By getting caught out in a shady assignation with you in the middle of the night, then creeping about my house at all hours of the day and night trying to pretend he hadn't spent most of them in your bed? You both have a very skewed definition of propriety if you think you've been behaving with anything approaching it,' Jack condemned without the usual leaven of lazy good humour in his eyes.

'Our so-called shady assignation was to discuss what Alex had managed to discover about Marcus's whereabouts without being overheard,' Persephone rushed to defend them both when she knew of old that she might as well stay silent once Jack had made his mind up about something.

'The rest was an accident,' Alex excused even more awkwardly and felt surprised when he saw some of the head-of-the-clan fury fade from Jack's eyes.

'I know from experience how those will happen,' he said mysteriously and Jessica blushed. 'What about your early-morning wanderings of late, then?' he went on sternly, as if only part one of the inquisition was over.

'What about them?' Persephone asked as if it was none of his business what she or Alex did when he was not about, as indeed it wasn't since they were plighted to each other from the moment they were discovered in the Queen's Apartments that night.

'They should never have happened, that's what about them,' he insisted.

'Don't be more of a fool than you have already revealed yourself to be, love,' Jessica chided and they were all secretly surprised to see the wolf who headed their particular pack pause and wonder if she might be right.

'Alex gave me his word he wouldn't seduce my cousin while my back was turned,' he insisted.

'They were married—what else did you expect a new-made husband and wife to do *but* make love to each other as often as their interfering relatives allowed?' Jessica asked as if she'd been present for their secret dawn nuptials.

'Married? How?' Jack bellowed as if discovering a dreadful family scandal.

'It's easy when you know how,' Alex said with mock-modesty. 'First you invest in a special licence, then you find a sympathetic clergyman who believes you when you say you cannot live without the love of your life much longer and desperately need to marry her out of hand. Since you are both fully of age and not bound to seek the approval of a barbarian who thinks it perfectly fair to condemn his cousin and friend to a purgatory of frustrated need for each other that makes a hypocrite of him, saving your blushes, Jessica, the rest is easy enough.'

'Why did you tell my wife and not me?'

'They didn't. The good reverend did it for them, as you would have seen yourself if you had not been so busy glaring at Alex as if you intended to tear him limb from limb if he didn't keep every single vow he made Persephone for the second time today. When he pronounced them man and wife, he mouthed "again" at them, as I suppose his conscience dictated he must, since their first set of vows were undertaken in the sight of God and already spoken as far as he was concerned.'

'Oh,' said Jack rather lamely, and Marcus and Antigone looked smug until Mr Warrender gave them a very stern look that told them two more weeks wasn't so very long to wait and he wasn't rising with the dawn again so they could jump the gun, too.

'I think it's very romantic,' Penelope said with a sigh that made her closest relatives eye her with disbelief. 'Even I can change my mind about the idea of love and marriage,' she said, as if excusing herself from all the times she had sworn not to fall in love and make a cake of herself like Jack and Jessica had over each other.

'One day I hope you find a man who will make you change it for good, my love, but for now you are a little too young to search for a husband and should very likely be in bed,' her mother said with implacable maternal authority and whisked her younger daughters off to bed before more unsuitable revelations could fall into their eagerly listening ears when the rest forgot they were there.

'It's true,' Jessica said even as two sets of newlyweds were wondering how soon they could follow without appearing ridiculously eager.

'What is?' her husband demanded a little grumpily, since he'd clearly decided not yet.

'It's been a very romantic summer for the Seaborne family, don't you think?'

'I will think so when you categorise yourself as one of us,' he replied, but Persephone thought he was using gruffness to disguise his true feelings.

'And it's not over yet,' she added, with a significant look at Marcus and Antigone that made them both blush and the rest of them think how young they were.

'But today is,' Alex declared and maybe part of his motive *was* to save the younger couple any more embarrassment, rather than only get Persephone to himself again. 'Since it's our official wedding night, you really will have to excuse us, because my wife and I have better things to do than sitting about gossiping.'

'Far better ones,' Persephone claimed without

even a blush and could hardly catch her breath for laughing as Alexander Forthin scurried his bride of two weeks up the ducal staircase for the official start of their honeymoon. 'I love you quite immoderately, my lord,' she informed him as they ran towards the old ducal suite, leant them for the night now its noble owner was downstairs making love to his wife in the splendour of what had once been the Queen's and was now the latest Duchess of Dettingham's Apartments.

'As you should, my darling, now we are an old married couple and you know for certain what a catch you made when you wed the Earl of Calvercombe one fine September morning.'

'That I do, my love, that I do indeed,' she murmured as he finally got them both naked in record time and fell on his bride with a ravenous ardour that seemed to build every time they made love, rather than diminish, as they came to know each other and what mutually pleasured them the most.

'I hope you don't expect such splendour at Penbryn, love? It's comfortable enough now, but it's no Ashburton, I'm afraid,' he told her as if she might mind not making love every night on the finest of velvet, lace and lawn when a rough blanket on a makeshift bed would do every bit as well as far as she was concerned, as long as he was sharing it with her.

'Having seen one of your properties, I shall be grateful if our bed could just have been clean and aired some time this century, Alex,' she said half-seriously.

'I think I can safely promise that, even at Calver, which is far more run down that Penbryn managed to become during the years my father and Farrant mismanaged it,' he gritted out somehow as she let her hands wander over his tautly muscled body and did her best to distract him from worrying about her future comfort.

'It's too late to have second thoughts now, my lord. We're married twice over and don't even think of leaving me here while you get your various houses in order.'

'If I lived in a pigsty, I doubt I could leave you long enough to make it less pig-like, my lady,' he responded and kissed her until they were both breathless.

'Love me,' she demanded blissfully as he finally admitted he couldn't bear to be parted from the wife he'd once promised himself he'd never have, and so he did.

* * * * *